I0654596

UNDONE

MIA KAYLA

MAM BOOKS LLC

Sometimes all we really need is for someone to say,
"I believe in you."
To my ride or die...
Thanks for always believing in me.

MAM BOOKS LLC

Visit my website at: www.authormiakayla.com
Cover Designer: Jersey Girl Designs,
www.jerseygirl-designs.com
Photography: Lindee Robinson Photography, www.
lindeerobinsonphotography.blogspot.com
Editor: Jovana Shirley, Unforeseen Editing, www.unforeseenediting.com
Proof: Mitzi Carroll, www.facebook.com/mitzicarrolleditor

ISBN: 978-0-9996757-5-5

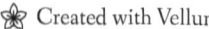 Created with Vellum

CHAPTER 1

"NO PEEKING. Keep your eyes closed, Angie." I framed my sister's tiny shoulders with my hands and led us to the door of Allswell, her boyfriend's restaurant.

The cool breeze had goose bumps rising on my bare arms, but I was used to being half-dressed to the nines when going out on a Saturday night. I wasn't the celebrant tonight, but that hadn't stopped me from rocking my silk halter and white jeans.

I released her and straightened my top and fluffed my hair, not a wrinkle in sight, not a curl out of its place. Perfection was my middle name.

"Tene, I don't understand why you got me all dressed up to go to dinner. I'm in a miniskirt, and it's cool tonight." She teetered on her borrowed four-inch heels. "And these damn strappy shoes of yours."

Angie Armstrong, my little sister, was conservative, practical, and still way underdressed for her surprise party. If I had allowed her to show up in jeans and a T-shirt, she would've killed me.

I knew she'd thank me later—after we entered the doors

and she opened her eyes to see all our family and friends and half of our town of Rosendell was there, ready to celebrate her promotion to partner in our real estate investment company.

Seven more steps to the door of Allswell. Once we were inside, we'd see purple and white balloons accenting every table, alternating in color, and a banner hanging against the far wall, screaming, *Congratulations*, in a girlie script. At the bar, a row of Angie's favorite desserts had been laid out, arranged by flavors and colors, just as I had ordered. Cade, Angie's boyfriend, had asked for help in planning, and I'd told him he wouldn't be disappointed. Plus, I'd do anything for my little sister.

Fine details mattered. In parties, at work, and in all aspects of life. Even my ten dainty pearls on the back of my stilettos matched my pearl earrings. The small features could make or ruin an outfit, a deal, an occasion.

"Hey, Christene. Wait up!"

I stopped mid-step, and my heart stuttered.

That voice. I'd remember that voice anywhere. Thick. Deep. Sexy.

It'd been months since I heard him or seen him in person. I'd viewed every movie he'd made, watched every YouTube video of his interviews, and listened in on my sister's conversations with her boyfriend just to hear what was going on in his life.

My pulse ticked up in tempo. *Tick. Tick. Tick.* Like a bass drumming on the inside of my wrists.

I froze, took a deep breath, composed myself, and turned around ever so slowly to find Jordan Ryder—the highest-paid actor in show business, Hollywood's hotshot, America's *it* guy—staring right back at me.

He was also Cade's adopted brother. Yep. My sister's

boyfriend's brother.

He blew out a breath of smoke and then flicked his cigarette to the side. A sizzle of electric energy surged between us, just like that very first day I'd met him months ago.

I took a step forward, and as though the world had suddenly tilted on its axis, I lost my footing. In slow motion, as if I were in *The Matrix*, my legs gave out, and I saw the ground, the gum on the concrete, the cracks in the foundation. One knee hit the concrete before I felt a pair of strong hands reach out to steady me.

My hands fell to his hips, and I thanked the heavens above that I hadn't totally wiped out. I thought I had been saved, saved by an angel. But just when I was about to pull myself up, my other knee gave out, and I face-planted. Not on the ground, but into his crotch.

Oh. My. God.

When I tried to push myself to a standing position, pain seared through my scalp. Because, like on an episode of *America's Funniest Home Videos*, I realized my perfect curls were stuck on his belt buckle.

"One second," Jordan said.

Is he laughing?

Shit. Shit. Shit. He is.

My sister was definitely laughing.

I peered up at her, and she had her phone out.

"Angie, what the hell are you doing? Help me!" Pain shot to the roots of my hair. Turning to look at her had only made my situation worse.

"I'm taking a picture; otherwise, no one will believe me."

"I hate you."

"How's the weather down there?" Jordan's deep

chuckle vibrated through my ears and my scalp.

"You're a jerk."

As they both worked to remove my hair from his belt buckle, Cade's loud voice boomed in the background. "Angie, why the hell do you have your hand on my brother's dick?"

"Hey, baby," she spoke as though this were normal. Her feeling up her boyfriend's brother and me basically on my knees, attached to Jordan's crotch.

"Oh crap, Tene. Some of your hair got stuck in his belt. I told you, your hair was too long."

"Shut up."

I'm going to die.

"I think I have to unzip." There was amusement in Jordan's tone. "Angie, can you help me?"

"Fuck if you will. Angie, step back." Cade's thick thighs came into view.

My focus was now on three pairs of shoes. "What the hell is taking so long?"

The sound of his zipper and laughter echoed above me, and then I was free.

My cheeks burned bright as I stood up, adjusted my halter top, and dusted off my jeans as though nothing had happened.

I frowned when I noticed a dark stain on my knees. Damn it. That would annoy me the whole night.

After I flattened my hair, my gaze met his.

Jordan's ocean-blue eyes locked with my brown ones. Wearing dark-washed jeans that hugged his thighs and a Henley that fit him perfectly, he looked as though he'd walked straight off a J.Crew billboard.

I was too embarrassed to smile, let alone acknowledge his presence.

"Seriously, I've never seen you fall ... like, ever. You can run in heels. Mom said you went straight to walking and skipped the crawling phase altogether," Angie said. "Did your heel get stuck in a crack?" She bit her lip to prevent her smile.

"Who knows, Angie? It happens, okay?" But not to me. My ears felt impossibly hot. Later, I'd have to confiscate her phone and delete that embarrassing picture.

"Jordan, what are you doing here?" Angie's gaze flickered between the brothers. "Did Cade invite you to dinner with us?" She blinked. Then, double-blinked. "Wait."

I could almost see the lightbulb flickering on in her head.

She glanced back at the restaurant, and the corner of her lips tipped up as all of Cade's plans to surprise her vanished into the chilly night air. "We're having dinner at his restaurant?" She popped out her hip, and her smile widened Crest-white style. Then, she pointed a finger in Cade's direction. "You're trying to surprise me. But for what? It's not my birthday. Unless ..." She tilted her head, seeming thoughtful, and tapped her pointer finger against her chin. "Unless it's for my promotion to partner." Her pitch increased with all-knowing confirmation.

Oh, great. Surprise ruined.

Jordan ran one hand through his blondish-brown hair, making it stick up on end, and stepped between Angie and Cade. "What? No. I was just in the area." His words flowed without hesitation; his face actor steady.

For a moment, I thought we were in the clear until Angie's eyes perused the area, spotting every single one of our family members' cars in the parking lot.

Shit. Busted.

Coming to her own conclusion, Angie clasped her

hands together and leaped up and down. She propelled her short frame into Cade's massive one, wrapping her arms around his neck. The muscle in his jaw jumped, and his eyes narrowed on Jordan.

The brothers were similar in height, but they didn't look anything alike. Where Cade was stocky with dark hair and dark eyes, Jordan looked like Barbie's boyfriend, Ken—lean muscles, tall stature, and blond. They were foster brothers turned adopted brothers, so I wouldn't expect them to look alike, but still, they were striking. No doubt, when together, they drew attention. I wouldn't know who I'd place my money on if they were both in the ring.

Probably Cade. Jordan was way too pretty.

"Thank you. Thank you. Thank you!" Angie squealed, hanging on to Cade's neck, her legs swinging from side to side.

His eyes softened, and his massive body melted into her when he placed her on the ground. It was the oddest and most heartwarming thing, watching this big, tatted-up muscleman cower into her tiny frame. It was as if she could break him with one look, one word, one touch.

Sigh.

I'd never known what it was like to hold that much power over someone. For someone to love me with such intensity that everything I thought, did, or said mattered to them.

He framed her heart-shaped face with his overpowering hands. "Congrats, my Angel."

My sister had been in love before but not like this, not where her whole being lit up at his words. My insides were doused with fiery envy. The good kind—where I didn't want to smother her in her sleep or wish her some incurable disease because she was happy, but one where I was genuinely pleased for her and ultimately wanted the same thing for myself one day.

"Why didn't you answer your phone?" Cade asked, turning toward me.

"Yeah. Good one. Answer my phone when I was trying to bring the girl of the hour here. That wouldn't have given away your surprise. Nope. Not at all." I rolled my eyes and shot him a look.

"I didn't expect asshole over here to take a cigarette break in front of the bar."

"Sorry, man." Jordan winced and held his hands up.

Cade swung an arm around Angie's lower back and brought her closer, his annoyance at the two of us gone. "Come on, baby. Let me take you inside. Just act surprised, okay?"

"Okay." Angie squealed, giddy, as she skipped into Allswell with Cade.

When the door shut behind them, I tilted my head toward Jordan. "You coming?"

His stare was directly on the door and filled with a deep set of emotions I couldn't place.

He leaned back against the building, one leg propped up against the brick wall. If I snapped a picture, I could sell the shot to some high-paying magazine.

He took out another cigarette and placed it between his lips. "I'm going to have another one of these. You want one?"

I peered into his baby-blue eyes. He seemed lost for a second, so I decided I'd stay.

"You know Cade's just messing around, right?" I took the cigarette he'd offered and rubbed it between my fingertips, hoping my mother wouldn't catch me out here. "He'll forgive you."

"Yeah, I know. But shit." He rubbed his free hand against his forehead. "He's been planning this for months. Everything from the decorations right down to the menu. It's all he's been talking about."

"But he'll still forgive you."

I bent toward the silver flip-top Zippo he held between us, so I could light my cigarette. The whiff of his expensive cologne was intoxicating, teasing, and begging me to lean in closer. He smelled of pine and an all-masculine scent. *Is it Creed, Tom Ford, Clive Christian?*

Whatever it was, I wanted to inhale it, taste it off his skin.

The wind blew the flicker of the lighter flame out. Spark but no light.

He placed his cigarette between his lips, and when the spark still didn't light, he cupped his hand around the lighter to light his.

I moved in closer, in the little corner right next to the door, to block the wind, and when he angled in, I placed my cigarette against his lit one.

We were so close that I could feel the warmth of his body radiating against mine.

He looked divine, smelled divine, and I needed divine intervention to stay far, far away from him. I didn't believe in insta-love, but lust? Yeah, that was a different story.

But given that he was the brother of my sister's boyfriend ... yeah, well, that automatically took him off my list. I liked my men uncomplicated and detached. Feelings and commitment and relinquishing control were things I stayed away from, ever since my last and only real relationship.

I took a long drag and anchored myself against the wall. I wasn't a regular smoker, just a social one, but the first drag of the cigarette was like the first sip of my morning coffee. It relaxed my muscles, eased my body, and cleared my mind.

If my mother caught me smoking, I wouldn't hear the end of it. Not like I cared. I wasn't the favorite, not by a long shot. That was Angie, but still, I didn't want to hear my mother's mouth run a Nile-mile marathon.

I peered toward the blue-eyed stud beside me. He was the Jordan Ryder from the big screen, and though our town was small, everyone most likely knew who he was.

His eyes perused the area as though he was waiting for something.

"Why are you so skittish?" I flicked off the ashes, the black and white falling to the ground, scattering in the wind.

"I came into town unannounced and want to stay incognito." He exhaled a puff of smoke, and I watched as the bubble of white fizzled into the air. "Safety-wise, I've got Dex. He's right over there."

"Who?"

"One of my bodyguards."

He tipped his chin toward the street where I took in an intimidating, wrestler-looking, bald-headed, over six-foot-tall male. A brick wall in an all-black suit, standing by the Lincoln. *How hadn't I noticed him before?*

"Are you famous or something?" My face was steady, straight, and without humor.

"You're killing me here, Christene. Do you really not know who I am?" He placed a hand over his heart, feigning hurt.

Too bad I knew he was acting. I bet he pulled this cute act on all the women. And the problem was, he didn't have to pull any act. He was charming just standing there, mute.

"I thought your sister would have told you by now."

I'd met him months ago when I was trying to find Angie. I'd traveled to Cade's hometown, and when Jordan opened the door, I knew immediately who he was. His face was plastered all over gossip rags and entertainment shows. But I'd decided to play coy at the time. Now, it was time to stop the game.

He was beyond recognizable. I believed I'd passed his billboard advertising cologne, on the highway.

"Okay, fine. Angie told me who you were, and I guess I did recognize you from somewhere."

This time, he smiled, dimple on his chin and all, and I was filled with a strange inner excitement.

"I knew it." He pointed a finger in my direction, smiling.

"But, honestly, you look better on-screen. You look so different, um ... in person." I laughed because of the way I'd said it, it sounded bad, but it couldn't have been further from the truth. He was like an Adonis in the flesh, but I didn't want to inflate his ego any further than it already was.

I tilted my head toward the meathead standing by the car. I'd lived my life flying free, doing what I wanted. I didn't find it surprising that Jordan had a bodyguard, just an inconvenience. "Can you leave without him?"

He took another drag from his cig, his cheeks pulling in. "Nope. Mobs of fans, stalkers—yes, plural—on the loose. Restraining order against one of them."

"Stalkers on the loose?"

"Yeah. Not about to go into it. Plus, it's more for the studio than me. They want their moneymaker to stay in one piece." He shrugged. "It's normal in my line of work." His tone was flat, monotone, as though that were the regular life for everyone—being watched, someone on your tail all the time.

I couldn't imagine it. I wondered if, in the same position, I'd take the money and fame and give up my privacy and my ability to be free. Nope. I couldn't do it.

Our eyes locked for a moment, and I blurted my thoughts out loud, "It sucks to be you."

He winced, a short, immediate reaction, and if I had blinked, I would have missed it.

"Some would say I live the life." There was no inflection in his voice, no heart in his tone.

"Of a prisoner."

He lived a life confined by his fortunes.

"I'm sorry. I didn't mean ..." I bit my cheek to prevent myself from being too honest.

His gaze clouded, his eyes going distant, and then he surprised me. "Yeah, sometimes."

I hadn't expected those words to come out of his mouth. I sensed we were built the same—cocky and with a lot of pride inside. My brain-to-mouth filter was emotion-proof, meaning I'd never reveal my true vulnerabilities. I guessed his wasn't.

He flicked his cig to the ground and stuffed his hands in his pockets. "Want to get inside?" Then, his lips tipped up into a confident smile, and it was as if I'd imagined that tiny, unprotected side I'd witnessed. "Because I want to get inside ..." His voice trailed off, seductive and alluding to things that made a shiver of pleasure run through me.

When his eyes roamed my body, I laughed and slapped his shoulder. "For an actor, I'd think you'd have more game."

The ovary-bursting smile made an appearance again, and I strolled past him to get to the doors of Allswell to join the rest of the party.

CHAPTER 2

THE MUSIC WAS BUMPING, and the restaurant was decked out in purple and white balloons, matching the white table linen and purple napkins, which were my sister's favorite colors. The ambience was perfect, just how I'd planned it.

Fine, the surprise had been ruined, but that didn't mean the rest of the night wouldn't flow effortlessly. It had to. Dinner would be served at eight p.m., dancing until nine forty-five, and cake and candle blowing at ten. After which, I'd be done and at home and in bed by eleven p.m. I had to be. I had an early morning meeting with a potential client to lease the Wells property. This had to happen. I needed to rent that property.

I greeted friends as I made my way to my family's regular table at the other end of the restaurant. It seemed as though Cade had invited the whole town. The restaurant wasn't closed to the public, but the majority of people were here for my sister.

When I glanced behind me, Jordan was a few feet away, but now, his cap hovered over his eyes, drawn low over his head to hide his high-profile self. I reached for his hand, ignoring the shock of his skin against mine and the warmth of our connection spreading down my arm.

I tipped his baseball cap and leaned in. "Let it go. No one will know who you are here in Rosendell. You might be big and bad and beautiful in Hollywood, but not here."

"I'm not used to a crowd this big unless it's for a work function, and then I'm there to do a job." He shifted with unease. "When I hang outside of work, it's usually just with my brothers."

I noticed that his bodyguard hadn't trailed him. Maybe he had given him instructions not to come inside. Who knew?

"Well, your brothers are here." I angled my head toward the long table on the side, taking in Cade and Wyatt—his adopted brothers—chatting it up with my parents.

My sister joined in the conversation with her overly animated facial expressions and hand gestures. I smiled. Man, did I love that little squirt. I had to make sure the DJ I'd hired had Angie's favorite dancing songs.

When Jordan didn't budge, I gripped his hand tighter and pulled him toward the table.

For a minute, I was a breathless girl of thirteen, palms sweaty, pulse pumping, and mouth dry. I was holding hands with Jordan Ryder. I dimmed my fangirl moment, but inside, my heartbeat raced.

Keep it together.

When Angie saw us approaching the table, she jumped up from her spot. "Tene! Jordan!" Her voice echoed throughout the room.

My mother's eyes were trained on Jordan and our inter-twined fingers. I couldn't read her face. Over time, she'd perfected the ability to remain stone-faced while her mind went into overdrive. Bravo for my mother. It was how I'd learned my poker face so well.

The stern look on Cade's face made it clear what he thought of our friendly hand-holding.

Jordan noticed, too, because he dropped my fingers as though I had some sort of hand disease.

The rejection pricked like a pin through my skin, piercing and sharp. That was what I got for changing up my tune and being nice for once. I'd been trying to put him at ease but no more of that.

Angie's arms wrapped around me first before embracing Jordan. "I'm so glad you came. I know your schedule is crazy busy with filming."

I pushed my way past them and went toward my nana. I hugged her fiercely.

"Tene, you dating that hot bod over there?" Her smile lit up my insides.

My grandmother—Nana—was the queen of celebrity gossip. She had subscriptions to every single celebrity magazine, watched every award show, and binge-watched practically every sitcom featuring all the hottest stars. Plus, she lived at the movie theater on the weekends.

"You know who that is, don't you?" I whispered, leaning into her.

She squinted and angled closer as though it would better her vision. She stared at the hottie talking it up with Cade and Wyatt, and I knew the exact second she recognized him. Her mouth opened, and her lips formed a small O.

Nana was the cutest, hippest, five-foot-nothing grandma. Other grandmas were knitting and going to bridge club. My grandma was memorizing star stats and going to the movies by herself to make sure she wasn't missing out.

"That can't be ..." Her wrinkled hand flew to her heart. She pushed her eyeglasses up her nose, bent forward, and squinted. "Jordan Ryder?" In the next beat, she stood. "Excuse me. I think I might introduce myself." Nana was a cougar on a mission.

I shook my head, amused, and then walked over to greet Wyatt, who was standing aloof by himself in the corner, ditching the crowd he'd been talking to. Wyatt Ryder. What could I say about him other than he was quieter than a mouse and easily as attractive as the other brothers? And I'd heard he was richer than the other two Ryder boys, combined.

His shoulders were slumped, his head downturned. If you didn't initiate conversation, Wyatt would stay to himself the whole night. A few months ago, I'd seen he was growing out a dark brown beard. Now, it was in full scruffy, lumberjack mode. It was pretty hot if you were into beards. Me? I preferred the good-looking, clean-cut types.

The brothers all had their separate, distinct characteristics. No doubt all gorgeous, but there was something deep and dark and hidden in Wyatt's soul. I had good people radar. And my radar read this man as someone who was still searching for who he wanted to be.

"Hey, Wyatt."

"Hey." He waved with his free hand while the other held a beer.

I followed his gaze to the ground. *What the hell is he staring at?*

"Have you been in town long?"

He nodded, his eyes focused anywhere but on mine. "Yeah."

"How long will you be staying?"

"For a little bit. I've started filming my documentary on

social situations." The corners of his lips tipped upward, and his eyes flickered toward me and then back to the ground.

"In Rosendell?"

Angie hadn't mentioned that Wyatt was in town long or that he was filming here. Wyatt had a bachelor's in fine arts with a concentration in film and cinema. Ironic, given the father he'd just met within the last few years, was the biggest media mogul in the nation.

"Yeah, it's nothing, really. Just in certain pockets of Rosendell. But I think it's going to be good." His smile widened. Whatever he was working on, he either enjoyed or believed in his project—or both.

"So, is this project for one of your dad's companies?"

His facial features dropped, the smile no longer on his face. "Yeah." He blew out an audible breath, and silence ticked on between us. "And just because we share the same blood, he's not my dad."

Noted. And awkward. "Yeah. I get that. Sorry."

I stared at him, noticing a scar I hadn't seen before at his temple. It was faint, but it was a scar, nonetheless. I wondered what building he'd jumped off, thinking he was Superman. I wondered what age he'd gotten that scar. And I wondered how I could change the subject and quick.

"You staying with Cade and Angie?"

"Yeah."

A man with only one-word answers.

And then the conversation was over, and I was done.

"Well, drink up, man. It's open bar." I slapped his shoulder, smirked, and then headed to meet the rest of the family —my father first, seated at the head of the table.

His jolly laughter had me smiling, and when he pulled me into his Santa Claus hug, I relaxed into him. The heart surgery that had happened a few months ago seemed to be successful, but he had retired permanently, and now, Angie and I were taking the reins of our multi-million-dollar real estate company—Armstrong Realty LLC.

He squeezed me harder, and my smile widened.

Where Angie was everyone's girl, I was Daddy's girl. He was the toughest on me, but only because he wanted me to succeed, as though he was always rooting for me, rooting for the underdog to win. That was why I'd made it my life-long mission to never, ever let him down. Tomorrow, I had to secure this deal and rent out the Wells property, which had been causing a bleed in our bottom line for too long.

When Dad released me, I turned to greet my mother.

"Tene." There it was—the flat, disparaging tone. Her way of letting me know I had just done something wrong, even though I'd only been in the room a few minutes.

"Mother," I uttered. My tone lacked its chipper mood. I scratched at my brow and fidgeted under her scrutiny.

She was still mad at me for breaking her dead mother's china last week at a formal family function. A single plate. *Did she care that it had been an accident? Did she care that I felt horrible? Did she care that I'd apologized left and right and up and down and in and out?* No. She never even liked Grandmother.

All she cared about was that I had done it, and she had someone to blame—me.

And I still had to hug her and pretend we had a perfect relationship because it would only upset my father if I didn't.

I leaned into her, and she pressed her cheek against mine, like the Europeans we weren't.

When she pulled back, she lifted an eyebrow, eyeing Jordan and Nana chatting it up. "So, is that the new man of the hour?" She adjusted her diamond stud earring and lifted her chin. "Isn't that Cade's brother?"

"I just walked in with him, Mom. I'm not dating him."

"You wouldn't want to ruin things between Angie and Cade, would you? Mess things up for them with another one of your flings?"

The ringing in my ears heightened, the sound of my blood buzzing behind my ears, something only associated with Mother dearest. I wished the noise could drown her out, but it never did.

"I'm not going to ruin anything Cade and Angie have." Tension rose to my shoulders and strained the veins in my neck. My hands clenched and unclenched, but my tone was utterly even. One quality that I'd inherited from her was self-control and the ability to master the poker face.

"That's good. Angie's promotional party was already ruined." She paused long and hard, staring at me as though it were my fault.

I rubbed at my temple and held back the colorful word on the tip of my tongue. Technically, Jordan had ruined the surprise.

She blamed me for practically everything—for the high-crime statistics, for the outcome of the election, for global warming. I could never get a break from this woman—ever. It wasn't like I'd done anything to her. I just refused to play by her rules, unlike perfect Angie. It didn't matter because everything I did would be criticized, along with every move I made and every breath I took. If there was a wrong way or right way to breathe, my mother would find fault in mine.

"And now, it's time for drinks." I pointed and headed to the bar, feeling her judgmental eyes on me the whole time.

I walked toward my sister and linked my arm through

hers, dragging us to our drinking destination. "Shots. Shots. Shots."

Cade was footing the bill, so the point of tonight would be to keep drinking and drinking to drown my mother's disappointing voice in my head.

CHAPTER 3

"OH, HELL," Tara, my sassy friend, spat out, draining the last of her beer.

I followed her line of sight to the door, and my stomach dropped and kept on going.

Of all the places that Logan could show up, it was at this restaurant on this night, where I couldn't escape.

"What's that asshole doing here?" She scowled in his direction. "Why couldn't he move to Mexico or to some remote island where we wouldn't have to see his face?"

God, did I love my friends. They always had my back.

"You sure you don't want me to stay?"

I shook my head. "No. It's fine. You told Emery you'd help her at JobOps."

Tara and Emery were my closest friends from college. But with life and jobs and family in the way, we hardly hung out anymore.

I pressed my cheek against Tara's. "Later, babe."

He strolled in, wearing his pressed dark slacks and signature favorite white polo shirt that I had bought him for Christmas.

Logan Price. The one. The only. The Ex.

The ex-boyfriend who had broken my heart but not "on purpose," as he'd said. Yeah, fucking right.

Camilla was on his arm.

Memories of heartbreak bombarded my brain. The breakup had once weakened me to a woman I didn't recognize. And it was all his fault.

I'd lost weight, lost my love of food, my love of laughter, my love of life. He'd done that to me with his betrayal. Grief and despair tore at my heart, and at times, taking my will to live. It had taken months to get over him, to get some semblance of normalcy back. Even now, I knew I'd never be the same after him. He'd taken a part of me—that innocent part of me that had hope; hope that believed in forever love.

Camilla stood right beside him—his first choice, the girl before and after me. And she merely stared, tongue-tied.

Camilla's blonde hair was tucked into a low ponytail, and her features screamed innocence, though she was anything but. She had known we were dating. The problem was, she'd wanted Logan back, and she'd won.

What I couldn't do on a night like tonight was lose composure, go psycho Tene, and cause a scene. Not on my baby sister's special night.

They both paused at the door and took everything in—from the balloons to the decor to the crazy-ass sign that my parents had made that said, *Congratulations*.

Maybe they'd leave. It wasn't a private event, but other patrons had left, knowing it wasn't a regular night at Allswell.

But Nana spotted them first and waved them over to my family's table. My mother stood to greet them, pressing her cheek against Logan's and shaking Camilla's hand.

My family thought we'd ended amicably. It seemed as

though my father knew better because he remained rooted in his seat, turned the other way, chatting it up with Wyatt.

I loved my daddy through and through.

My mother had loved Logan because she thought he was the perfect man to tame my wild self. When we had broken up, she had been relentless with the unending questions of *why—Why isn't he coming around anymore? Why are you broken up?*

The answer I never gave her was the truth. He didn't want me. I wasn't good enough.

"You going to drink the night away?"

The stark, familiar blue eyes raked over my face, and I shifted on the barstool, focusing my attention on something new—Jordan.

"There's nothing like having a good time." At times, I believed I got drunk on purpose for my mother to see. To be more defiant. Or maybe ... maybe it was to forget about her entirely.

"Baby, I'm all about a good time, but there's also something called alcohol poisoning."

His smile was actor beautiful—too good to be real, too impossible not to fall for. I bet he paid to have his teeth whitened daily.

My eyes teetered to the far end of the restaurant, where my family was chatting it up with The Ex, and I shrank into myself, not wanting to be seen.

"What's the sour face for?" Jordan raised his hand to the bartender to get another drink.

I tipped my chin to the left, and Jordan followed my line of sight to our families congregated at the other end of the restaurant.

"Who is that?"

"The Ex," I spat out like acid was at the back of my throat.

"And I take it you two didn't end well." Jordan eyed Logan across the room.

"Nope." I tipped back my beer, feeling the cold liquid hit the back of my throat. "That's his first girlfriend. Let's just say, she never got over him and begged him to come back—literally, on her knees."

He threw a few bills on the counter and grabbed his beer. "Literally?"

"Yes. I caught him with his pants down. Her on her knees." I laughed without humor.

"Ouch." Jordan flinched.

"It's fine. He was never over her. It was like he was only half in with me."

I should have trusted my gut. It'd started with innocent texts, her asking him if he still had her stuff. Their families were intertwined, and we'd see Camilla at family parties. I couldn't get over the way he looked at her, as though they weren't done.

"They're coming over here," Jordan said.

Nana pointed in my direction, and when our gazes met, Camilla and Logan waved.

And I waved back, clenching my teeth in a fake smile, my jaw locked.

"Why are they coming here?" I whispered under my breath. "I don't want to deal with this shit right now." I seethed, still smiling.

Logan approached, holding Camilla's hand within his, swinging their arms between them.

"Tene." Logan's smile wavered.

"Hey." *Oh, God. Not today. Please.* My hand fisted

around the cold beer bottle, and I willed it to cool the heat rising within me.

I didn't want to fake it in front of these people. I wanted to call Logan out for being the cheating bastard he was.

The last time we'd spoken six months ago was when I caught them in the most compromising position. I still had his toothbrush and his teddy bear that I had stolen from his bedroom, the one his grandmother had given him.

He'd asked for it back via text. I hadn't bothered replying.

"I had no idea there was a celebration here tonight." Logan's voice was low, nervous.

His eyes teetered between Jordan and me. I guessed he didn't recognize the star, given that Jordan's baseball cap was drawn low over his eyes.

"Yeah. It's a long time coming. Angie was ready for partner last year." My heart beat loudly against the chambers of my chest. I couldn't for the life of me stop picturing the last time I had seen him with her, like a bad porno playing over and over in my brain. The heat spread behind my eyes, rage brewing below the surface of my skin. I was so angry that I wanted to cry.

"Tene, the last time we saw each other—" he drawled out.

I lifted a hand, not wanting to relive the moment I could never forget—the moment he'd betrayed me. "You know what? That's water under the bridge." My voice shook, barely under control.

The gush of air that escaped his lungs was audible. "Thank God. I just wanted to explain—"

"No need to explain. I saw everything. Remember?" I stood and lifted the beer bottle. Taking it deep into my mouth, I tipped it back and released it with a pop, smiling blatantly at Camilla.

Her cheeks flushed red, almost as red as they had been when I walked in on them.

"Hey." Jordan slipped off the barstool and wrapped a warm hand around my hip, pulling me close.

My whole body was wired stiff, and I almost fell backward.

"I'm Jordan, by the way." He flipped his hat backward, showing off that beautiful, recognizable actor face.

What the ... I'd thought he was going incognito.

Logan blinked, and his mouth slipped ajar. He took in a sharp breath of utter astonishment.

"And you are?"

Logan and Camilla were stunned and tongue-tied. Camilla might as well have had emoji hearts in her eyes. Starstruck was an understatement.

My shoulders eased, and I relaxed against his lean, muscled frame. The scent of cigarettes and beer and a cologne that was all masculine filled my nostrils.

Goodness, I could kiss Jordan right now.

Logan had nothing on Jordan—not his height, his build, his good looks, or his millions of dollars. My insides soared.

Let them think what they want.

"Jordan ... Jordan Ryder?" Camilla asked, her voice shaky. Her trembling hand flew to her lips.

"In the flesh." His voice was cocky, confident in a way that oozed sex appeal.

I pictured him pounding his chest like a caveman.

Camilla's smile spread across her face, and she hopped on her toes, but Jordan's focus was on The Ex.

"I'm sorry. I didn't get your name." He took a step

forward and firmly shook Logan's hand. The veins in his forearms protruded.

"Logan." Logan motioned between Jordan and me. "So ... you two ..."

"I'm just using her for sex," Jordan said, which made me want to throat-punch him.

I angled away, and the look I gave him had him pulling me in closer. *Was that the only thing I could ever offer a man? Was that the first impression I always gave off?*

He peered down at me with a glint of teasing in his eyes. "I'm kidding." He nuzzled my neck, and his warm breath sent tingles down my back. "It's just the beginning, but I'm determined to know everything about her. I'm already impressed by her independence, smitten with her beauty, and entertained by her smart mouth."

I blinked.

Wow.

He was good.

No wonder this guy won awards.

If we were doing a scene on a set, he'd be totally believable.

He brushed my cheek with his thumb, and I sighed silently, melting into him because he was just that beautiful.

Our eyes locked for far too long until Logan cleared his throat.

"Yeah, it's good that she's found someone."

His words snapped me into the present.

I gritted my teeth and flipped back to face him. *Did he think I wouldn't?* "Nice seeing you, Logan." My voice was cold and lashing. I turned on my heels, dropped my hand into Jordan's, and stomped away.

I heard him calling after me, "Tene, I didn't mean it that way."

"One man's loss is another man's gain," Jordan yelled back. Then, he pinched my ass, and I slapped his hand away.

"Hey, Jordan, do you think we can get an autograph?" Camilla yelled above the noise.

My heels dug into the floor. I wanted to sink into the ground, disappear, drop from the earth. Better yet, I wanted to take off my stilettos and chuck them at Logan.

"So, I guess that would be a no to the autograph." Jordan chuckled. He hooked an arm around my neck and brought me closer.

"Don't even think about it," I grumbled. My feet led us back to the table where our families were congregated. "Let's just help Nana finish that bottle of wine."

———

An hour later and after a bottle of wine, we were at the bar. Logan Price was long gone and had been replaced by the *People*'s Sexiest Man Alive award recipient—Jordan Ryder.

Sigh.

If he was the last thing I looked at for the rest of my life, I'd die a happy woman.

My cheeks warmed, and I knew I needed to pace myself, or I'd complicate my life by sleeping with the male in front of me. And he was definitely off-limits.

Uncomplicated, detached, easy relationships. Especially after all I'd been through. That was all I could handle right now. And Jordan was choice D—none of the above.

"Aw, poor baby boy, who I can probably outdrink. Did you want me to order you a Cosmo or buy you a lemon drop shot? Let's live on the edge today, shall we?" I sassed.

He laughed, but in the next second, he leaned into me,

so close that I could smell his last cigarette. I needed one. A drag, but this time, from his mouth.

"I used to live my life on the edge. Haven't been there in a while, but ..." He licked his lips. "... I'm tempted to do it again." His eyes combed my body, dipping lower before making it back up my neck and landing on my lips.

He was flirting, definitely flirting. And I drank it all up. All of it—his attention, his firm hand on my hip, and his scent that I could bottle up and sell for thousands on the black market.

The air sizzled; unspoken words were shared between us. His gaze was beyond intimate, and I had to tear my eyes away for a second so I could breathe, formulate my next thought. I wondered if this was natural for him like he could never turn off this heat.

I got more than my share of looks from fine men, but it was usually the good-boy kind who were attracted to me. The ones I could tease and tame and train. Jordan seemed all bad boy and gorgeous—like my twin but in the male form —and that unnerved me.

The lull in the room was broken when "SexyBack" by Justin Timberlake burst through the speakers.

I placed my beer on the bar and stood. "Let's dance."

He smirked. That panty-dropping, party-stopping, pant-inducing smirk. "I don't think you can keep up."

Oh, boy. A challenge? Did this guy just throw a challenge in my face? Does he not know I was on the varsity poms squad in high school?

I flicked his shoulder. "You might just be a pretty face. Let's see if you can actually dance or if I prefer you just standing there mute."

His stare wavered between the dance floor and me.

"You know what? I wouldn't want to outdo every guy on that dance floor. Let's sit this one out."

"Um ... no." I grabbed his hand, ignored the electric fire that coursed through my veins at his touch, and pulled us through the crowd to the middle of the dance floor.

He wrapped one arm around my waist, pressed himself flush against my body, and then whispered in my ear, "Were you born on a farm?"

I reeled back, already smiling. "What?"

"Because you really know how to raise a cock."

I rolled my eyes and laughed. *Press release: Jordan is a certified dork.* "Don't tell me you use that on those models you date. I would've thought you had better lines."

"I usually don't have to think of lines to impress the ladies."

I wrapped my arms around his neck. "Does that mean you're trying to impress me?"

"Maybe."

The rhythm of the music blasted through the speakers. The pounding of the bass shook my feet, forcing me closer to Jordan. The strobe lights flashed around us, and I swiveled my hips, shaking my body to the music. The way his body was pushed up against mine was electric. Fire and heat coursed through me, through him, through both of us.

His eyes darkened, and when his hand made its way to my hip, I knew I, the devil temptress herself, had succeeded in drawing him in.

He stepped into me, our hips and our chests in sync with the bumping beats in the background. My breathing matched his. Slow, shallow, and seductive. He angled closer, his gaze making my heart and pulse and ears pound, sending a dizzying current through my body.

He dropped his mouth to my ear. "Damn, you're sexy."

"Not bad." I was talking about his line, not about how sexy I was.

A small smile touched my lips, and I turned around and slowly backed into him. With one hand pressed to my stomach, he pulled me against him, and I felt the hardness of his length thicken. I guessed I had been born on a farm.

A ball of sexual tension formed in my gut. It had been a long time since I had sex. If three months was a dry spell, I was experiencing a drought.

When his nose grazed my ear, my nipples pebbled against my halter top.

"You smell like fucking strawberries."

I angled my head, so he could hear. "You want a taste?" A lick to sample some of my sweetness. Because every part of me wanted to taste his lips, feel his tongue against mine.

Throwing away all self-control, I turned around and wrapped my arms around his neck. The sizzle between us, the electricity around us, was heightened by the closeness of our bodies and the warm breaths shared between us. His heavy-lidded eyes locked onto mine, and the world around me stood still.

Beautiful was an understatement. His blue eyes sparkled against the strobe lights flashing across the room. His face had been made to be on the big screen. His chiseled jaw and his kissable lips—the bottom lip fuller than the top, the bow shape on his upper lip, inviting women to kiss him. And that dimple on his chin, there as if to say, *My lips aren't enough; lick farther down.*

When he dropped his head, I lifted my chin in response to his silent question. Closer and closer, one more centimeter and our lips would finally and blissfully meet. My eyes fell shut, and I inhaled deeply and breathed him in before—

"Hey!"

Jordan jumped back at Cade's booming voice like he had been doused with a cold pail of water. The move was so abrupt that I nearly fell over and stumbled on my heels. Again.

If Cade was going for the scary factor, he was winning.

Cade's lips thinned, and his eyes narrowed, zoning in on Jordan. "Hey." The music was loud, but Cade was louder.

The crowd around us made room for him to pass as though he were Moses parting the Red Sea. Strobe lights worked the room, highlighting the planes on Cade's face, making his features seem mean and menacing.

"I know how to throw a good party, right?" Cade's voice heightened above the music, but there was no lightness in his features.

Jordan adjusted himself, his boner sticking out like a jumbo dog at the ballpark. "Yeah. Good party."

In the sea of dancing bodies, we were the only ones standing utterly still.

Angie trailed behind Cade, her face transparent, mouth downturned and pouty, just like when she had been younger and would throw a tantrum. Her silent hostility was aimed toward her boyfriend.

Cade's tone was light, but his eyes burned with annoyance, and the vein in his temple throbbed.

Jordan ran one hand through his light locks, fisting them at the top of his head. "You know what? I think I'm going to call it a night. I had a long day. Tired and all of that."

Angie's jaw tightened. "Don't be ridiculous. This is my party, and I say you stay and have fun. You guys go ahead." She motioned between us with her pointer finger, encouraging us.

We both blinked at her, unmoving, stoic—which only caused the frown on her face to deepen.

She shook her shoulders in what seemed to be a dance move. "Keep dancing, and don't mind Cade over here."

She tugged at his shirt, but Cade didn't budge, didn't move, didn't breathe. He simply stared at Jordan with a brewing hostility.

What was his problem? Did he want to kiss Jordan instead? Anyway, I thought I needed to get Cade a shot of Calm the Hell Down.

Angie's face scrunched up and hardened, her usual soft features vanishing. "I'm going to get another drink." And then she stormed away, unsteady in my heels. She'd break my shoe—or worse, break her ankle—the way she stomped the heels into the ground.

Cade cocked his head, and then he focused his attention on his retreating girlfriend. "Fucking A!" He threw Jordan one aggravated look and pointed a finger in his direction. "See, it's started already. We're having a chat later." Then, he stormed after my sister.

Okay ... that was weird.

Jordan pinched the bridge of his nose, dropped his head, and blew out a deep breath. Then, he moved to the side of the dance floor.

"What was that about?" I asked. My eyes bounced between Cade and my sister at the bar and then to Jordan.

"Your sister overheard Cade and me talking."

"And?"

"It was a warning."

"About?" I lifted an eyebrow.

"Rules, per se." He smiled and ducked his head, looking sheepish for once.

Aw, isn't he cute?

"Get on with it," I prodded, hands on my hips.

"His exact words were, 'You'd better not fuck Angie's sister, or I'll fuck up your face.' And I like my face. I've been told I have a good one. And this face ..." He pointed to said beautiful actor face. "... pays the bills." Jordan stared at the floor, avoiding eye contact. "It's more than that, but I'd rather not go into it." When his gaze met mine again, his tone turned serious. "I'm sorry about earlier. I shouldn't be flirting ... not with you."

I wanted to tell him that it was a little late for that, given I'd felt his boner pushing against his jeans.

Clearly, he intended to follow the rules, like a good brother. I tipped my chin up, refusing to show my disappointment because, clearly, there was an attraction here. Coloring within the friendly lines was probably for the best because we wouldn't want to complicate things by screwing.

"Well, if you're following the rules, we must do so while drinking. Otherwise, where's the fun in that?"

He tilted his head, assessing me. Then, after a beat, he tipped his chin toward the bar. "After you, my lady."

I grabbed his hand and tugged him toward the bar, where we downed more beverages.

And a-drinking we shall go.

Our drinking-fest was interrupted by a two-foot cake topped with sparklers as candles. The music died down, and Jordan and I moved closer to the center of the room, by our families. When the DJ gave Cade the microphone, he tapped it twice, and the crowd quieted to a hush. From

Cade's devastating grin and the way he gazed at my sister, I knew they had made up from their spat.

Part of me wondered if this was it … if this was the moment where he got on bended knee and proposed. *He'd have told me, wouldn't he? I mean, I'd have helped him pick out the ring, right?*

Jordan bumped his shoulder against mine. "Don't worry. He's not going to do it now. I know when and how."

My face scrunched. "And why don't I know?"

"Oh, you will. It's going to be a family event."

People crowded around, glasses in their hands, eyes intent on Cade.

"I just want to thank everyone here for coming. For Angie, she's all about celebrations. She makes it big and grand for everyone else. I don't know if you know this little tidbit about her, but she bakes each of her family members a cake on their birthdays." His eyes shone with pride, and a giddiness a man of his stature never usually showed pushed through. "And for once, I wanted to make this party just for her. Just because. I mean, it's a celebration for her promotion. But … really, a celebration of her."

He brought her in by her waist and angled her toward the sparklers lighting up the cake. The illumination highlighted the unshed tears in her eyes.

When he took her hand in his, my heart bubbled with happiness for my sister. Right now, at this moment, they were the epitome of true love. If I captured this on camera, it could be a cover on one of those romance novels.

"It's not your birthday or anything," Cade began, his eyes shining. "But I know you like to blow out candles."

Angie swiped at her eyes. Any moment, it'd be a full-out water fest because she could never help it.

"Blow out the candles, little sis!" I yelled above the crowd. "Wish for that big ring you want!"

Angie narrowed her eyes and pointed a finger my way. The crowd laughed, and I blew her a kiss.

The sly smirk on Cade's face widened. "It's not my birthday, or else I know what I'd ask for."

Her eyes flipped to his, and her smile dimmed. I knew they had talked about it before. Though they'd only been together for a short time, they were destined for one another, and they both knew that. Marriage was inevitable. And now, Jordan had confirmed that it was on Cade's radar. I'd have to ask him later about Cade's timeline.

"Go ahead," he urged.

She smiled up at him, and in typical Angie fashion, she clenched her eyes shut, just how she'd done when she was a little girl, and then she blew out the candles. The crowd clapped and hollered. Then, Cade tipped his tall frame and kissed her five-foot-two one. He picked her up and hugged her fiercely against his body, and I sighed out loud, practically gushing.

An intense longing surged within me, a longing for what they had, a longing for that forever type of love. But I knew deep in my gut that true love and a happily ever after was not in the cards for me.

Logan had taught me that. He'd never gotten over Camilla. I'd always been the second choice. The rebound girl when I'd thought I was *the one*.

It was as if I was always forced to play the understudy— second best in the family, second best in relationships.

I gritted my teeth.

Never again. I refused to be anything less than first.

My parents and Nana had left, leaving only the hard-core partiers.

After drinking for a few hours, Jordan and I were alone at the bar while Angie fell asleep in the booth in the far corner.

Cade approached us. "Hey, I'm about to take off in a minute. Kristy will be closing up tonight. Lightweight Angie over there had a little too much fun." He peered behind him at his sleeping, drunk girlfriend, who was sprawled out on the leather booth on her stomach—legs and arms hanging over the sides.

"You heading out soon?" His question was meant for Jordan, not me. Cade's words formed a question but sounded more like an order from the deep set of his tone.

"Yeah, going straight to my hotel." Jordan tipped his beer toward his brother in some sort of agreement.

After a nod of his head, Cade pulled me in and kissed the top of my forehead like I was five. "Stay away from this guy, okay?"

"You should be warning him instead of me." I winked. "Take care of my baby girl."

"Always." His voice softened into a tenderness that was so familiar every time he talked about Angie.

I watched Cade stroll over to the booth. He paused before touching her face, hovering over her for a few seconds before lifting her in his arms.

"He has it bad," Jordan said behind me.

"Yeah, but she has it worse." My heart dipped a little, that same longing swelling in my chest.

"I'm happy for him," Jordan added. "He deserves it."

"She does too." I turned to Jordan, a smile heavy on my face. "So, let's continue this party, shall we? But let's get out of here."

CHAPTER 4

I KNEW I had to get up at the crack of dawn tomorrow because I had a meeting with one of the top investors in the nation—Geovani Tolintino. He could essentially end the bleed of our company if he agreed to sign a lease and rent out our property.

But the haze of the liquor and the handsome male in front of me caused a detour in my plans for an early night.

I'll get up on time.

It wasn't like I hadn't done it before—partied before a very important meeting. All I would need was an extra shot of expresso in my coffee to start tomorrow, and I'd be fine.

I walked out of the bar, arm linked through Jordan's. "We're taking this party to the next bar."

Two cars whizzed by, and a few patrons strolled out, leaving Allswell.

Jordan wasn't nearly as toasted as I was. My body was warm from the liquor, and I had a good buzz going.

He eyed me, the beginning of a smile tipping up the corner of his mouth. "I don't think that's a good idea.

Staying low-key, remember?" He lowered his baseball cap for emphasis.

I rolled my eyes. "I told you, you're not that famous; trust me." I unwound my arm from his and linked our fingers together, dragging him down the street to Clive's Bar. "I think we should test my theory."

"I don't know about that." He tipped his chin to the wrestler-looking guy trailing us, his bodyguard. "I want to keep Dex's night uneventful."

My face scrunched, showcasing how unamused I was. *Did the brick wall follow him everywhere?* I threw dirty looks his way, and he maintained his composure and distance behind us.

"New plan." I sprinted down the street, dragging Jordan behind me. I didn't get very far as he walked at his normally slow pace and weighed a ton. I felt like I was dragging him.

"Fine." I dropped my hand. My feet clicked against the concrete, the wind blowing past my hair and face and bare arms. I ran as fast as I could in my four-inch heels. I was a pro at that; nothing slowed me down.

I heard him yell my name behind me, but my arms pumped, matching the pace of my feet, racing toward who knew what.

"Christene, come on," he snapped.

I was smiling so hard, my cheeks hurt.

"Tene!"

When I turned around to see if Jordan was gaining speed, my body knocked into someone, causing me to teeter on my heels.

The burly male, who was three times the width of me, steadied me with his thick hands, one wrapped around my center, the other by my ass.

"Hey." I schooled my features, lifted my chin, and tried to jerk away, but his hold wouldn't relent.

"They said love would hit me right in the face." The man's breath stank of hard liquor and cigarettes.

Both of my hands pushed at his chest, but before I had a chance to snap some sharp remark, Jordan's voice echoed behind me.

"Kindly step away from my girl." He used the word *kindly*, but the deep set of his tone was anything but meek.

When Dex turned the corner and approached Jordan's side, the burly man gently placed me on my feet.

"Someone might steal this one away from you. Better watch her more carefully."

"I plan on it." Jordan stepped into me, wrapping an arm around my waist, bringing me into him.

When the man was out of view, Jordan turned to face me.

The moonlight highlighted his beautiful face, the sharp lines of his masculine jaw, and the ocean blue in his irises. And he wasn't a happy camper. "Are you trouble in a beautiful, brunette package? Because it seems as though trouble follows you everywhere you go."

I raised a finger. "I would have gotten out of that situation if you weren't here. Don't worry." *Trouble? Where did he get that?* I used to welcome excitement in the form of drama in my younger years, not so much now. "And I'd like to say, I kept tonight pretty tame. Remember Logan? I maintained my composure and was pretty proud of myself. I wanted to kick him in his balls so hard that he and Camilla wouldn't be able to procreate." I smiled.

"Yeah, given what you told me, I'm quite impressed by your ability to keep it together."

"If I didn't love my sister as much as I do, I would have

caused a scene worthy of one of your movies." I pushed a finger into his chest. "Me, trouble? I think I'm looking at trouble with a capital T. I saw that bar brawl you caused on *TMZ*."

"Yeah, that." He scratched at his temple. "Let's just say, I don't like people messing with my family."

"I guess we're built the same then."

"Must be." He brushed a strand of hair away from my forehead and tucked it behind my ear, leaning closer, so close that I got a whiff of his masculine cologne.

My eyes flickered to his lips—his delectable, kissable lips. But I couldn't, I shouldn't, and I wouldn't.

"We've established we're both trouble." I laughed. "Okay, where are we heading next?"

"To cause double the trouble since we're trouble squared."

And I led us to our next drinking destination.

CHAPTER 5

THE CARS BLURRED PAST US, and the sounds of horns honking, sirens blaring, and drunk people laughing on the street filled my ears as I led us toward Clive's Bar, which was quite the walk down the street. Jordan and I, we stayed completely silent, our buzz slowly wearing off. When I looked behind us, Dex had disappeared.

"So. Logan ..." he began.

This was the last topic I wanted to revisit.

"Thank you, by the way. For back there. At Angie's party." A nervous laugh escaped me, and I fidgeted with the end of my shirt. "Did you see Logan's face? Or better yet, how about hers?" I bumped my shoulder against his, trying to diminish my uneasiness. My smile dimmed a little, and I focused on the crowd forming a line in front of Clive's Bar.

When I'd been with Logan, we'd had sex all the time. Our relationship had not lacked passion, but maybe he thought that was all I was good for. A sudden chill came over me, and I wrapped my arms around my middle.

"Screw him and Camilla," I blurted under my breath.

I needed a drink—bad.

"I asked about you," he said, breaking me from my thoughts.

"What?"

The overhead lamppost shone above us, highlighting his five o'clock shadow.

"After that first time we met." He stuffed his hands in his pockets as we both shuffled down the street to the line forming in front of us. "I thought you were funny—not to mention, extremely hot," he said with a sly smile. "So, when you went home, I asked Cade about you, and he basically shut me down."

"Oh." My normal flirty response got stuck in my throat. "I never did thank you that night, for lending us your jet and arranging everything so we could get home."

Months ago, my father had needed emergency surgery, and Jordan had gone out of his way to lend Angie and me his jet to fly us home. He had also organized transportation when we landed.

"It was nothing," he said with a slight smile.

I stopped to face him in the middle of the sidewalk, people moving past us because his comment couldn't have been further from the truth. "It was everything." My voice was soft but powerful.

His kind gesture had meant everything. Truly.

Angie and I had been on such high alert after our father's heart attack that when the doctors found out there was another blockage, we couldn't function. We'd been hours away from home, and Jordan had saved the day by speeding up our arrival.

His gaze unfocused, he stared at the line in front of us. "Even though I don't know my real parents, Cade, Wyatt, and my adoptive mom are everything I have. Family is important. I know this as much as anyone." He turned to face me and pinched the bottom of my chin. "And I love that you're close with your family." He paused and then quirked an eyebrow. "But what is up with you and your mother?"

Another topic I didn't want to visit. I cringed inwardly. "Nothing. Why?" The thought of talking about my mother tempted me to ask Jordan for another cigarette.

He smiled, and the dimple in his chin appeared. "If there had been any more tension in that room between you two, it would have started World War Three."

"You're exaggerating."

"Does that mean you're not elaborating?" He lifted a curious eyebrow, but I wasn't about to elaborate on my mother's and my dysfunctional relationship.

"Yep." I flicked his side.

"So, your mother and Logan are non-discussable?"

I smiled and rolled my eyes. "That's not even a word."

He shook his head. "Evasion. Okay, note made. I guess I'm getting nothing."

My hand found his again. "Nope, that's where you're wrong. You are getting something. Another round of drinks from *moi*." And I pulled us to our drinking destination— Clive's Bar.

CHAPTER 6

DRINK AFTER DRINK and laugh after laugh, we kept pounding the beers back. Minutes and then hours ticked by, and my body buzzed from the liquor that coursed through me. We talked about our love of music and our favorite shows. Actresses and actors who were hard to work with and those who were nicer than they seemed online. I wished I had a recorder, so I could replay our convo for Nana because I knew she'd be interested in the Hollywood gossip.

Soon, my words slowed, my vision blurred, and, yeah, conversing was harder to do.

"You're drunk, and you're not driving home." Jordan's voice rang in my head as my eyes fell shut.

We were outside now. The brisk air brushed against my bare skin, but my body temperature was elevated from one too many drinks.

My arm was slung around his neck. His arms were wrapped around my waist, but he shifted his stance.

Me, drunk? That was funny. He wasn't in much better shape.

"Where do you live? I'll take you home."

"Oh, soo," I slurred, "you're going to take me home now. After all you said about Cade making me off-limits and your conviction to listen to him." I leaned into him, pushing my chest against his side. "I'd love for you to break the rules and take me home." My voice was seductively low, all inhibitions gone.

Jordan sighed, hesitating.

He smelled good. Really good. Like all-man, sex-god good.

I wrapped my other hand around the back of his head and dropped my head in the crook of his neck. "Am I not up to par with all the models you're used to dating? You're bruising my ego here."

"Fuck, Tene. We can't." His voice sounded low and tortured. His breathing hitched. "He said I'm not ready." His voice was whisper soft, and my mind was so mushy that I didn't question what that exactly meant. His hands wrapped tighter around me, and the heat of our bodies pressed against each other. "We just can't. I promised." The ache in his voice was evident, no doubt mirroring the ache in his blue balls from earlier.

I brushed my nose against his. "I promise I won't tell," I said, my voice husky. My rule about no complications flew out the door in my uninhibited state.

"Christene ... " his voice pleaded with me, "... don't start something I can't finish."

He turned and led us to the SUV at the end of the block. I was vaguely aware of Dex walking behind us. When we got to the car, Jordan pushed me against the side, steadying me next to him so he could open the door. His whole body was pressed beside mine, his hard flesh against my softness.

I peered up. The blue in his eyes was highlighted by the moon shining down on us. They flashed to my lips.

"We just ... we can't." He opened the door and glided me in.

Somehow, the more he said no, the more I wanted him.

His driver shut us in, and his bodyguard hopped into the front of the car.

"What's your address?" Jordan asked.

I pinched my fingers together by my lips in a lock-it-up motion and giggled.

"Christene ..."

When more laughter escaped me, he motioned to his driver. "Take us to the hotel." He reached for my purse, grabbed the keys inside, and tossed it to Dex. "Bring her car to the hotel."

"Mmm." I ran one red-painted fingertip down his chest. "So, you've had a change of heart."

"No, I just think you need to sleep it off and sober up."

"I'll sober up faster with drunk sex."

When I slipped my hand underneath his shirt, he stiffened. In the next beat, he grabbed my wrist, held it between us, and slid a few inches away.

Damn this man and his self-control, but the thing about Christene Armstrong was that she loved a challenge. Especially when it came in a hot and handsome, blond-haired, blue-eyed, alpha actor package.

We entered through a tunnel, and darkness surrounded us. We were in the garage of the hotel, some sort of back entrance. Before I knew it, Jordan's bodyguard was escorting us inside an elevator and into the penthouse suite. He held us back before we entered and did a full sweep of the room.

When the door shut behind us, I kicked off my shoes

and admired the Presidential Suite of the Rosendell Grand Hotel. Floor-to-ceiling windows walled one side of the room, which overlooked my breathtaking city. I walked to the window and pressed my nose against the glass.

"I think I can see my apartment from here. And Callie's Coffee Shop, and there's Allswell ..."

I always knew that my small town was beautiful. But from this view, from the little twinkle of lights from the neighboring building that I recognized, it was breathtaking.

"I love Rosendell." Words spoken out loud and mostly to myself.

"Me too," Jordan replied, a water bottle in hand. "It's this quaint town with little pockets of character everywhere. It's no wonder Cade made this his permanent location." The way he leaned against the bar, ankles crossed, and hair untamed with that water in his hand, it was as if he'd stepped into a commercial selling water. All he needed was his shirt off and maybe to pour the water over his head, shaking the droplets from his hair.

Commercial?

Yeah, right. What I was picturing was more of a porno.

I strolled to the couch, tucked my feet under my bottom, and fell to the cushions, patting a spot on the couch.

His mouth curled as if on the edge of laughter.

My eyes were tired, my body was tired, but my mind and libido were wide awake.

He strolled back toward me, unsteady in his swagger, and handed me bottled water. "Drink this."

I tipped back the bottle to take a sip, and it dribbled down my tank top, spilling on my pants. I placed the bottle on the center table and smiled up at him.

He groaned, walking toward the bar. "Just sit still." Jordan came back with some paper towels and dabbed at my mouth and down my chest. His profile was strong and rigid and painfully beautiful. "Can you please just stay still?"

"Bossy pants, aren't we?" I laughed. "And why is it so cold in here?" I threw my legs to the floor and rubbed my hands over my arms to warm myself.

My stomach flipped from the abrupt movement. Confirmation: I'd had too much to drink. Oddly enough, I could usually throw the liquor back.

"Because you spilled water everywhere." He rubbed at his temple, his eyes glazing over. "Now, please drink this."

He reached for the bottled water on the table and placed it to my lips. Honestly, he didn't look like he had it all together either. He wanted me to sober up, yet he needed some sobering up too.

"Are you this bossy in bed?" Up close, I could lick the shadow of stubble forming on his jaw. *Damn, he was good-looking.* "Because I think I'd like that better."

"You're worse than me," he huffed under his breath and placed the water bottle on his side table, dropping on the couch in a big thud.

"I can't believe you're not even trying," I complained.

My ego was badly bruised. I wasn't sure why I was surprised. He wasn't without lots of propositions. Ladies probably dropped their panties on the daily for him. But I wasn't used to someone being immune to my charm. It made me want to work harder, flirt more, turn up the attraction volume. That was how I ticked, how I worked. If there was a challenge, I stepped up and womanned up. And I wanted to climb the Jordan Ryder mountain. That was the next challenge on my list.

"You're such a loyal brother. Loyalty is the sexiest trait there is." My finger caressed the line of his neck by the collar of his shirt.

He side-eyed me and laughed, inching away toward the edge of the couch. I watched him with sleepy eyes as he twisted the cap of the water bottle, brought it to his lips, and downed the water in three long, satisfying pulls.

"I think I'm officially wasted."

A giggle bubbled from my mouth. I stood on unsteady legs and walked to where my purse was at the end of the hall, by my shoes. "The best way to sober up is to ..."

"Yeah. Not going to happen," he stated.

I reached in my purse and shook my head. "I'm not reaching for a condom, crazy man. The best way to sober up is to play cards."

I pulled out a deck, held together by my black hair tie.

"Cards?" He tilted his head, and that little cute dimple made an appearance.

"Yes, cards. Gin." I plopped down beside him, divided the pile of cards, and shuffled.

When he groaned again, I pinched his side and got nothing. Man, did I want to see his stomach, his abs.

"Come on, Jordan. It's either play cards or my first option for how to get sober." I wiggled my eyebrows in a suggestive motion and held out his portion of the cards.

After reaching for them, he fanned them out, smiling. "You should really practice your poker face."

After a bit, I leaned back against the plush leather couch, resting my head against the comfy cushions.

"I don't know why I need a poker face when I'm going to win." I sighed.

"Long day?" he asked.

"Very long." Every day seemed to drag on longer and longer. No wonder I was exhausted.

"Do you want to tell me about it?" He reached for

another card, and I smirked. "Does it have anything to do with your mother?"

I wrinkled my nose. "Nice try. And don't distract me with your mindless small talk. I'm going to win."

He laughed.

"It's other things too." My fingers rustled at the soft silk of my top. "Before the surprise party, I had a prospective tenant for this restaurant I've been trying to rent. The Wells property." I reached for another card and placed it on my stack.

"Restaurant?" His turn now.

"Yeah, I'd forced our company to buy it."

I'd sworn to my father it was in the new up-and-coming area and that we needed to jump on the property. I should have known it wouldn't rent out when there was no one else bidding on it. I had known the history of the location but thought that wouldn't stop people from renting it.

"Cade did mention you guys were in real estate."

"Mmhmm." Man, was I going to win this game. One more card, and I'd have gin.

"We're investors too," he said, "but Wyatt and I are just on the financial end. Cade makes all the acquisitions for new restaurants. Anyway, did they sign on to rent the restaurant?"

"No." I bit my pinkie nail, waiting for him to put down his cards.

"Why not?" He stalled.

"Because they're stupid. It's your turn."

He laughed, a deep rumble in his chest that vibrated against me.

"Why didn't they sign?" he asked again.

"It's crazy talk, really." I tipped my chin toward the cards in between us on the couch. "Your turn."

"Is it haunted or something?"

I peered up at him and tilted my head, assessing him. "Did you hear about the Wells property?"

News had spread through every media outlet when it'd happened.

He shook his head.

"Murder. Twenty years ago. Michael and Michelle Wells. And people still swear their ghosts haunt the property."

He made a comical face. "Bullshit. What happened?"

"A wife and husband owned the restaurant. When the wife found out the husband was pounding more than meat in the kitchen after hours, she got her revenge."

"So, now, all of a sudden, it's haunted? Pfft."

"I know, right?" I didn't believe in that stuff, but it didn't matter because the majority of Rosendell did, and now, I couldn't rent the restaurant out even with a *first month free* incentive. "Business blows. I'm always on the go—acquiring, maintaining, and renting out facilities. The more we grow, the harder it is. And this property ..." I blew my bangs from my face. " ...it's only slowing me down." I placed my cards on my lap, thinking of the early morning meeting that I had tomorrow. The responsible adult in me should call an Uber, head home, and get in bed, so I could wake up bright and early tomorrow morning.

"It's like you're living my life."

"How so?"

"The *always on the go* life. Always filming or on a press tour. I'll be in Hawaii for a few months to film my next movie."

He was complaining about Hawaii?

I narrowed my eyes. "What? You don't like the life of the rich and famous? Where bodyguards open your doors, people fall at your feet, you can attend every high-profile function, you have an assistant to shop for you and get your food, and you don't lift a single finger?"

"You didn't mention the fact that I work for this." He flicked at my nose. "Acting is work."

I pretended to bite his finger. "Well, yeah, there's that."

"I'm always wondering when the high will be over. And I want to get more gigs, win more awards, but the more I want, and the more my life surpasses my expectations, the higher the bar is raised."

I got that. I functioned the same way—trying to beat last year's profits, trying to always stay ahead of the real estate curve.

"Gin." He placed his cards down and smiled victoriously.

That blows. I scrunched my face. "Ugh. I'll have you know, I'm not a gracious loser." I stood and dug my feet into the plush carpet. "Well, now, I need another drink."

"I thought we were sobering up." He scratched at his temple.

"Change of plans. We're going to play another game." This time, I was determined to win.

CHAPTER 7

WARMTH.

Pure warmth encased my body. I was floating against soft one-thousand-thread-count Egyptian sheets, sheets that I'd only slept on. Though my eyes were closed, my body moved against the soft-as-satin sheets, enjoying how every single inch of me was fully relaxed. Every muscle felt as though it had just experienced a two-hour massage.

I'd had the best dream ever, one where I'd had the greatest steak dinner and wonderful conversation with the perfect man, ending in multiple orgasms that lasted forever and ever until my body was limp with satisfaction.

I writhed against the sheets. Warm hands wrapped around my belly, a body spooning me from behind. Spooning ...

Spooning felt like heaven.

Spooning was only for intimate, serious relationships.

Spooning only happened in my dreams, in complete unconsciousness.

I sighed, but when a man's long sigh echoed behind my

ear, I was instantly wide awake. I flipped around and found a familiar pair of blue eyes staring back at me. Surprise seemed to hit us both at the same time. My eyes went wide, and my mouth dropped open. I tugged the sheet to cover my body as he tugged the same sheet toward himself.

"Shit," I screeched.

"Fuck," he muttered at the same time.

He lost the tug-of-war.

I yanked the sheet toward me, revealing him almost naked and at full salute with morning wood. He covered his package with both hands while I wrapped the sheet against my body, noting that I still had my bra and underwear on. *Thank goodness.* All he wore was one sock.

His entire upper body was a mural of tattoos. A dragon and Chinese characters made up most of the art on his chest and upper arms. Sexy as hell.

"Nothing happened," I stated.

I doubted it had since I was fully clothed, but shit, where the hell is the rest of my clothing? And why did he only have one sock on? My head pounded with a dulling pain, and I rubbed at my temple.

It wasn't like I'd never had a one-night stand before, but I would like to remember if it had been with *the* Jordan Ryder.

With one hand, he gripped the top of his hair, squinting against the light shining through the window. "No, 'cause I'd remember." He scratched the top of his head, and his eyebrows furrowed. "I do remember bringing you in here, so we would be more comfortable, but I don't know why I only have a sock on."

I nodded and bit my lower lip, debating my next move. *Run? Hide? Escape? All of the above?*

"Why am I only in my underwear and bra?" I slapped my head as memories of the night filtered through like clips from a movie—playing gin, making drinks, and then, of course ... strip poker.

Well, considering he had one piece of clothing on—his sock—and I had two, I'd won.

"Strip poker," he confirmed, no doubt reliving the same scenes in his head.

I slowed my breaths, though my heart raced, and my pulse thrummed hard on the inside of my wrists.

I wasn't surprised that I was in a hotel room. What shocked the shit out of me was that I had fallen asleep in his room, in his bed, and in his arms. And we hadn't had sex. Worst of all? We had been freaking spooning.

Spooning!

What in the ever-loving shit is going on? That never happened. Ever. Not in my lifetime, at least. Not since ... the man I no longer thought of.

We blinked a couple of times, and I cocked an eyebrow.

"I'm not used to sleepovers." He double-blinked. "So ... yeah." He almost sounded as though he was in denial.

We were built the same after all.

He tipped his chin. "Hey, I'm getting a little cold here. Can you throw me the sheet from the floor?"

My eyes scanned the room. The pillows were neatly stacked against the bed, but the covers were scattered on the floor. It was how I woke up every morning—by myself—with the covers littered everywhere. I move around like crazy when I'm sleeping.

I really should be in the hospital right now with the amount of alcohol I'd had last night. One drink. Too many drinks. The card game. The laughter that had lasted for hours, our deep conversations I vaguely remembered, and the sweet touches ... the way my heart had pitter-pattered against his chest right before he went in for that kiss on my forehead that seemed to last forever.

And then we had fallen asleep together.

He gave me a look of impatience. "I know I'm one glorious specimen to look at, but I'm hard as a rock right now. Morning wood and all. So ... unless you're going to get naked, too, can you please throw me that sheet on the floor?"

Crap. What time is it? I glanced at my watch on my wrist, and my heartbeat doubled in speed. *Wells property meeting. Shit.*

My shaky hands quickly picked up my pants and my silk top. I slipped into my clothing under the sheets and chucked the other sheet toward him.

I grabbed my purse from the ground, pivoted, ready to leave, but the look on his face stopped me.

He flushed a deeper shade, and then he pulled the blanket over his knees, covering himself to mid-chest.

"So ... yeah ..." I searched through my purse and pulled out my keys. "Like I was saying, I really had a great time last night. Thanks for everything." It sounded as though we had done the deed, and I was taking the walk of shame.

I stifled a laugh in my throat as he pulled the sheet closer to his neck.

"Uh ... yeah, me, too?" He didn't sound too sure.

For once, Jordan Ryder seemed to be at a loss for words, but I was too discombobulated and ready to run to contemplate it further.

I inched backward toward the door, and my legs shook as I waved at him.

A wave? Really? Were we in high school again?

"So, I'll call you, yeah?" I said, knowing I wouldn't.

He pulled the sheet closer to his chin now. "Yeah ... call me?" His voice cracked puberty-style, and then he furrowed his brow. "You have my number, right?"

I laughed nervously. "Yeah, sure, I have your number." Another wave.

I did not have his number. *Could it get any weirder?*

Good God, I need to leave.

"Christene?"

"Yeah?" My hand was on the doorknob.

"Your pants."

I glanced down and noticed that my white pants were inside out, and my shirt was backward. This man had thrown me for a loop. I didn't know which way was up or down or left or right. "It's the style. They're supposed to be like this."

He gave me a doubtful look but didn't reply.

"Okay, bye." Another awkward wave.

Right before I turned, I heard him ask, "You're going to call me, right?"

"Yeah, yeah. Sure." Then, I slammed the door and raced down the hall. My brow, my breasts, and the back of my neck were damp from sweat.

I punched the down button on the elevator and stole glances toward his door.

Punch.

Punch.

Punch.

Dang it. Open. Open. Open.

My foot tapped frantically against the floor as I hoped and prayed that the doors would open.

One thing I knew for sure: there was no way I was going to call him even though he was *the* Jordan Ryder, Academy Award winner and *People* magazine's Sexiest Man Alive.

I needed to put this behind me and pretend we hadn't crossed the spooning line.

CHAPTER 8

AT THIS RATE, there was no time to go home to change and still make it in time.

When the elevator pinged open, I rushed into the crowd of people standing inside. *Just my luck.* Internally, I groaned.

They had to scoot a little to make room. Everyone gaped at my attire. The older, retired-looking couple, the young twin girls and their parents, three bachelors with a set of golf clubs ready for the range—all of them stared.

The lining from my pants was on the outside, and the tag was evidently displayed, as my shirt was too short to cover it. I'd have been staring too.

I threw on a relaxed smile through the longest ride down, even as the elevator stopped and let people out and in on every floor.

Through the lobby, I walked at a leisurely pace as though I were walking the catwalk in Paris. My hair was a mess, my shirt was wrinkled, and, yes, my pants were on inside out.

A group of older women passed by, whispering among

each other. As the bellboy opened the door for me, I sensed his eyes watching the curvature of my ass as I strolled past him and pressed the unlock button of my apple-red BMW M3 convertible.

Fast was her first name; Furious was her last. She was fast and furious, just like I loved to live my life.

As soon as I shut the door to my car, I let out a low, jagged breath, and my body went on high alert.

Destination: Wells property. Time of arrival: ten minutes too late. Damn it. I needed this tenant like I needed coffee in the morning, but the coffee had to wait. This tenant could not.

I pressed the pedal to the metal and headed to my destination.

At a stoplight, I looked into the visor mirror and wiped the black eyeliner from my eyes. It looked like someone had punched me in one eye, and because they hadn't wanted to leave out the other eye, they'd punched that one too. Sunglasses would have to do, for now, so I put them on.

It was days like this. I thanked the heavens for my high cheekbones and unnaturally pink lips, looking as though I were wearing a sheen of lip gloss. If there was one thing that God had graced me with, it was a beautiful facade—a curse and a blessing all at once.

I pretty much got everything I wanted with one look and my ability to sweet-talk my way through anything in life. But on the other hand, everyone thought that since I was a looker, I had no brains.

I'd graduated and earned my MBA at Wharton School and was heir to the biggest real estate company in Rosendell. When I'd first started working for my father, I'd had to prove to everyone that I was capable of handling my father's day-to-day business. Slowly, I had proven my worth.

If I were a man, there was no doubt I'd have been treated differently.

Screw the people who thought there was nothing on top, and I used everything on the bottom to get what I wanted.

My phone buzzed in my purse, and I perked up. I glanced inside, hoping to see Jordan's number but also terrified at the same time.

My mind was indecisive, and it bothered me because I was the most decisive person on the planet. I didn't know if I should be happy if it was him or crazy scared that he was calling me so soon.

When Angie's face popped up on the screen, my shoulders dropped, and a tinge of disappointment coursed through me.

There goes that.

Goodness, Jordan had screwed up my brain in more ways than one, and nothing physical had even happened between us.

I picked up on the third ring, sending the call to my car's Bluetooth.

"Hey." Angie's voice came through my car speakers. "What time are you meeting the Tolintino clients? You're showing them the Wells property?"

"Yeah. Meeting them soon."

Angie didn't need to know I was already late to one of the most important meetings this year.

"I'm fully booked this morning too. I need to check on a few clients and get over to the Carina property. They're going to sign the lease later on today."

"Angie, that's amazing." *Man, if I could only have the same luck.*

"You're coming over to check out my curtains, right?"

"I'll be there right after."

My sister was obsessed with home decor, ever since she'd moved in with Cade.

"Did you get home okay last night?" Her tone was soft, cautious, as though she were dipping her toe in water, testing the warmth. This was where all the small talk had been headed.

"Yeah. Why?" I tried to tame my voice, though my pulse raced, drumming against the inside of my wrists.

Jordan and Cade were brothers. I had to remember that. And Cade was not too keen on our friendship.

"Didn't someone take you home?" Her tone sounded suspicious. Look at that; her foot was now completely submerged in the water. "Did you leave with Jordan?" she asked. And now, she had jumped in, headfirst.

I laughed over the phone. Angie was my sister, but we couldn't be more opposite. I would've asked the question straight out.

"He did. But don't worry. You can tell Cade that nothing happened. I was just over there late."

"Like, late, *late*?"

"Angie, if you're asking if I slept with the infamous Jordan Ryder, then the answer is no."

"You didn't?" Her tone increased with incredulity as though the thought were impossible. "What did you do then?"

I shifted in my seat, stopping at the next light. What came out of my mouth sounded impossible. "We talked, played cards, and fell asleep." *And flipping spooned.* Somehow, that was more intimate than getting naked, rolling around in the sheets, and playing Poke-a-Girl-Go.

"Now, I totally don't believe you."

"I'm a little offended here." If she wasn't my sister, I

would have hung up on her. "You should believe me because Jordan is hella scared of your boyfriend. I would be too. I've seen Cade angry."

She huffed loudly, her tone sharp. "Honestly, Jordan deserves a good girl, and I just told Cade to let things be."

"Me, a good girl?" Sarcasm leaked heavily in my voice.

I slammed my horn. People really needed to learn how to drive. And I needed to get to the Wells property fifteen minutes ago.

"Yes, despite your crazy lifestyle choices, in your heart, you're the best girl I know."

I gulped. That wasn't what my mother would say. To my mother, I walked on fire with a pitchfork next to Satan himself.

"After all Jordan's been through, he deserves happiness. It's been forever since he's dated anyone seriously. Years even."

I laughed. "So not true. He just had Jezebel what's-her-face on his arm last month."

Victoria's Secret models all started to blend together. I'd seen their picture together on a tabloid in the grocery store checkout not too long ago.

"I'm talking a serious relationship," she said. "His last serious girlfriend was Candice, and that was years ago."

Curiosity pushed to the surface.

Angie's voice quieted to a hush. "I didn't tell you because it wasn't my business, and ... it's a sensitive subject."

"I have Google-stalked him, but not everything can be found on Wikipedia." I flicked on my turn signal and turned right onto the highway.

"Candice was Cade's biological sister."

"I already knew that."

The beginning of traffic began to form in front of me. *Could my luck get any worse?*

"Cade's sister was killed in a car accident, remember?" Angie's voice was somber. "Well, Jordan's last serious relationship was with her."

I blinked. A heavy feeling in my stomach settled, and a sudden coldness hit me. I pulled over to the side as cars whizzed past me.

"Tene?"

Why hadn't I connected the dots earlier?

Candice.

I had known he'd dated Cade's sister when I met him.

"Tene!"

"Yeah?" I said, distracted and not feeling so well.

"Are you okay?"

"Yeah." *No.*

I guessed as carefree as Jordan seemed to be, his life had been plagued by tragedy.

I pulled into a spot in front of Wells, and my car screeched to a stop. In front of our property stood Geovani Tolintino, heir to one of the nation's largest coffee chains. Tolintino's famous coffee combined chocolate and high-end coffee to rival's Starbucks' white chocolate mocha. And I needed them to rent this spot and essentially entice bigger tenants and bring in more clientele, but, more importantly, to stop the bleed in our company. Since we'd bought it six long months ago, the property has been vacant.

I grabbed my purse, slipped on my overly large sunglasses, and scurried out the car door.

Seventeen minutes late. That was a first. I'd never been late before.

I lifted my chin, smiled, and walked at a normal pace to where Geovani stood six feet tall, sporting his cowboy hat with its tall crown and wide, flat brim.

A redhead in a fitted black minidress stood beside him. It looked like she was ready for a party. This wasn't Mrs. Tolintino or the second Mrs. Tolintino.

And I should know. I had a twenty-page report on Geovani at my office. I even knew how he liked his steak—medium with a little pink on the inside—which I planned on ordering for him over lunch to sign the papers for him to lease Wells.

I stuck out my hand first and tipped up my chin. "Christene Armstrong. You must be Mr. Tolintino."

A faint sense of nausea hit me directly in the gut. I didn't know if it was the liquor from last night, the fact that I hadn't eaten breakfast, or nervousness because I needed this win so badly.

His lips pressed in a fine line. He paused a bit, eyed my hand, and shook it. "You're late." His deep Southern accent was filled with disdain.

I smiled, wanting to vomit. "You're early." I glanced at my watch. "Our appointment is at eleven thirty." My voice exuded confidence—a tactic I used on others to push some doubt in their heads.

"I'm not," he snapped.

Sweat formed at my brow. There was no bullshitting this man. I wondered why I'd even tried.

"Oh, honey. Your pants are backward." The redhead dipped her chin and gave me a once-over from the top of her sunglasses, making matters worse.

Fuck. My damn pants. I forgot about my freaking pants. "It's the style. These pants are from Italy."

"Oh." She smiled and tipped her head. "I think I saw that in *Cosmo*. I'm Kat."

Geovani's mouth slackened as he was unbelieving.

I swallowed hard.

This was going to be a long morning.

CHAPTER 9

DAMN IT.

I chucked my Hermès purse in the back seat of my car and slipped in.

"You were late, which is highly unprofessional, and is this how you dress for all your meetings? Is this how Armstrong Realty does business?"

Geovani's scathing words still rang loudly in my ears.

If he knew that he wasn't going to rent the property, why did he make me go through the motions?

I slumped against the steering wheel.

It had all been for show.

All for his girlfriend, Kat.

She'd done her research, and when I keyed into the impeccable place with newly-shined floors and polished countertops, I knew instantly that they knew it was supposedly haunted. She was hanging on Geovani as though she were entering a real, live haunted house—the kind you paid to get into at Halloween, and at the end, a masked madman would chase you out with a chain saw.

Maybe he had been initially interested in renting it, but she'd come for a show.

My phone rang, bringing me back to the present. A picture of my father with me on his lap, smiling my cheesy smile, lit up my screen.

I inhaled deeply before I picked up. "Hey, Dad."

"Hey, sweetheart. I just wanted to see how your meeting went. Is it over yet, or do you want to call me back?"

I rested my head against the headrest. My father never gave me guilt for my failures. He never pressured me with extra goals. He loved me for who I was and pushed me to better myself within my own constraints, but shit ... he wanted this property rented more than I did.

I debated. *Should I lie? Should I tell him it's rented and work my ass off to find a renter before I have to tell him the truth?*

I couldn't. I wouldn't lie to my dad. Not him.

"It's a no-go." I let out a frustrated growl. "I'm trying. It's cursed, Dad. I have a few more showings later this week. I hate that I pushed you to buy it. I'm so stu—"

"Tene." He stopped me mid-sentence. "Stop. It's part of the business. We'll get it rented, but we need to give it a deadline, or else I want to put it up for sale. I don't want to take a loss any longer."

I closed my eyes, hating that I had to let the only man who had ever believed in me down. "I totally get it. Give me until the end of next month." Disappointment settled in my gut, weighing me down like an anchor. I rubbed at my temple. "But, Dad ... if we list it, we're not going to get what we paid for it."

"I know, honey." He sighed. "We'll just have to take the hit."

I rested my head against the headrest, focusing on the street in front of me. A couple of upscale retail places had set up within the last six months. A doughnut shop, an old-style theater. I'd thought for sure this would be a winning buy.

My gut had never been wrong before, but I guessed there was a first time for everything. Case in point: my night of non-sex, conversation, and spooning with the hottie.

"It's the best thing to do." His relaxed voice was meant to calm me, but it didn't.

"You're right, Dad." I threw my hands over my eyes and sighed. "I'm going to try my hardest to market this property, and after the month's through, we'll let it go."

"Tene, don't be too hard on yourself." His tone was soft, soothing, one that was so familiar, coming from my father.

"Hmm." My stomach clenched.

Silence ensued, one where I'd bet he was wondering what to say and knowing there was nothing that could be said.

"All right. You going to Angie's today?" he asked, changing the subject.

I was more than okay with that. I pushed enthusiasm into my tone for his benefit even though my father, of all people, would know I was faking. "Yeah, she needs to pick out new curtains, and, well, you know Cade. He's indifferent, or more likely, he wants to give her whatever she wants. So, now, I've got to help her decide."

"Okay. Drive safely."

"Thanks." A lump formed in the back of my throat. "Love you."

I hung up the phone, and for a few seconds, I let my head hang while my hands were on the steering wheel. The hot leather seared through my skin. I had a month. I didn't want this to be my first failure. This was Angie's and my future, our legacy. I couldn't start making mistakes this early in the game.

Please, please, please, God, I need an answered prayer. I need this unit rented.

Desperate times called for desperate measures.

After I'd gone home to change and freshen up, I stopped in front of Angie and Cade's new apartment building—a two-bedroom condo, walking distance from his bar.

When Angie opened the door, and I walked in, I hadn't expected to see Jordan sitting on the couch. I hadn't expected him to be super fine and looking at me through his sexy, endless ocean-blue eyes. Most of all, I hadn't expected him to still be in Rosendell.

The tension was instant, the spark between us so palpable that I could taste it, feel it, inhale it.

My usual sassy words were stuck in my throat. "Hey ... guys!" I croaked out with forced cheeriness.

"Teeeeene," Cade hollered, watching the baseball game, his hands in a popcorn bowl.

Wyatt tipped his chin from the couch. Jordan gave me an awkward wave.

That wave should be our signature greeting.

Everything about our situation was weird, and I never did weird.

I wanted all this awkwardness between us gone. Enough was enough. I pointed a pretty red-manicured fingernail in his direction. "Jordan Ryder ...," I tilted my head toward the corner. "... can I talk to you?"

His eyes slid to Cade and then to me, as though he was unsure of what he should do. "Okay."

He followed me around the corner, and I walked

straight out the door, knowing Cade and my sister would be eavesdropping.

When I flipped around, his gorgeous half-smile was on display, making my heart race, my breathing hitch, and my whole world stand still.

Why is it that, whenever I'm around this man, he makes me feel like a teenage girl with her first crush? I was a responsible, levelheaded, grown woman. Well ... most of the time.

His hair was styled back, his skin evenly tanned. His jeans hugged his nice, fine ass, and his shirt clung to his muscles like they were cold. And boy, did I admire them.

"So, I know nothing happened last night ..." I started, trying not to stare at his bulging biceps.

"It didn't," he confirmed.

"Then, why does it feel so ... so strange?" I motioned between us. "It's like the day after drunk sex, where there's this awkwardness around us, but the thing is, we didn't even have sex."

He looked relieved I'd just said it out loud. "I feel like it would've been better if we did have sex. Less awkward."

I pointed to him. "Exactly."

There was a silence suddenly. Thoughts of him and me and sex ran rampant in my mind, and I could see something similar on his face.

Did he want to? Would that make it better?

He cleared his throat. "But we can't."

By the sound of his gravelly voice, I knew the same thoughts had been running through his head.

"Of course not."

With his schedule and what Angie had said earlier about his old girlfriend, he had baggage. He was complication wrapped up in a pretty bow. Another ticked box why

I shouldn't date him. I couldn't and wouldn't repeat the past.

"Well, now, since that's settled."

I stepped to move past him, but he grabbed my wrist. The warmth of his skin against mine sent a jolt through my body that made me stagger.

"Tene, wait." He held my stare for far too long. Seconds felt like minutes. "I want to make you a proposition."

Proposition?

My mouth felt dry, and I sucked in my bottom lip. I'd take it.

As though he could read my mind, his dimple appeared. "Remember what you said about that haunted restaurant?"

I blinked. "Yeah."

"Well, I think I have a solution to your problem. It's a temporary solution, but it'll help in the meantime." He shoved his hands into his pockets and leaned against the doorframe. "So ... I haven't brought it up to the production team yet, but my last film is on a project deadline, and we have to do a lot of reshoots. The premise of the story is, we're being held hostage by terrorists at this restaurant. Only the restaurant we originally filmed at is no longer available. I was going to suggest that ..."

I jumped into his arms, gripping his upper body. He caught me mid-flight.

"Omigod! Omigod! Yes! Yes! Yes!"

It was like the Almighty had answered my prayers in the form of a Hollywood star.

He wrapped his hands around my waist, and we were jumping up and down together.

The door flew open, and Cade, Angie, and Wyatt stood in full view. Angie laughed, Cade watched warily, and Wyatt looked straight-up amused for once.

When the jumping died down, I placed both hands on my chest, trying to catch my breath, and pointed to Angie and Cade. "You guys were eavesdropping, weren't you?"

"Maybe. A little," she cooed in her angelic way. "And when you started screaming, 'Yes! Yes! Yes!' I wanted to see the show."

"Funny." I tugged at the end of her hair. Then, I walked past them and back into the apartment.

"Glad that nonsense is over," Cade grumbled.

She shot him a look and then faced me. "Okay, what was all the screaming about?" Angie placed both hands on her hips, smiling. She never did like secrets.

"It's the Wells property." I grinned. "Jordan is going to film there!"

He raised a hand. "Wait a minute. I haven't even asked the production team yet, and there's a process and logistics to these types of things. We'll see, okay? I'll ask them today. I wanted to run my idea by you first."

I slugged his arm. "You so have this. You're their money-maker. I dare them to say no." My mouth couldn't keep up with all the things going through my head. "I'll cut you the best deal, and filming in Rosendell is great. I'll help with the permits, and the city will give you incentives. Tons of them. Plus, after you're long gone, that will be the appeal. The nation's biggest heartthrob filmed his movie here. It'll be great." I squealed, and it took all my restraint not to jump up and down again.

I didn't miss Jordan's cocky grin.

"So, I'm America's biggest heartthrob?"

I slugged his arm again. "Funny." I turned to Angie, my cheeks hurting from my excitement. "Anyway, this is exactly what we need, so I don't have to sell the place."

I gave him a playful shove. "Call them."

He frowned at me. "I doubt they'll pick up."

"Leave a message." I reached for his hand and squeezed. "Come on. Please."

He would soon learn that I was a persistent little thing.

After a beat, he retracted his phone from his back pocket. He raised an eyebrow and stepped around me. "Hey, Ryan. When is the production supposed to begin ...?" He walked out to the balcony where I couldn't hear a word.

"This is great, Tene," Angie said, beaming.

"Yes, girl."

We high-fived, but my eyes were trained on Jordan pacing outside.

Angie knew how stressed I'd been with the haunted-property dilemma. She held my shoulders and angled me toward her dining room. Swatches of fabric were scattered on their long glass table.

"You ready to pick curtains?"

"Now?" I was so distracted. I swiveled and eyed Jordan.

"Yes, now."

I scoffed. Angie was almost as persistent as I was. Good thing I adored her.

"All righty then. Show me what our choices are."

CHAPTER 10

THE NEXT FEW DAYS, it was back to the grind. I hadn't heard from Jordan's camp. The anticipation was causing bags to form under my eyes.

The moment I opened my door and stepped out of my air-conditioned car, the humidity had my hair fluffing out.

Why is it so difficult to maintain good hair? I'd worked on it all morning.

I huffed and slipped on my sunglasses, slinging my bag over my shoulder. The first of the month meant I was going to visit our bigger clients, show my face, see how they were doing, and pick up some checks. As a family-owned business, we prided ourselves on good customer service. Some of our tenants had been with us for over ten years, and from that landlord-tenant relationship, we'd formed a trusted bond.

My phone rang from my purse, and I hitched it on my hip and dug to the bottom to pick it up on the second ring.

"Hello?"

"Hey, it's me." Jordan's sexy voice echoed through the receiver—throaty, deep, and signature him.

"I'm sorry, who?"

He laughed. "Jordan."

"Oh, hey." My heartbeat picked up.

"You didn't recognize me because of the number of men who call you on a daily basis?"

I forced a carefree laugh. "You could have been a client."

"Now, I am."

My heart stopped, and I stepped under a canopy, flushing myself against the door of Cupcakes Galore, shielding myself from the sunlight. "Really?" I tamed my voice, keeping my emotions at bay.

"Potentially, if you can convince our location director. What're you doing this afternoon?"

"Really?" I jumped in my heels, practically scaring the people walking out of the cupcake store. "Don't kid around. Do your people know the history of the restaurant?"

"They do. Our director wants to chat and tour the place before we sign."

"Today?" I squealed, unable to tame my excitement.

"Yes, today. He wants to get things moving."

I lifted one hand to the sky, praising the heavens above. "Thank you! Thank you! You're a godsend. I love you." I stilled. "Uhh ..." I slapped my forehead the moment those words had fallen from my mouth and winced. "I mean ... I love, uh ... I loved that you helped me with this."

He chuckled. "It's okay. I'm used to women saying that. They send me love notes or write how much they love me on their underwear. Sometimes on their skin."

I rolled my eyes, completely cured of my embarrassment. "I get it; you're beautiful. Anyway, at three o'clock at Allswell?" I teetered on my heels, letting the excitement bubble up inside me. I glanced at my clock, noting I had more than enough time to visit the rest of my tenants and make it back in time.

"Yeah, see you there. And, Tene?"

"Yeah?"

"I love ..." He stopped, and my heart stuttered. "... that you're doing this for us." He let out a low chuckle.

"Shut up." I hung up the phone and fist-pumped in the air, not even caring if anyone was looking. *Yes!*

I needed this. I had faith that after filming, I would be able to rent the space with no problem, given Jordan's feet had graced the building.

Before I stuffed my phone in my purse, it dinged with a text. Three hearts showed up on my phone, followed by a smiley face.

This guy ...

I couldn't deny the girly smile that pushed to the surface, just seeing his name on my phone with hearts.

Boy, oh boy, was I in trouble.

———

The morning flew by in a blur, and by the time I slipped into Allswell, I was bone-tired, but my skirt suit was still pressed to impress, and my hair was slicked and styled to perfection in a low ponytail.

The restaurant was packed with its usual busy crowd. There was never a true lull at Allswell. It was either busy with people grabbing lunch, or at non-lunch hours, they were grabbing drinks. My eyes searched the tables and booths, but Jordan was nowhere to be seen, so I strolled to the bar when I saw Cade.

He spotted me, said something to the bartender next to

him, and then hopped over and greeted me with a half hug. "Are you stopping in to eat?"

"No, I have a meeting." My eyes continued to search the vicinity. "Didn't Jordan call you?" My eyes perused the room, but he was nowhere to be found.

Cade pulled back and assessed my face. "No. Why?" His jaw twitched, and I sensed he was working something in his head.

"I'm meeting him and his location director here today. That's weird. I thought he'd make reservations."

Cade cocked his head and then slowly shook it, his eyes fixed firmly on mine.

"Do you have a table for us? It's pretty packed over here. They should be here in ten minutes." I frowned at the crowded room and the lack of empty tables.

Cade rubbed at his brow and then hollered behind him to someone at the bar. "Carrie, can you make sure nobody sits in thirteen?"

Cade grimaced, seeming lost in thought, and then he gripped my elbow and ushered me toward the corner like a parent would do to scold a child. "Listen, Tene, whatever's happening between you and Jordan ..." He let out an exasperated sigh and then tipped his chin to get in direct eye contact. "... it has to stop. You don't know his history. He's not ready."

My hand went to my hip, the way it always did when someone was trying to dictate what I had to do with my life. Yep, *no bueno*. And I knew his history. I wasn't thinking a relationship with Jordan. I was thinking ... I'd finally get to rent out Wells.

I lifted an eyebrow. "Really? Are we having this conversation?" My toe tapped against the floor. "I'm not going to break his heart if that's what you're worried about."

Because they were brothers, and with the loss of Candice, I had no doubt Cade had seen Jordan go through heartbreak.

"That's not what I'm worried about." He rubbed the back of his neck, his face scrunching. "I'm worried he'll break yours."

I laughed out loud, so loud that the patron having a drink at the bar glanced our way. My hand flew to my chest. "Me?" I'd learned my lesson the hard way, and I was never, ever going to repeat the same mistake again. "I'm sorry, but really? I'm a big girl. I can take care of myself." I patted his shoulder and smiled.

Look at this guy, trying to protect me and getting it all wrong. Jordan was the one who needed protecting.

He shook his head and scratched his temple. I could already tell when Cade was annoyed. He'd been with my sister long enough. They were so comfortable around me that when they got into arguments, they sometimes forgot I was in the room.

His posture turned rigid, and his eyes narrowed. "No. This is how it's going to go down. He *will* break your heart, and I don't want to see that happen. I love him. I love you. But above all, I fucking love your sister. And the fallout from you two will mess with what Angie and I have." He gave me a pointed stare. "Don't mess this up for me, please? I've warned him, but I'm also warning you."

I gulped. I hadn't thought of a serious relationship with Jordan. We lived miles apart; it wasn't even a possibility.

From the corner of my eye, I saw Jordan stroll in with a taller male. The guy reminded me of a suave teacher—dark hair was parted to the side, glasses, skinny frames, electric-blue polo, crisply pressed khakis.

I patted Cade's burly arm to placate him. "Don't worry. We're both adults. I'm sure we'll be fine."

"He dated my sister," Cade blurted, like a last warning.

I couldn't help the sympathy on my face. "I know."

"He hasn't gotten over her."

I kept my features casual, though it stung a little when I thought about it.

"He's still in love with her," Cade continued. "Her damn name is tattooed in Chinese characters over his heart."

I tried not to let his words affect me, but a heavy feeling settled in my stomach. It wasn't that Jordan wasn't allowed to still be in love with her; it was that I'd told myself I would never settle for second. Not again. Not ever.

Jordan approached us, smiling casually. "Hey, guys." His gaze pinged between us. "Is this a good time?"

I lifted my chin, gaining my strength. Nothing was going to get in the way of me getting this damn restaurant rented. "Yes. Perfect timing." I plastered on my business smile and put business Tene on display.

Jordan motioned to the guy behind him. "This is Ryan. He's in charge of sets and locations for the studio."

I stuck out my hand. "Christene."

Ryan took my hand in his, and his grip lingered a while longer. He sported a Crest-strip smile—all white, no gaps, and beautiful—but my mind couldn't help but wander to Jordan.

He's in love with a ghost.

When did she pass? How long ago? I wondered if she and Jordan had been together long. Most of all, I wondered why I cared so much.

I bit the inside of my cheek and forced myself to focus on securing the deal.

Ryan's hand was still on mine, and Jordan noticed. He immediately turned toward Cade. "This is my brother. Ryan, Cade. Cade, Ryan."

Cade took his hand. "Nice to meet you, man. I'm going to have to lead you to your table and then cut out and assist with the after-lunch rush. I reserved that table on the far end." He pointed to the only table vacant.

Jordan tipped his chin. "It's all good. We can take it from here. Do what you have to do."

Jordan stepped in front of me and proceeded to the table, but then Ryan touched my elbow and said, "After you."

"Thanks."

I could feel Ryan's eyes on me the whole time, and I didn't miss Jordan's irritation. It seeped out of him like sweat—in his rigid stance, the visible tension in his neck, in the way his eyes narrowed when Ryan paid me attention.

When we got to the table, Jordan scooted into the booth and patted the seat next to him. "Sit here, Tene."

The use of my nickname did not escape me. *This guy ... trying to establish that he's known me forever in front of Ryan.*

I couldn't help the stubbornness that flared up inside of me. *Sit? Like a dog? Did he just order me to sit?*

He eyed me expectantly, and a little part of me wanted to sit by Ryan just to spite him, but I let it slide.

I slipped in next to Jordan and raised my hand to the waitress to order a bottle of red Château Montrose, my favorite wine from Cade's menu.

The wining and dining is where I shine. I was used to the sales part of my job because I knew how to close the deal.

I started the conversation. "I've already looked, and

Rosendell has great incentives and tax cuts for your film." I leaned in as I spoke to Ryan, never breaking eye contact, business and seriousness in my tone, in my stance, in my every move. "We can negotiate the rent, depending on how long you think you'll be at the location."

The waitress delivered the wine and poured our glasses. I didn't miss her eyes making their way to Jordan multiple times or the way her cheeks flushed pink.

I forced my attention back to Ryan, the one who could seal my fate when it came to this property.

Ryan nodded. "It'll probably be no more than three weeks, but we'll rent it for the month. We really just want to reshoot a couple of scenes because we have a release date that's creeping up." He tipped back his wineglass. "The key is to not get behind schedule. I saw the pictures online, and it looks fine. If everything checks out at today's walkthrough, then I can have our production crew move in and set up, and we can start filming within three days."

I blinked. *Three days. Holy crap.*

The filming would be the talk of our town. I made a mental list of all the newspapers and media I needed to contact. The more publicity it had, the more exposure for my property.

"We have the place, and all you need is the main star right here." Jordan patted his chest and then placed a hand on mine.

I quirked an eyebrow.

This boy is staking a claim on me. Really? Right now, when I am trying to get this deal done?

"Perfect." I kept my smile even, not sure if I should be annoyed that his caveman tactics were distracting me or flattered by Jordan's newfound jealousy.

"So ... Christene, how long have you been working in real estate?" Ryan leaned into the table.

I noticed the speckles of green in his brown irises. I also noticed Jordan inch toward me, his thigh by my thigh, his hand never leaving mine.

"All my life." I let out a low laugh and tipped back my wine. "Armstrong Realty is family-owned. My granddaddy was the one to get it started. I remember doing rounds with my dad, going to our tenants, and picking up rent checks. One of our customers was a cupcake bakery. One of my earliest memories is getting cupcakes every time my father collected rent."

A wave of nostalgia hit me directly in the chest. My granddad had a special chair for me in his office. It was where I would sit when he was making his morning calls or taking meetings with Dad. While Angie was always with my mother at home, I was out in the field with Dad and Granddad. It was why I knew the business so well.

"You guys ready to order?" The waitress took out her notepad and directed her question only toward Jordan, not the table.

"I had a heavy lunch, but, gentlemen, you go ahead."

Only then did her focus make it my way. *Cute. Wavy blonde hair. Younger than me for sure. Maybe his type, but why should I care? I shouldn't care, right?*

"You started right out of college?" Jordan asked, filling up my glass of wine after they decided they weren't hungry either.

"Yeah. My dad ..." It was hard not to feel the pain when I thought about it. "He got sick not too long ago, and I had to step up." I remembered the past year, not knowing if Dad would still be here in this world. Just the thought of losing him gutted me. "He's not as active in the company as he used to be, so my younger sister and I do most of the work nowadays."

Now that Angie was partner, we'd be splitting the responsibilities fifty-fifty, so my workload would ease up.

Ryan's eyes perked. "Oh, yeah. Your sister is dating Jordan's brother, isn't she? I have to talk to him later. We weren't able to have a wrap party, so we'll have one after this second take. Maybe we can throw it here." He motioned to the room with his hands, his eyes scanning and seeming pleased with what he saw.

Ryan reached for the wine bottle, but in the process, he tipped my glass over. I jumped up and stepped out of the booth, the red liquid spilling over my black suit dress. Thank goodness it was black!

"I'm sorry," he said immediately. "I'm such an idiot."

In the next second, Ryan was by my side, helping me wipe down my dress. He rested one hand on my shoulder as he dabbed the white cloth napkin across my stomach.

"It's fine. I can do it," I said, my face heating.

He gave me the napkin, and his fingers dropped to my back. "I'm sorry." His ears turned red, and his chin dropped toward the floor, as he was visibly embarrassed.

I forced a chuckle. "No, it's fine. It happens." I wasn't going to tell the guy who was about to change the cards for my haunted restaurant that this was my favorite suit. I dabbed at my dress with my own napkin.

Jordan stood and reached out to me, gripping my upper arm, the force not too tight, but firm. His face was unreadable, his jaw taut. He nodded toward the other side of the room. "Tene, why don't you go to the restroom and clean yourself up?"

My eyebrows rose to the ceiling. I wasn't used to people telling me what to do. I was usually the one giving orders, but I had to admit, I kind of liked it—Jordan and his authoritative, jealous ways. I wondered if he was the same in the bedroom. The thought heated my insides.

I nodded. "Excuse me, Ryan, Jordan. I'll be right back."

I felt their eyes on my ass as I strolled across the room and made it a point to swing my hips a little more.

When I exited the restroom, Jordan was the only one at our table, standing.

"What was that all about?" I needed another glass of wine, so I lifted my glass, and Jordan proceeded to pour me one.

He whispered something under his breath, but I was unable to catch it.

"What?"

Jordan shook his head and muttered, "I thought Ryan was gay. Obviously not."

Speaking of Ryan ... "Where did he go?" I frowned.

He tipped his head toward the bar where Ryan was talking to Cade, most likely about the wrap party. This could potentially be a win-win for both businesses if I could get this done.

I laughed. "Does it make you jealous that I have his attention?"

"Yes," he said, no hesitation, eyes firmly set on mine.

I blinked, surprised at his honesty. "I think you've made it pretty clear that nothing can happen between us. Maybe ..." I glanced over at Ryan. "Maybe I think Ryan's cute." I was baiting him, and I could tell, based on the look on his face, he didn't appreciate it.

He pulled me in, his five-finger grip on my hip, his nose by my ear. "Just because it can't happen doesn't mean I don't picture turning you around, lifting your skirt, and slamming into you to tell everyone to back the hell off."

I almost fainted from the heat. And there went my dirty mind, playing back his words. I bit my lip while everything south tingled, begging Jordan to fulfill his promise.

Our eyes locked, lustful, longing. Seconds ticked by. I told him with one look what I wanted, and I could read the same through his blue irises.

Then, he backed away, the abrupt movement robbing the air that I breathed.

He ran one aggravated hand through his hair. "And now, we're going to have to work together, so it's an even bigger reason we can't."

I let out a long, disappointed sigh. This back-and-forth between us, this tug-of-war, was giving me whiplash. "Too bad." I playfully licked my lips. "Because I'm sure it would've been a fun ride."

I tapped the table twice and walked toward Cade and Ryan, who were still speaking in the corner, all the while trying to calm my raging pulse.

I didn't know how I was going to do this, live through all this sexual tension, now knowing I had to deal with him for the next few weeks.

CHAPTER 11

RYAN AND JORDAN had ridden together to the restaurant. I had driven separately. When I stepped out of the car, I could feel Jordan's eyes on me. On my bare legs, on my neck, on my skin. The sexual tension between us was at an ultimate high, and I squeezed my thighs together to keep the ache from spreading. I needed a tall glass of water to cool the heat rising within me or a few more glasses of wine to loosen the strain in my shoulders. I hadn't had enough to drink earlier.

I keyed into the Wells property, and he held the door open as I strolled in.

"Here it is." I strolled over to the wall, searching for the light switch, my heels clip-clopping on the black-and-white tiles. When I switched on the lights, they flickered before fully turning on, and a shiver ran down my spine. Although I didn't believe the building was haunted, I couldn't force my body to calm whenever I walked inside, just knowing what had happened here.

"So, it is haunted," Jordan joked.

I laughed and rolled my eyes. "Well, what do you think?"

Ryan surveyed the room, his eyes taking in the round wooden tables, the booths against the edges of the room, the trendy chalkboard that spanned one wall that would list the specials, the lights hanging over the booths, the black stools that surrounded the bar.

If I closed my eyes, I could hear the chatter of patrons. Plates sliding against the counter, the sizzling of the frying pan in the background, the business of a once-well-established restaurant.

I watched Ryan pace the floor, holding my breath the whole time. I couldn't remember a time when I had wanted a win so badly, more so I wouldn't be a disappointment to my father than a letdown to my ego.

After what seemed like forever, Ryan turned my way. "It has character. And just the right size to fill the terrorist scene."

"Terrorist scene?" I dimmed the excitement on my face because it wouldn't be professional to go all starstruck gaga right now.

Jordan grinned. "Yes. Terrorists are holding the patrons at this restaurant hostage. Guess who's going to save the day?" He pounded his chest with one hand. "This guy."

I laughed, but really, this was insane. In a few days, this town and my restaurant would be bustling with A-listers. I couldn't help how my stomach fluttered with excitement.

"Jordan and Kay are working for Interpol and entering this restaurant as spies, knowing the owner is involved in smuggling illegal drugs into the United States." Ryan ran his finger against one of the tables.

"Kay Sterling?" I bit my lip to prevent my overly cheesy smile from escaping.

Ryan spun around on his heels. He formed a square with his hands, squinting his eyes, envisioning the terrorist scene most likely. "Yes, the same Oscar-winning Kay."

I blinked, and this time, I couldn't hide the smile from my face. Kay was stunning and beautiful, and one of the actresses Nana and I loved watching on the big screen. We just knew that every movie she starred in would be a good one.

"That is pretty cool." *Cool?* My twenty-six-year-old self had said *cool*, which was crazy not cool. I flattened my hands against my skirt and cleared my throat, trying to sound more mature. "Your presence in this town will benefit us greatly."

He turned to me, and with a tip of his chin and a small smile, he said, "I'll have my lawyers review the papers you gave me and send over a check. We want to be in here before the end of the week, so we need to keep everything moving."

Cha-ching.

I wanted to jump for joy, scream for Santa. I couldn't believe this was happening. After months and months of searching for a renter and failing my father, again and again, I was getting this place rented.

"It's a pretty standard contract," I said, my tone even. For never having rented out our spaces for film, my real estate lawyer had to draw up a new contract. I'd read it over last night. It had the customary language and stipulations included.

The sooner they filmed and finished, the sooner I could advertise this place and get a permanent tenant in this spot. I had no doubt it could be rented for top dollar after the filming.

I needed to check this one off the list and move on to bigger and better things for Armstrong Realty.

"All right, I have to get the ball rolling. Christene ..." Ryan tipped his head and placed a hand on his chest. "... it was a pleasure." He stayed rooted in his spot and didn't bother to shake my hand as though he were afraid to touch me, and I wondered if Jordan had said something to him in the car.

I smiled. "My pleasure, and thanks again."

"Tene, do think you can drop me off at my hotel?" Jordan turned my way. "Ryan is flying out to LA tonight, and I'm a little tired."

I quirked an eyebrow. Did he say something to Ryan?

"Sure."

Who knew that the A-list actor had a jealous streak in him? On other men, it would be a damning quality, but on Jordan Ryder? It was quite sexy.

With one last salute, Ryan was out the door.

Jordan stepped closer, just a few feet away, and my breathing hitched.

"So, where did it happen?"

"What?" I shifted in my spot and pulled at the edge of my suit jacket. I knew what he was talking about, but I didn't want to address his question.

The logistics of how Mr. Wells had been murdered had been plastered all over the papers, and the case had played out on the news.

"The murder."

He inched closer, and just the sight of him had my mouth watering and my mind going blank. If he was a stranger and wasn't my sister's boyfriend's brother—and if he wasn't so hell-bent on staying on the no-sex side of the

fence—I'd be making a play to make a movie of our own—
the X-rated kind.

"Where did it happen?" he asked again, his cocky grin
telling me he knew how he was affecting me.

"In the kitchen, in the back. It's been renovated since
then." I took two conscious steps away from him, trying to
collect myself and get air in my lungs.

"Take me on a tour, pretty girl." His sexy smirk was on
display, the one that sported his cute chin dimple. His face
had been sculpted from the gods, and just to make him stick
out, they'd added a dimple for good measure. It was so
unfair.

Tour? "Okay." My tone was without its usual steady
confidence.

I turned to lead him in that direction, but he stepped
into me, and my breath caught.

Mental slap, slap, slap.

What was wrong with me? I had never been *that*
teenage girl, the one with a crush. I had skipped those
awkward years altogether—never nervous, always confident
in my own skin—until now. *What the hell?*

"I'll stay really close in case you're scared." Jordan's
voice deepened into a macho man bass tone, and his hand
suavely caressed my hip.

I sidestepped him, needing some semblance of control.
"I can handle myself," I said, walking toward the kitchen.

I didn't know what his game was. His flirting unnerved
me and threw me off-kilter.

As we stepped into the kitchen, that same eerie feeling I
always got swept over me. My back snapped to attention, and I
flipped on the switch, turning on all the lights. A chill came
over me once I proceeded farther in. I didn't believe in ghosts.

The fact that someone had been murdered in this room, however, did fill me with a little unease. Not enough to keep me from buying the place. I'd had this place cleaned and stripped and renovated. It was in a killer—no pun intended—location.

"What's the story?" Jordan's flirty demeanor dimmed as he walked around the kitchen, hands stuffed in his pockets as though he didn't want to touch anything like he was in a crime scene.

"Love story gone wrong. When the wife found out he was cheating, she went into a fit of rage and cut him up into pieces. Tortured him." I shivered. "It was her best friend, a partner who had equity in this restaurant."

"What happened to the mistress?" Jordan moved to the center table and grimaced, probably imagining the night it had all gone down.

"Nothing, really. She testified against the wife. But there was no question who had done it. The wife's DNA was everywhere—on his clothing, on his body ..." I shuddered at the thought. "It wasn't premeditated."

I knew he'd been killed in the kitchen. My imagination was vivid enough to picture it—the blood, the gore, the pain.

I wrapped my hands around my arms and rubbed them to dim the chill within me. "It's cold in here. I swear the air isn't even on."

He smirked, the flirting back in play. "Is this your ploy to get me to come over? 'Cause, baby ... all you have to do is ask."

"Please." My tone oozed with sarcasm, but Jordan took it as an invitation to come toward me.

"Begging is not necessary." He backed me against the wall, his arms over my head, and I gasped.

"What are you doing?" I peered up at him, my strong

knees feeling weak. Sudden dizziness took over at his closeness.

"You did say please." The playful seductiveness was back in his tone.

And when I stared up into the endless sea of electric blue, I lost my ability to think, to utter my next words.

I pushed at his hard, overworked chest, chuckling. "I meant, 'yeah, right—please' or 'please; don't flatter yourself.'"

"Sure." His hands dropped to my sides, sliding up and down my arms to warm me. "Feel better?"

Goose bumps prickled my skin, but they weren't caused by the cool air around me.

I laughed to cover up my nerves. "Sure," I said, mimicking his word. I was that breathless teenage girl again with a crush, and I hated it. My breathing slowed at his proximity, and beads of sweat formed on the back of my neck. "Wh-what are you doing, Jordan?"

He angled toward me and ran his thumb along my bottom lip. "I don't know."

"That's not an answer," I breathed out, dazed and confused and mesmerized by his stare.

His lustful blue eyes locked with mine, but something in his expression made me wonder if he was thinking deeply, contemplating something more.

"I like you," he said, his voice a hoarse whisper, a tender brush against my skin.

Goose bumps spread down my neck, and my heart staggered to a stop.

"I bet you say that to all the girls."

"I don't." His eyes never left mine, indecision reigning.

My mind was like mush. The way my body reacted to

him was undeniable, but the way my heart reacted was unprecedented.

Losing control again, Tene. Get it together.

His lips brushed against my cheek, moving closer to my mouth.

"Jordan, I'm asking you again." My hands gripped his sides. I wanted to push him away, but I was unable to. "What are you doing?"

"Getting as close as I can get without going too far."

"How is this making it any better? Do you like walking around with a case of blue balls every time you see me?"

His warm chuckle vibrated against the tender part of my neck. "No. It's physical torture, being this close to you and not being able to do the things I want to."

I angled my lips toward his. "Is that so?"

"Yeah."

Suddenly, the air-conditioning blasted on in the background, and I jumped, grabbing his biceps and pulling him closer. My nerves were shot around this man and not because of the eerie feeling in this restaurant.

"Don't be scared. No ghosts are going to hurt you." He playfully wiggled his eyebrows and offered a bemused smile.

My goodness, he smelled so darn good. It must be his aftershave. The masculine scent filled my nose, and I wanted to swallow it up, bottle it for tomorrow, and sell it on the black market.

"I'm not going to let anyone hurt you. The only person you need protecting from is me." He sucked in his bottom lip, which had to be the sexiest thing I'd ever seen. It took all my energy not to take a bite myself.

As I peered into his blue irises again, I decided, *this is it.*

I was done pretending I didn't want him. I'd never *not* want him. Then, I figured out the solution to my problem.

I needed him out of my system. Avoidance wasn't the answer.

Why didn't I think of this sooner? I needed to sleep with him to gain my sense of normalcy back. Scratch the itch. Then, this teenage infatuation would be flushed out of my system, and I'd have my life back. There wouldn't be any complications because no one else would know. No one had to find out.

Decision made.

I fisted his shirt and crashed my lips against his. His eyes widened as he was surprised at the contact. I thought he was going to back away, but he molded himself against me and gave in to this kiss—our kiss. It was exquisite, an unleashing of pure, uninhibited passion. He tasted like mint and cigarettes and all alpha male, and I couldn't get enough. I never wanted it to stop.

My fingers threaded through his hair, and his hands gripped my hips, pushing into me. His lips released a thousand fires inside of me, and flames of heat coursed down my neck to further forbidden parts.

Pure sexual attraction was unleashed and poured into our lips, mashing against each other. He took control, just how I liked it, just how I craved.

His lips progressed into a slow dance. He sucked on my bottom lip, teasing it between his teeth before moving to my upper lip. Tease, lick, nip, and suck. The gentle, sensual rhythm of our lips increased the temperature in the room, the heat in my body boiling the blood in my veins. I pushed my breasts against his chest and moaned into his mouth.

When I tried to change the kiss into a clashing of teeth and a tangling of tongues, he slowed and dropped his lips to my neck, kissing a steamy path down to my collarbone. I was held captive, but it only increased my want, my need, my lust for him.

He was driving me insane.

Absolutely insane.

I wrapped my fingers around his neck, grinding against him. He gave in to the power of my lips again and opened his mouth. I was rewarded with his slick, soft tongue against mine. I knew I'd let him take me here, clothes off, passion high. But I also knew he wouldn't do it. His hold, his posture, his restraint were like chains around his crown jewels.

He wanted me, but he was holding back. I could sense it in the way he wasn't letting go and giving in to our kiss fully.

Abruptly, my phone rang in my purse on the counter, but I didn't care. I only cared that Jordan Ryder did not stop kissing me.

"Are you going to get that?" His lips dropped to my neck, sucking, tasting, teasing.

My panties were a foregone conclusion, wet and lacy—and if I had my choice, tossed across the room.

"No," I groaned. "I'm sure it's not important. I want you," I breathed, sounding pathetic and unlike myself. I'd never waited this long to get what I wanted. It was agony, my insides on the verge of combusting from sexual frustration. "Jordan ..." I moaned as he rubbed me in all the right places.

My hands flew to the buckle of his jeans. He grabbed one to stop me and rested his head against mine, eyes closed, his chest heaving.

"Tene ... we can't."

"Why not? He doesn't even have to know." Desperation

overrode any reason. All I knew was I wanted him, and I knew we'd be explosive together if we did this.

"He'll know. He's my brother, and he'll know." His self-restraint was shot, his eyes heavy-lidded, but his mind was stronger than his body. His hands dragged down from my shoulders to my arms as he put some distance between us.

I pulled away, the rejection like a splash of cold water to my face.

He reached for my waist, but I shoved at his chest.

"Tene, don't." He scrubbed a heavy hand down his face and released a long sigh.

"You're such a tease." My expression pinched, and my hands clenched into fists. "That's like someone going down on me, getting me *this close* to orgasm, and then stopping to jam a bowling ball up my vagina." I threw my hands up. "What was the point of that? You can't start cooking a raw chicken and stop midway."

"I'm sorry." He pulled me closer and placed one hand on my hip. "I'm sorry because ... I couldn't resist." He wrapped both hands around my waist, bringing me closer. "Can you blame me? Have you seen yourself in the mirror?"

He smiled, trying to break my mood with a compliment, but it didn't work. He'd started this and refused to finish. Where was the integrity in that?

I full-on pouted and pushed his chest, my hands a hard barrier between his holy hotness and me.

He dropped his head closer, whispering so softly that I strained my ears to hear him, "I'm sorry." An inch closer. "Do you forgive me?" Another inch closer. "I'm so ..." Closer. "... so" Millimeters apart. "... sorry." He closed the gap between us and pecked my lips. Once, twice, three times.

I peered up at him, utterly frustrated from the waist

down. "You're the only man I know who doesn't want to give in to what you want ... what we both want."

"Because I promised," he groaned.

"I've heard that one before."

He held me in the silence. "And because I want to be sure."

I reeled back, studying his features. *Sure of what?* I wanted to ask him, but I was interrupted by my phone ringing again in the background.

"You'd better get that."

My question would have to wait. For now.

I straightened my skirt and walked back to the counter, pulling my phone from my purse.

"Tene, where are you?" Angie's voice echoed through the receiver.

"At the Wells property," I told her, my voice tight and annoyed.

Jordan's eyes were still on me, and he was rocking one hell of a boner. Good. His choice, not mine.

"Dad and Mom want to try that new tapas restaurant downtown. It's right by Allswell. Wanna come?"

I shifted from one foot to the other, tapping my heels against the ceramic tiles. I wanted release. This was bad. I was like a dog in heat.

"Sure, text me the address." I hadn't meant to sound so clipped, but I couldn't help it.

Jordan stood there, watching me, his eyes unreadable. I remembered I was his ride home. Guessed he was coming to dinner.

"Add Jordan to the reservation."

"Jordan?" I could hear the questions in her voice.

"Yeah, he's with me right now. I have some good news to share tonight."

"About you and Jordan?" My sister's voice pitch hitched with excitement, but I only had the truth for her.

"For the millionth time, nothing is happening between us. But I did rent out this place."

She squealed over the line, which made my sexually frustrated insides ease up.

"Yes. I've got the place rented. Don't tell Dad. I want to give him the good news."

"Okay."

After we said our good-byes, Jordan walked toward me but remained a few feet away this time. "So, we're going to dinner?"

"Yeah. Tapas place." I tipped my chin in his direction, my eyes dropping to his pants. "You want me to give you a few minutes to take care of that situation?"

"No, it's fine." He adjusted himself and grimaced. "It'll calm down in a few minutes. I'm used to this situation whenever you're around."

I slipped my bag over my shoulder and laughed under my breath. "Suit yourself."

CHAPTER 12

THE DRIVE to the restaurant was slow and torturous. He rocked the boner in the car until I pulled up in front of the Tapas Bar and shifted my car into park.

He shifted in his seat and adjusted his pants. "Better?"

"Nope." I was still highly annoyed with him starting something he didn't want to finish. And I absolutely loathed feeling off-balance whenever he was around.

"It's getting better." He motioned to the action happening in his pants.

If that was him getting soft, I wondered how he looked at a full salute. I squeezed my thighs together at the thought.

"I know how to make it better," I said, swiping at my bottom lip.

His pants tented up again. I was going to make his balls so blue that he'd be walking funny for the rest of the day.

"Tene, you're killing me here," he groaned.

"Don't even start with me." I opened the door and threw my keys at him. "Don't jack the hammer in my car. I'll be thoroughly pissed if your jizz is all over my seats. Calm down first, and then come in."

I would've gladly eased his ache if he wasn't playing Blocko My Taco.

I touched my lips, reliving the amazing kiss we'd had at the restaurant. God, was he an amazing kisser. His lips had to be from the Almighty above.

After I entered the double doors of the restaurant, my senses were bombarded with the scent of meats and spices, my ears were filled with the beats of a Latin drum, and my eyes took in the colorful decor of the Tapas Bar.

Red velvet couches outlined the outer walls, and the yellow and orange decor was lit up by the lights hanging above us and the wall lamps anchored to the wall.

I spotted my family and Cade at the far end of the room and raised a hand.

Angie rushed toward my side. "Tene, where's Jordan?"

"Nice to see you, too, Ang. He's parking the car."

Where Cade was purposely pushing us apart, I believed Angie wanted us together. This couldn't be the healthiest thing for their relationship.

When I approached the table, Nana and my father simultaneously asked where Jordan was, and I refrained from rolling my eyes. I wanted to tell them I had caused a major hard-on that prevented him from walking in without limping, but that would be inappropriate. I debated on it just to see the epic disappointment in my mother's eyes.

I made my rounds, bending to kiss my father and Nana.

My mother lifted her head. "What took you so long?"

"Work."

She nodded and then dropped her stare to the menu.

Unluckily for me, the only two spots that were empty were the two seats next to her.

After slipping my purse over the chair and scooting in,

Jordan strolled through the doors, walking at a slower than average pace—the blue balls swagger. His fault. His choice.

Nana practically jumped up to greet him, followed by my father, Angie, and even my mother. Even though my mother didn't want to admit it, I knew she was a little starstruck. She had to be. I'd caught her reading a magazine with Jordan on the cover.

Cade's eyes followed him as he sat in the only vacant seat—beside me—and his jaw ticked.

"Jordan, so glad you could join us," my grandmother cooed over my mother and me.

I swore her eyes had heart emojis.

"So, you guys were hanging out today," my mother stated, her tone low and judgmental. "Was Christene here showing you a good time?"

I hated how there was an insinuation with every word that came out of her mouth. *Will she ever have faith in me? Think of me as anything other than her bimbo daughter?*

I straightened my back, pushing up my nose a tad, my body tense as a wire while the waitress dropped some appetizers at our table. "Actually, we secured a deal today." My tone perked up, and my eyes avoided hers and instead went to scan the faces of the rest of my family members. "I finally rented out the Wells location."

My grandmother and father clapped, their praises known as I continued, "Yeah, it worked out perfectly. Jordan's team is going to rent it and film there. And once filming is over, I don't think it'll be a problem to lease it out."

My gaze made its way to my mother, who showed no reaction, and my whole body tensed.

Jordan placed his hand on my knee under the table. It wasn't a sensual hold but a gesture to calm me. He squeezed my knee once, and the tension in my shoulders eased up.

"During my last movie, we weren't able to perfect a couple of scenes. It was horrible, actually. We're way behind production. I asked Tene if we could rent out the restaurant to finish up those scenes. I had to clear it with our production crew and the studio, and today, it was finalized by the set manager."

My father's beaming smile from across the table had my mouth ticking up in response. "That is the best news I've heard all day."

Angie smiled over her drink. "Like there was any doubt Tene would get the job done."

Cade tipped his head, but his eyes were still cautious.

"Good thing you finally got that thing rented out. It's been such a money drain. What's going to happen after filming?" My mother's voice broke me from my happy cloud.

I didn't understand why she had to be such a Debbie Downer in life like her whole focus was to torment me and bring up every negative aspect in every situation of my existence.

My smile was tight. "As a matter of fact, Mother, I believe this could be the end to the renter drought. Once filming wraps, it'll be a tourist spot. I'll have renters jumping at the property. I'll probably have a bidding war on my hands." I motioned to the Hollywood star beside me. "All because of this man."

"I hope so." My mother stuck her fork into the little plate of patatas bravas, one of my favorite Spanish tapas dishes. Too bad I was no longer hungry.

My mouth snapped shut, and I fisted my hands in my lap, heat rising to my ears. *This woman! Would anything I do ever be good enough?*

I opened my mouth to speak, but Angie's stare warned

me off. I bit my tongue hard enough to taste blood and slowly breathed in through my nose and out my mouth.

Sensing my mood, Jordan changed the subject. "I'm a double agent in this one. It's based on a best-selling book." He leaned in, resting his elbows on the table. "We're stuck in a restaurant because there are terrorists in the place. We're playing regular patrons sitting in the booths when the action goes down."

He continued talking about the film, and I noticed everyone around us was engrossed in his tale. Nana's smile was so wide that I thought her false teeth would fall out of her mouth. I'd seen it happen once. We'd been at the movies, watching an old Chevy Chase film. She'd been laughing so hard that I thought she was going to go into cardiac arrest.

Jordan's phone buzzed on the table, but he didn't pick it up. When it buzzed a second time, his eyes dropped to the phone again. The name *Larry* blinked on the screen.

Jordan's eyebrows pulled together, and his story slowed to a stop. He raised a finger and stood at the same time. "Excuse me. I have to take this." He smiled before moving across the room.

My family continued to talk about the upcoming filming at Wells, but my eyes followed Jordan, watching him pace, one hand on his hip, the other hand holding the phone. He wasn't speaking, mostly listening. He rubbed at his brow, and his face creased with worry.

I eyed Cade, who was focused on Jordan, his eyes probing and curious. As soon as Jordan hung up, Cade stood and was by his side. It took every ounce of self-control to stay in my seat. They exchanged some words, Jordan mostly speaking a mile a minute. Cade put a hand on Jordan to calm him, and that was when he shut his mouth.

When they returned to the table, they took their seats and were silent, their demeanor melancholy—so different from only moments before.

I discreetly asked Jordan, "Everything okay?"

He smiled, but it didn't reach his eyes. There was a depth of worry behind the blue irises staring back at me. "Yeah."

My bullshit meter was on high alert, ringing loudly and pointing an arrow directly at Jordan. I narrowed my eyes at him. *You're lying*, I mouthed.

He shrugged and put his hand over mine, rubbing his thumb over my fist. Everyone saw—including my mother and Cade.

We locked eyes for a brief second before he addressed everyone at the table, "Sorry, guys. The crazy studio execs need me to be available at all times. I'm going to have to cut this dinner short."

My nana groaned in disappointment from across the table.

"I'm sure I'll see you guys around. You're more than welcome to come down for the filming, which should begin soon. I'll be sure to let you guys know when."

That brightened Nana's mood as she straightened in her seat and beamed a Nana false-toothed grin.

I turned toward Jordan. "Aren't you hungry?"

"No, I'll pick something up on the way to my new hotel."

"New hotel?" I frowned. "What happened to your old hotel?"

"I'll be transferring hotels tonight." He averted his stare and bit his lip to prevent himself from speaking any further.

"All righty, ready to leave?" I was the one who'd brought him here, so I assumed I was taking him back to his hotel.

"No, Larry and Dex are headed over here." He tipped his chin to the two overly burly guys standing by the exit.

They both wore the same suit—black, custom-fitted. All they needed were sunglasses, and they'd be on the set of *Men in Black*.

"Who's Larry?"

Another bodyguard? I knew he had one, but now two?

"What's going on, Jordan?" My voice was tight, cautious.

Whatever it was, he obviously didn't want me to know because he clammed up.

He let out a long sigh, and his eyes found Cade's across the table. My eyes ping-ponged between them, and the whole table went silent.

Curiosity piqued within me, and I vowed to find out what was going on. I stood, pushed out my chair, and smiled. "Ready to get going?"

"Tene," he argued with a small shake of his head.

I heard my mother murmur something under her breath, but I ignored it.

"We still need to discuss a couple of things regarding the rental." I clenched my jaw. If he denied me and embarrassed me in front of my family, I'd never forgive him. "Just tell your bodyguards to meet us at my place."

When he didn't answer, and his eyes showed he was debating his next move, I pressed him further. "Let's go." I maintained strong eye contact, brooking no argument.

"Tene ..." Cade called from across the table. The big-brother tone was back in his voice, but too bad he was Jordan's big brother, not mine.

"No, it's okay. I've got this." I grabbed my thin jacket and kissed Nana and my father. "I'll meet you by the door."

My mother's sharp tone stilled me. "Tene, his body-guards are picking him up. Why do you have to leave?"

"Because I want to make this night more enjoyable for you, Mother," I snapped, my whole body going rigid.

Our staring contest cut through the air until Jordan cleared his throat. "I apologize again for leaving so early." He reached for my elbow and walked us toward the door, ignoring Angie calling me back to the table.

As we were leaving, Cade and Angie caught up with us.

"Jordan, this isn't a good idea. It's not safe," Cade said.

I threw up both hands. "What is going on here?"

"Cade?" Angie peered up at her man, pulling at his shirt, forcing his attention her way.

He grabbed one of her hands. "I'll tell you later."

"Why don't you tell us both now?" My patience was running out. I was hungry, worried, and tired.

"I won't let anything happen to her," Jordan promised.

They held each other's stare. For one, two, three seconds too long.

Cade gritted his teeth and planted his feet far apart. "Just tell them to pick you up here."

"Quit playing big brother here," I argued. "We're leaving, and his people are meeting us at my place." My voice was stern, and my patience at this point was nonexistent.

Jordan reached for my hand and intertwined our fingers. It was the first time he'd done it deliberately in front of Cade. His hold was fierce and firm as he pulled me out the door. Cade murmured something under his breath, but before I could decipher what he'd said, we were outside.

Jordan pulled my keys from his pocket and unlocked the car, which was parked by the curb. He opened my door, and I didn't even argue about him driving. I slipped into the passenger seat, pressing the navigation to my apartment.

When he shifted the gear to drive, my mouth spat out the questions roaming around in my head. "What's going on? Who called you back at the restaurant? Why are your bodyguards here? Why do you have to switch hotels? Why aren't you telling me what's going on?"

My questions fired out like a machine gun, fast and unrelenting.

But he changed the subject on me, trying to distract me like it'd work. "Is it always that volatile between you and your mother?"

"What?" My face scrunched up because I knew what he was trying to do here. I was the queen of diversion. "No. I mean, I don't know." My mother was something I never wanted to talk about. "Don't do that." I jabbed a finger at his shoulder. "Don't change the subject on me. What the hell is going on?"

He pulled to the side of the busy road and shifted the car in park. The abrupt movement had me bucking forward, the seat belt tightening against my chest.

Jordan's nostrils flared as he exhaled. "They think my stalker is in town ... in Rosendell."

The color drained from my face, and I blinked. *Stalker?* "What?"

"I have this obsessed fan." He shook his head. "I mean, I have quite a few obsessed fans, but this one ... this one is unstable. I have a restraining order against her."

My eyes widened adrenaline pumping through my veins. *His stalker is here?*

"I'm a big guy, and I'm not afraid, really. If anything were to happen, I'm sure I could protect myself. But the studio, my team, wants to make sure I'm safe, which is understandable. I'm more concerned about the people around me. Those I care about the most." His knuckles brushed my cheek, and I felt the touch everywhere.

"How do you know she's here?"

"My security team informed me." He sighed and ran one frustrated hand through his hair. "I'm pretty careful. I didn't think anyone would find me. I'm not from around here, and I tried to stay incognito. I'm just visiting my brother. Maybe someone spotted me and posted it on social media. With filming at Wells—eventually, it would have come to light, but security is tight on the set."

"But you haven't been to that many places, and you've haven't been in town for long."

"I did sign an autograph the other day when I grabbed some cigarettes."

I leaned in, worry creasing my normally calm features. "I could have bought some for you, Jordan." I needed to know more. I needed to know what he was up against. "Who is this girl? What do you know about her?"

He shifted with unease and tapped his fingers against the steering wheel. "It's not something I like to talk about."

"But it's me," I said, placing both hands on my chest. "And I want to know."

A sweet smile touched his face. "It is you, and you are one tough cookie." He blew out a long breath. "I just hate that I'm reliving this nightmare." He focused on the passing cars in front of us, his stare going vacant. "At first, she was normal, sending me underwear, naked pics of herself."

"That's normal?" I raised an eyebrow, and as soon as the words left my mouth, I knew it was the stupidest thing to say.

Of course, that was normal in his line of work. He was *People*'s Sexiest Man Alive. The Brad Pitt and Tom Cruise of our current generation.

"Then, it got a bit freaky. She found out my personal email address and started sending me love letters, but they were really disturbing ones. Ones that indicated that she'd been where I had been, restaurants I'd been to, places I'd been hanging out with my friends."

My heartbeat picked up, the hairs on my neck standing on end.

"She knew things. Where I worked out, what I ate for lunch."

He rubbed at his brow and stared at me, searching my face for something ... fear, maybe? So, I forced the eerie feeling away and kept my face steady.

"Then, it got fucking scary. She knew who I was with." He tilted his head to the side, easing some of the tension in his neck. "When I was briefly talking to Celine, someone I used to date, the stalker would mention her. Her emails would get angrier and more cryptic."

I swallowed the bile forming in the back of my throat.

"I increased security. I wondered if I should hire security for the girls I was seen with or those that I worked with. But I was never with a girl seriously, or for more than a couple of weeks, and the stalker has never contacted them."

"That's crazy," I said, my voice a tremulous whisper.

"Yeah, you can say that again. I thought I could keep it under control if I beefed up security." He paused, and then after a beat, a shudder ran through him. His stare was vacant, somewhere else. "But last year, she jumped the fence to my place and was outside my door."

My hand flew to my mouth. This time, I couldn't hide the fear in my eyes. "They need to find her."

He nodded. "She can't get within three hundred feet of me because of the restraining order, but that doesn't stop her from being in the vicinity."

Automatically, my fingers flew to the door to lock it. "Aren't you scared?"

"No." His response was firm, his eyes steady, and I believed him.

He shook our intertwined fingers, which were breaking all the rules. "I told you, I'm only worried about the people that I care about. That somehow, they'll be collateral damage. Cade, Wyatt ... you."

"I'm scared for you." For myself, sure. But for him too. Words that were in my head and weren't meant to be said. Four words that revealed my vulnerability and that I cared for him more than I'd led myself to believe.

His eyes bore into mine, so steady, so fierce, so right.

My stomach fluttered with butterflies, and without warning, for the second time in the day, he leaned into me and met my lips. Slow and seductive was long gone and replaced with a fiery passion. He kissed me with a raw, animalistic need, so intense that my whole body tingled. Lips on lips, tongue on tongue. His hand was clasped against my neck, keeping me in my spot.

A fire ignited in my belly like an engine roaring to life. Our kisses intensified, and the windows fogged up. I wanted him more than I wanted my next designer bag, and I was addicted to designer bags.

I hopped over the console and straddled him, my hands threading through his hair, our lips never breaking contact.

"What are we doing?" I asked when he peppered kisses down my neck.

"Kissing," he said, which made me laugh. "We should stop." He lapped kisses up and down my neck, his words saying one thing but his body wanting another. "Because this won't stop at just a make-out session."

His lips met mine one last time, and with one last peck,

he slowed our passionate tempo to a stop. "When I touch you, I don't want to stop." He cupped my face, his eyes tormented but beautiful at the same time. He ran one hand through my hair and massaged the base of my neck. "We haven't eaten yet."

I wanted to tell him that I wasn't hungry for food. "Well, we can't exactly go out to dinner now. Not after what you told me." I inhaled deeply and exhaled a shaky breath, trying to catch my breath and get my pulse back to a normal beat.

He laughed, but there was no humor in his tone.

"Do you want me to cook you something?" I asked.

"I don't know. She's in town, and I don't want to lead her to your place."

"I'm a big girl. I can take care of myself. I figure you'll be filming soon, and you'll be pretty busy. Plus, when was the last time you had a home-cooked meal?"

"Not in a long while." He nodded once, his eyes showing amusement. "Fine, but let me call my security team."

He tilted his head toward the passenger seat. "I need to grab my phone in my back pocket, but I'm a little constrained right now by this beautiful girl straddling me."

"You mean me?" I said, feigning innocence and touching my heart. I hopped over to my spot, holding his stare while he pulled the phone from his back pocket.

I couldn't care less anymore that he wanted to stop. I needed him out of my system, and Christene Armstrong always got what she wanted.

And tonight was the night it was going to happen.

CHAPTER 13

WE WENT a different route to my apartment, double- and triple-checking that no one had followed us. What normally took fifteen minutes to get to my place took us thirty.

Jordan was neurotic and relentless. He'd wait until the street was empty before making turns. He'd pull over and stall for no reason, and then two cars would flash their lights. One drove in front of us; the other waited for us to pass. His security detail trailed behind us and followed us home.

What seemed like twelve years later, we finally ended up in front of my place.

It was silent as we got out of my car, but the air was charged with energy. The same energy I felt every time we were in close vicinity to one another. Electric, passionate, undeniable.

A minute later, a black SUV pulled to the front and parked by the street. The same tall bodyguard that I'd seen at Angie's birthday party stepped out of the car and walked to the passenger side. "Mr. Ryder."

Another one stayed in the driver's seat.

Jordan smiled. "Dex, just wait out here."

Dex replied with a tip of his chin.

"Do they follow you everywhere?"

"Basically," he answered. "More so now."

I gulped. She was here in Rosendell—not at my apartment—but here ... in my hometown.

I rubbed at the back of my neck, unease heavy in my gut.

I started to walk into the building first, but he rushed toward the door and opened it before I stepped in.

"Such a gentleman."

From the moment I'd met him, he'd been respectful and courteous, opening doors, pulling out my seat, letting me walk ahead of him. Chivalry wasn't dead after all.

"I wasn't always like that, but my mother taught me well." He was talking about his adoptive mother.

Sometimes, I forgot he was adopted. Cade, Wyatt, and Jordan looked nothing alike but still acted like siblings when they were together. The banter, the disagreements, were the same for Angie and me. But I wondered about his biological parents, and it made me realize there was still so much I didn't know about him.

Right before we walked in my building, he pulled a baseball cap from his back pocket and placed it on his head, pulling it low over his eyes.

"You okay?" he asked.

His intense gaze, the glimmer in his eyes, didn't waver from my face, and I swallowed hard, unable to speak. The roof of my mouth felt like sandpaper, and I could sense the uptick of tempo in my pulse.

What the hell is wrong with me? Why do I turn into a puddle of goo whenever he gave me that look?

I shifted in my spot. The heat of my cheeks rose to my ears. "I'm so fine."

He slipped an arm around my waist and pulled me against him. "That you are. So, dinner and drinks?"

"I said I'd cook you dinner." I tapped my finger against my chin. "But last time we drank together, I ended up practically naked in your bed."

"Nothing happened," he reminded me.

I tilted my head, wondering why.

"But if I'd had my way, lots of things would have happened that night." He leaned in and kissed the tender part of my neck. "My brother never said anything about kissing you. He just said I couldn't ..."

This man is such a tease. "Do you always listen to whatever everyone tells you?"

"If it's my family asking, yes." He slowly pulled away, dropping his hands from my sides. The loss of contact and warmth was like a shock of cold water. "I had nothing before them, and I have everything because of them. What I do now, who I am, is all because of them."

His fingers trailed lightly down my arm, and goose bumps followed.

"And if all I can do is kiss you, then I'll take it. I'm going to kiss you every chance I get, but know that I'm using all my self-restraint to not go beyond that."

My lips pinched together. He made no sense.

"What's the point? You're getting me all hot for nothing, and you've got a bad case of blue balls."

"Because I like you, and I want to kiss the crazy-beautiful girl with a smart-ass mouth." His gaze flickered to my lips, up to meet my eyes, and then back again to my mouth.

And there was that look again. My stomach flipped, my palms were sweaty, and my whole body heated.

My gaze dropped. I hated and loved the way he affected me. I was glad he wasn't immune to my charm either and that he was using all his self-control. They were very admirable qualities, loyalty and respect, but the fact that he was loyal and respectful only made me want him more.

"Okay, dinner next," I said

He intertwined our hands.

I let him hold my hand, and suddenly, I realized I'd missed the intimacy of hand-holding. The gentle touch of skin against skin, intertwined fingers, the connection wherever you went, walking hand in hand.

"We're breaking all the rules here."

He smiled, and his eyebrows scrunched. "Cade said I couldn't sleep with you. Right now, I'm going to take those words literally, so we're not breaking any rules." His voice trailed off as though there should be a *yet* at the end of his sentence.

"Good plan," I said under my breath.

He pulled me closer when we rode the elevator up to my penthouse suite.

"So, have you lived here long?" he asked.

"It was my first buy out of college." An eighteen-story high-rise. I loved this place, and obviously, I lived in one of the penthouse suites that occupied half of the top floor and had the best view of Rosendell.

When the elevator pinged open, he held it, so I could walk out first in front of him. My heels dug into the plush beige carpet of the hallway. He placed a light hand in the middle of my back.

"Does this ever stop? Your gentlemanly behavior?" I peered back behind me, smiling.

He shook his head. "Nope. Mom taught us two things—manners and how to cook. Wyatt has always been a nice guy, but it took me a while to get used to her rules because I was always the troublemaker."

"That's hard to believe." My tone was laced heavy with sarcasm. I was sure Jordan had been born with *trouble* written on his birth certificate.

He ran one hand through his hair, his face thoughtful. "Before the Ryders took me in, I was in and out of juvie." He paused and eyed me before he continued. "That seems like a long time ago, but I remember when I almost killed someone with my fists." His eyes turned distant, but in the next second, he shook it off. "That was a long time ago. I promised Mom I'd never end up in jail. Cade and Wyatt too. I owe it to them for helping me stay on the right side of the law."

His admission shocked me. Looking at his clean-cut demeanor, the Rolex on his wrist, and his newly pressed designer jeans, you would never guess he came from the wrong side of town.

"Seems like you cleaned up nicely."

"It wasn't without help." His fingers brushed against my elbow, ushering me toward the door. "Ladies first."

"I could get used to all this gentlemanliness."

He chuckled and then wiggled his eyebrows. "How do you know I'm not letting you go first, so I can see that tight ass of yours bounce?"

I twerked my ass mid-step. "I knew it." I pointed a finger in his direction. "You're an undercover bad boy. So deceiving. Face of an angel, but I know the truth now."

One of his hands dropped to my waist, and he tightly pressed four fingers into my skin. The contact was so sensual that my nipples pebbled against my shirt.

"I never said I was a good boy." His breath was warm

against the shell of my ear, and my breathing staggered. "But it's too bad because you're never going to find out."

I flattened my hair and composed myself. This situation was out of control, and I needed to seize the reins, or I'd never feel steady. "I wouldn't be so sure about that," I whispered under my breath.

"What did you say?" He laughed.

I spoke up louder, "I said, I'm sure about that." I pushed the key into my condo door and flicked the lights on before stepping inside.

Jordan trailed behind me, and I could feel his every move. We walked down the hallway, passing pictures of my girlfriends and me on vacation; my family and me in NYC on New Year's; Angie and me with smiling faces—all preserved in black frames that led into the main room.

The tension between us tightened like a double-knotted rope.

"Nice place." He strolled to my kitchen island, and his hand brushed against the marble.

An array of fruit sat in the center, and overhead, pots and pans hung in order of size on a rack suspended from the ceiling. Otherwise, the kitchen counters were bare—the KitchenAid mixer, toaster, coffee machine hidden in their intended spots. If he opened the cabinets, he'd see all the dishes stacked in their respective piles. My cloth napkins were all folded, tucked in the drawers, and sorted by color.

One thing I prided myself in was hard work and the finer things in life that my hard work paid for.

His eyes widened, taking everything in. "I love your place."

Floor-to-ceiling windows accented one wall of my living room, leading to my patio adorned with my mini bar and Jacuzzi.

"I hired this interior decorator because I wanted a professional opinion."

He nodded and ran his hand over my Taurus custom-made dining room table that I'd had shipped from Italy.

"You own this building?"

I walked to the kitchen, grabbing two wineglasses. Wine first, and then I'd have to figure out what to cook for dinner since we hadn't eaten yet. "Yep. Basically, every one of the surrounding buildings on this block belongs to Armstrong."

"Your family is self-made." His eyes assessed me with approval.

"Well, it was really Grandpa who started everything. He bought one house, renovated it, and flipped it. One house turned into three, which turned into apartment buildings, which turned into strip malls and now tiny skyscrapers in our tiny town of Rosendell."

"I'm impressed."

"You should be." I placed the glasses on the counter. "Grandpa, now, he was one cutthroat businessman."

The kitchen, living room, and dining room were one big open space. The only separation was the kitchen island stove with a stainless-steel mount range hood hanging from the ceiling. I strolled to the counter and picked up a remote that lifted automatic blinds, exposing my view that overlooked the city.

"Nice view."

"Thank you." I surely paid for the view.

"I wasn't talking about what I see outside." There was a mischievous sparkle in his eye, and my stomach flipped like a pancake.

When I turned toward him, his eyes weren't focused on the twinkling stars or lights from the windows from the skyscrapers on the horizon. His baby blues were directly on me.

My cheeks warmed. They never warmed, and I never blushed. I made men blush. I hated this feeling.

"Wanna drink while I cook?" I strolled to the mini wine cooler and pulled out the bottle of wine.

"What are we having?"

"Madeira. It's red, and I bought it from Portugal." I lifted the bottle and tipped my head toward the stove. "And for dinner, I think I'll make some pasta. Let's be Italian today, shall we?"

"Sounds good to me. If you're serving, I'm partaking."

I hid a smile. Little did he know, before the night was through, I'd be serving more than he ever thought he'd be taking.

CHAPTER 14

THE STARS TWINKLED in front of us as we sat at the table on my rooftop balcony, enjoying the breeze, good conversation, and finishing off our second bottle of wine. I was admiring the way the moonlight accented the hard planes of his jaw and the blond in his hair but more so the bluish gray in his eyes. My chicken fettuccine Alfredo pasta had been a success, and I was about to work on my second piece of cheesecake. Frozen cheesecake was a must in my freezer. That and mocha ice cream.

I took a swig of my drink and angled closer. "What do you mean? So, you were doing a love scene, and they had a little cover on your penis, and you got hard?" I coughed up my wine as laughter bubbled up my windpipe.

Just when I thought nothing would top his stories, he'd pull out another one to make me laugh harder.

My cheeks and ears were warm from my buzz.

"I couldn't help it." He tipped back his glass and smiled his Oscar-award-winning smile. "She had the nicest rack. I mean ... I did apologize afterward. It was pretty awkward, but there's a certain way you're supposed to position yourself to act out a love scene, and how she was positioned was directly above my cock. She was rubbing against my dick, and ... well, you know ..." He averted his stare, seeming sheepish. It was kinda cute on him.

More laughter escaped me. *Oh, the joys of working in Hollywood.*

"So, what happened after? Did you take her off the lot for a test drive?"

He coughed, choking on his wine. "The lot? Who talks like that?" Reaching for the napkin, he dabbed at the dribbles of wine that had slipped from the corner of his mouth. "And no. She was married. I don't date married women."

I quirked an eyebrow, curious about all the action this man had gotten. "You have quite the playboy reputation." I lifted my hair and pulled it into a bun on the top of my head. It must be the muggiest night all summer, gauging by the way my hair had been stuck to the back of my neck. "Always with a model," I said. "Never with the same girl twice."

"Stalker," he coughed out, covering his mouth with one hand. "Should I file a restraining order against you too?" he teased.

I chucked a napkin at him. "Please. This is widely known. If you walked through a grocery store aisle and looked at all those tabloids, you'd be confused about your love life too. So ... I want to hear it from the source."

He leaned in and brushed a finger against my cheek. Goose bumps formed down my neck, turning into horny bumps traveling farther south of the border.

"I only date beautiful ones. Plus, why stop something you're good at?" He winked and offered a bemused smile.

I rolled my eyes, but shit, if I didn't want a piece of that action too. Yes, I did. I'd raise my hand and volunteer as tribute.

Enough of this nonsense.

I stood, placed my wineglass on the table, and sauntered over toward my hot tub. I untied the top, took off the cover, and turned it on. The hum and vibrations of the tub came to life.

This party was just about to get started.

I was going to turn up the heat and relieve some tension —the tension that should have been eased nights ago.

At least, that was my goal.

"What are you doing?" His tone lowered, his breath husky, nervous and hella turned on.

"I'm taking the party into the Jacuzzi."

I pushed down my slacks and unbuttoned my shirt, slipping it off and exposing my black lace thong and matching bra. His sharp intake of breath cut through the night sky, and then his mouth slipped slightly ajar.

I bit my lip to hide my smile.

I threw one leg over the edge of the hot tub, careful not to fall, and slipped right in. Throwing him a sinful glance, I asked, "You joining me or what?"

He lost all ability to speak, and for once, I was grateful that the tables had turned. This was exactly what I needed. *Now, look at who is all out of sorts.*

He swallowed. "Uh ... I don't think that's a good idea."

My look was playful, seductive. "Did Cade specifically say you couldn't get in a hot tub with me?"

What did his brother dating my sister have to do with me? If anything, my sister was trying to drive us together, pelvis to pelvis.

His eyes searched the vicinity—who knew for what? Divine intervention? There was no escaping this she-devil.

"No, he never said that, but ..." His voice was shaky and lacked his normal confidence.

"Or maybe you don't have as much self-control as you think you do."

Automatically, he stood, bringing the bottle of wine and wineglasses and setting them on the edge of the hot tub. I could read him like an open book, clear and predictable. He was the male version of myself. When someone challenged me, I always, always womanned up.

My mouth watered as he lifted his shirt above his head and threw it on top of the chair. Next, he pushed down his jeans, and I might have drooled a little at the sight of his six-pack leading to the happy trail that was covered by boxers.

Goodness gracious, his great balls of fire were thick beneath his boxers. And for the love of all that was holy, he wasn't even hard.

"Move over," he commanded, his voice rough and guttural.

"Okay." I scooted over, making room for him.

He slipped, and the water slushed against the edge of the Jacuzzi. The air was charged with so much energy that I could almost taste it. The invisible spark, a line that I felt from his eyes to mine, intensified, and that sizzle was undeniably there.

"Let's work on finishing that bottle." I poured him a glass and passed it to him and then poured myself one. *Then, you can finish working on me.*

Once the wine touched his lips, he relaxed, spread his arms over the sides of the tub, and leaned his head all the way back as he closed his eyes, his whole body going limp in the water. "This actually feels good."

"Mmhmm," I hummed, wanting to tell him what else would make him feel good.

"I bet you use this often." His eyes remained closed, his breathing steady and even.

"Yeah, when I first moved here, Angie and I were out here almost every day. Lying out during the weekends mostly." Now, those nights were far and few with Cade in her life. "I kinda miss our sisterly Jacuzzi and Netflix nights."

His eyes flicked open, meeting mine. "I love how you love. How you love your family. How passionate you are about your job."

His words caught me off guard.

"You and I are more alike than not." His eyes fell shut again, and he sank farther into the water. "We love wholeheartedly, and we'd do anything for our family."

Silence spanned the space between us, and I relaxed against the Jacuzzi, admiring the view.

The firm set of his shoulders, his square jaw, the shadow of a beard on his baby face. His profile was sharp and confident, and oh-so attractive.

This time, I wanted to see if he tasted as good as he looked, so I inched over, and his eyes flew open. He straightened and sat taller, and the water swished between us.

His eyes flicked back as though he was debating whether or not to get out. Considering I was about to turn up the volume on this party, maybe he should.

"Did you know when I was younger, I always wanted to be an actress?"

"Really?" His pitch heightened.

If we weren't in the hot tub, I'd imagine the beads of water on his upper lip and cheeks were sweat.

"Yes. A Disney actress."

I undid the bun I'd put up earlier, letting my locks fall

into the water, causing ripples to fan out. There was too much space between us, and when I moved closer, he stiffened, the strain in his neck visible. I placed my wineglass on the edge and stood. My breasts were level with his face, and a shiver ran through me.

"I think I've seen this scene before in one of your movies." My voice was barely audible against the gurgling of the hot tub.

His eyes were cautious, and he purposely gripped the edge of the hot tub, leaning back as far as he could.

"Remember *Love and Lust in Vegas*?" I asked.

A nervous laugh escaped him. "You saw that? That was one of the first films I made."

"And I loved that movie, especially the hot tub scene." I stepped in closer, dropped to eye-level, and wrapped my arms around his neck.

"Tene ..." There was worry, indecision, and want in his eyes that mirrored mine.

"Did Cade say we couldn't act? That I can't replay a scene?" I sucked on my bottom lip, pushed against him, and pressed my aching breasts against his chest. Heat flooded every molecule of my body, searing my skin, bubbling in my veins.

I needed this. I wanted my sanity back.

Droplets of water cascaded down the hard planes of his toned chest, and I angled my face toward his.

"How about we say this is an acting lesson?"

"This is a very dangerous acting lesson." His hands moved to my shoulders, and his fingers trembled, just like the rest of him.

I knew he was using every ounce of self-control to keep steady, and I was using every ounce of mine to not strip and attack him.

I decided to turn up the heat and wrap my thighs around his waist, pushing myself flush against his body.

He was hard, and a small moan fell from his lips. "Tene ..."

"So, you said that the last time you got hard ..." I pushed my pelvis against his thickening bulge. "... she was rubbing you wrong."

The water splashed between us, and the sensual friction caused my insides to burn with an intense need that was unbearable.

His hands dropped to my waist to still me, but I positioned myself against him. My breathing sped up as I rocked farther into him, teasing him.

My nipples pebbled into hard nubs, and every inch of my body prickled with sensitivity.

"You're playing with fire here, Tene." His breath was warm and throaty and horny against my skin.

"This is just an acting lesson," I reminded him. "I just want some tips from the best."

His eyes darkened as we rubbed against each other, and he grabbed my ass in a ten-finger hold and pushed into me. One. Two. Three times. My eyes fell shut as our breathing became labored.

My hands threaded through his hair, and I tilted my head to peer down at him. "Cade never banned you specifically from this."

His fingers moved up, lightly skimming my stomach, cupping my breasts, and landing on my face. "I'm done talking about Cade."

Our lips crashed together in an overpowering, hungry kiss. A kiss that sang through my body and sent shivers of desire through me. He flicked the seam of my lips and kissed me openmouthed, our tongues meshing together in a sensual dance. He ravished my mouth, hard at times, soft at others, the perfect arousing rhythm.

"You taste so good," he whispered, dropping his mouth to my neck, peppering kisses back up to my mouth. "You're beautiful. You're perfect."

"All lines," I breathed.

"All true," he said breathlessly. "I want you so bad. You just don't understand."

My insides soared. It had been a long dry spell. Well, months with nothing but my vibrator was a long dry spell for me. I needed him. All of him buried deep inside me.

When I stood, his fingers gripped my hips, and his mouth hovered over my stomach, his tongue dipping into my navel. He peered up at me through horny, hooded eyes as he flicked his tongue over each of my nipples. When his large hand squeezed the swell of one of my breasts, my head flew back, and my eyes fell shut from the sensation.

I gripped his slick, damp hair with both hands and pulled him up. I was done with nice and slow and careful. I wanted hard and fast and dangerous.

I wrapped both hands around his neck and crashed my lips against his again.

"Fuck it!" He stood with one arm around my waist and the other holding the edge of the tub for support to get us out.

The water dripped against the concrete, our undergarments soaking wet and clinging to our bodies like Saran Wrap.

Our lips met together in a fiery hold, and I met him head-on, mouth on mouth, tongue against tongue.

He gently laid me on my patio table and slid my panties down my legs.

The battle he was fighting against our attraction had been lost. This time, the white flag was replaced with my black lace underwear as he waved them and tossed them to the side.

When he dropped to his knees and his tongue touched my center, my hips bucked forward.

"Relax," he soothed.

Relax? There had been no lead-in, no warning, just a flick of his tongue against my clit. And this man wanted me to relax?

Loud moans escaped me. I wasn't a quiet woman. If something felt good, I'd let my man know it, and oh goodness, his tongue was mighty skilled and long and thick and—

Ahh!

My eyes fell shut, and he only lifted his head when I let out an exceedingly loud moan.

"Baby, you've got to be quiet, or we'll have your neighbors calling the cops."

I lifted my head and shot him a look that made him laugh. "I live in the penthouse for a reason."

There were only skyscrapers on the horizon that were higher than my building. No one would be able to see us unless they were working at two in the morning and had binoculars.

He slipped two fingers inside me, and I exhaled, dropping my head back on the table.

"So, you've done this before? Sex on this balcony?"

I breathed through my next words, desperate for release. "No, that's not what I said."

When I moved against the friction of his fingers, he stilled.

"Jordan ..." I moaned.

The smile on his face was blinding and playful, but, most of all, annoying.

"Did you need something?"

I lifted my bottom, wanting more, desperate for release. "Yes."

Warm lips trailed kisses along my ankle and up my leg to my inner thigh, ending where he'd begun.

I lifted my hips, needing to get closer, needing more friction.

"You're so sexy. So sweet." He flicked and teased my center, his hands rubbing up and down my thighs.

I gripped a good chunk of his hair. Enough foreplay. I wanted the real thing. "I need ... need you in me." I wanted to feel the fullness of him when I came.

He kissed me fiercely with the tenderness of his mouth, and I could taste myself on him, exciting me further. His hardness pressed against my stomach through his boxers. I knew we'd be explosive together, and I was done waiting.

My hands dropped to the waistband of his soaked boxers, pulling them down just a tad and holding his thickness between us, feeling the expansion of his hardness between my fingertips.

His hands fell at my thighs, and our mouths found each other under the moonlight once again.

"Condom," I commanded.

He pulled back and dropped his forehead against mine. "I don't have one."

I searched his face and stopped. "What? In your jeans?"

He backed away, and my fingers dropped from his cock.

He strained his neck to the sky, his breathing labored and erratic, his chest heaving. "I doubted my self-control, so I ..."

I hopped off the table, steady on my feet. My body

zinged with no release, and my emotions were all over the place. "Well, I have some inside."

His fingers dropped to my wrist, stilling me. "Tene ..."

My eyebrows flew to the open night sky. "What?"

"I can't. We can't. And I shouldn't have, but you're ..." His eyes scanned my body. "I just needed a taste. Lie on the table; let me finish you off."

"You're serious, aren't you?" It was as if I had been doused with a bucket of ice. No. Pelted with ice. In my face.

When he didn't answer, I knew he was dead serious, and my face reddened. I dropped to my knees and reached for the waistband of his boxers, which were slick to his skin.

"Tene ..." His words trailed off, going poof into the air as I took him deep into my mouth. I took him in as far as I could take him without gagging and watched his eyes fly to the back of his head. "Sh-shit."

Within minutes, I could hear the guttural sounds that escaped his lips. He held on to the table, his fingers trembling, clutching my table for support. I sucked and tasted and flicked my tongue against his thickness, possibly giving the best blow job I'd ever given in my life. I could tell he was close, given the tightening of his balls and the loud noises escaping him.

Then, I stopped.

Abruptly.

I pulled back, stood, crossed my arms over my well-endowed chest, and smiled.

He lifted his head, his face red, eyes showing confusion.

Take that, Taco Blocker.

Then, I turned, leaving him a standing, boner-pointing mess.

In one swift movement, he grabbed me by the waist and

lifted me under the knees. "You're right; he never has to know. Where's your room?"

I pointed in the direction he needed to go.

"You don't like when I play cockblocker, but you totally can?" I huffed out.

He shut my words down with passionate kisses and led us through the patio door and to my bedroom.

CHAPTER 15

WITH KISSES ON LIPS, hands on hips, our bodies crashed against each other. Mine was crazy hot, the flames spreading like a wildfire underneath my skin. What I needed wasn't water. What I needed was release. He gently guided me onto the bed, his eyes deeply hooded, thick with need and heavy with want.

My body was on the verge of combustion, and I mirrored the same need, but I backed up against the head-board, playing the cat-and-mouse game. He'd started it, and I would decide when we finished it.

He smirked, and the deep blue in his eyes darkened. "Is that how you want to play it?"

I sucked in my bottom lip. "Maybe I don't want you as much as you think I want you."

He lifted an eyebrow, and his dick twitched beneath him. He peered down at his package. "Well, I know one thing—this guy knows what he wants." He leaned forward, tipping his dick in my direction, a direct line to me. "And it wants you."

He reached for my feet, and I squealed, laughing and

wriggling against his hold and against my purple satin sheets.

He caged me in, his arms by my head, and kissed me with reckless abandon, steady and seductive and sensual. His hardness pressed against my stomach, my wetness touching his skin.

"Beautiful," he whispered through sweet, peppered kisses. "God, you're exquisite." Words of worship escaped him. He planted a kiss between each word, on my shoulders, my neck, my face, and back to meet my lips.

I quivered at the sweet tenderness. And besides the desire building inside of me, a little sliver of my heart opened for him—for his words; his kindness; for the love of his family; for the gentle way he'd taken care of me the other night when no one else really did.

My hands ran through his hair as he lowered his kisses to my neck, my collarbone, the swell of my breasts, worshipping me with his lips. He took my nipple in his mouth, and his tongue tantalized the swollen bud, making my body arch and wriggle beneath him.

His hand seared a path down my abdomen, onto my thigh, and between my legs. He slipped a finger inside of me. First one and then two.

My eyes closed at the contact. The sensations coursing through my body, and moans of pleasure escaped as he continued to tease me, rocking my world.

The crazy sensations were all too much to take. I rested on my elbows, out of breath, and reached for his hardness, beginning to stroke his length. "Please ..."

I turned toward the side table, opened the drawer, and grabbed a condom. The crinkle of the wrapper against my fingertips was like running toward the goal line.

When I turned to face him, there was no indecision; his eyes told me this was going down.

He grabbed the condom from me and ripped the side with his teeth. My mouth watered at the sight of him, his length at full-fledged vagina salute.

He knelt before me and dropped his body against mine. "Is this what you want, Tene?" His gaze traveled over my face and searched my eyes.

"Yes," I breathed.

With a tenderness as though I could break, he cupped my cheek. "First, I've gotta do this."

He pressed his lips against mine. The kiss was surprisingly gentle, but it still sent my stomach plunging like a wild roller coaster. I exhaled, my heart pitter-pattering against my chest. His tongue traced the fullness of my mouth, sucked on my top lip, and then as though he didn't want my other lip to be forgotten, he paid attention to my bottom one.

"There's nothing like kissing you, Tene." He kissed my cheek and my neck, and then he peppered kisses on my earlobe, before returning to my lips.

Kissing seemed to last forever, yet it wasn't enough.

He could kiss me for hours, and that was all I would ever need. Even without foreplay or penetration, I would be satisfied with the sweetness of his kisses.

Inwardly, I sighed.

When he positioned himself above me, I was struck by the sad notion that his kisses had stopped, but when he entered me, and I felt the fullness of him inside, I knew it was exactly what I needed.

Touchdown.

We both groaned at finally feeling our bodies molding into one.

It took me a second to adjust to him, the width of him, the strength of him.

He peered down at me with a look I hadn't experienced in forever. It wasn't a look of lust, want, or utter sexual need, as I'd seen time and time again.

It was a look of longing, and that sliver in my heart opened just a tad bit more.

When he began to move above me, my mind was mush. His words and his movements overtook every thought in my head. I was completely filled with Jordan Ryder. Not just my body but also my mind.

"Baby, you feel ... amazing."

Our breathing was labored, and our skin clung together from our sweat as the scent of pure passion permeated the air.

Thrust after thrust, he whispered sweetness into my ear. How good I felt. How beautiful I was. How much he liked me. And it was exhilarating.

Dirty talk was good, familiar, but this ... what was happening? I wasn't used to this.

It went deeper. Touched deep in the chambers of my chest.

"Baby, are you almost there?"

"Yes." I wrapped my legs around his waist, bringing us even closer together.

He pounded against me, harder and faster and sweeter. "I'm not going to last long."

The vein at his temple pulsed, and I locked eyes with him, loving the feel of him, his hands, and his movements above me. He was beautiful—from the tips of his dirty blond hair to the irises of his baby-blue eyes to the strength of his body—but that was nothing compared to the softness in his heart.

The tingling began at the base of my spine, warning that I was close—so close.

He cupped the side of my face and then bent down to kiss me with a tender passion that I felt everywhere. "Come for me, baby."

His thrusts became urgent, his breathing ragged. He was on his last string, and I was there. Right there with him. The ripple of feeling tingled up my spine, the pleasing, pounding pressure building.

"I'm coming," I breathed.

His look was one of ecstasy but also thoughtfulness. He was waiting for me. Me.

And with that one gesture, it overtook my mind and stopped my body. Because as his thrusting became urgent and his movements turned erratic, one clear thought pushed through.

I like this man.

I liked him for who he was, not the guy on the big screen, not his actor facade. I felt a connection with him, a connection I had only ever felt with Logan.

He leaned back and grabbed my hips, his movements commanding. His chest was glorious, and a sheen of sweat highlighted the black ink against his muscles, moving down his defined abs.

Then, I remembered.

The entire room stopped, and everything stilled in my chest.

The ink on his heart, black and thick and visible there. In small Chinese characters, just as Cade had told me, her name above his left pec. Candice.

And just as that one thought filtered through my head, it threw my whole world off-kilter. To cover my unease, I bucked my hips and screamed his name, faking it like my life depended on it.

He pumped one last time and stilled inside of me, and I was robbed of my own climax with the most beautiful man on the planet.

A feather of kisses descended on me, on my eyelids, on my cheeks, ending on my lips. My body tightened like a coiled wire ball.

When he pulled back, lying through my teeth, I said, "That was amazing."

The silence and passion were gone, and all that was left in its wake was a lie. Though he was inside of me, on top of me, I'd never felt so far away from someone.

I squirmed beneath him, not knowing what to do, not knowing how to act. After a beat, I lifted my chin to meet his lips with one final peck and pushed at his chest.

His hold didn't relent, and he rested his head against mine for one split second. He closed his eyes and exhaled deeply, falling into me. "You're amazing."

It took three whole breaths for him to move above me, five to six seconds that seemed to last hours. Then, he finally got up, disposed of the condom in the trash can by the window, and hopped back into bed.

Without words, he pulled me into him, and we did more than spoon. We nooked, which was ten times more intimate than spooning. With my neck tucked into his, he fell asleep with me in his arms. We were entangled together, my breathing matching his, and my heart and his heart beating as one.

And I didn't get an ounce of sleep that night because I couldn't stop wondering if I was the woman on his mind or if it was the one forever etched on his chest.

CHAPTER 16

MORNING LIGHT PEEKED through my window, and I gazed up at the tiny cracks in my ceiling. Earlier I'd focused on the time in red digital numbers on my side table, watching it tick slowly away.

When I tried to move from the entanglement of Jordan's arms, his soft snores ceased, and it scared me to be still.

The sheets rustled when Jordan turned over, and I held my breath, knowing this was my chance to slip out. I hadn't slept the night before. My body was a wreck—on edge like an exposed electric line—from not getting my own release and from thoughts of Candice. I wondered what she'd looked like when they had started dating, if he was still in love with her.

When soft, even sounds escaped him, I knew he was dead asleep, and I slipped out of bed and decided to fry some bacon and eggs to try to relax my nerves.

It was rare that I didn't come. I knew my body, and I knew how to hit the right area to induce my own spots behind my eyes.

And if I was honest with myself, I knew why it hadn't happened last night.

It was my mind over my body.

It was Jordan and his crazy, kind self.

And the fact that I was utterly *in like* with this man.

It was Candice's flipping name over his left pec, right above his heart.

And, yes, in our moments of passion, Cade's face, his brother, had ruined my orgasm. His words of warning playing over like a bad song in my head.

I gritted my teeth.

We were supposed to do the deed, so I could finally feel steady and in charge of my life again. And now, sleeping with him had done the opposite.

It unhinged me.

Now, everything was shit.

It was flipping worse.

Ten million times worse than before.

I slammed the pan against the stove.

"Hey."

I jumped, feeling my whole body tremble from the mere sound of his voice.

I turned around and pushed an awkward smile to the surface.

"Hi." I waved from the stove. A wave. A flipping wave like he was a stranger, and we hadn't bumped uglies the night before.

He carefully eyed me, watching my movements and, more noticeably, my eyes. I turned away and focused on the stove, as though there was nothing in the world more interesting than cooking bacon and eggs.

Yes, so interesting. Especially how the eggs were forming together into a solid.

Inhaling deeply, I took in the scent of bacon grease and eggs and tried to calm my erratic heart.

I knew my face would tell all. How I had faked it. Even worse, how I liked him.

My whole life was in shambles now. I even doubted my ability to lie with a straight face.

His arms wrapped around my center, and I forced my body to relax.

"I missed you this morning. Waking up next to you."

"Mmm."

His lips found the tender part of my neck, and I tensed.

It would have been so easy to just melt in his hold, just give in to his arms around me, but I felt even more unsteady as though the earth were shaking beneath my feet.

"Aren't we getting domestic now?" His words were muffled against my skin. He was hard, the thick bulge in his jeans pressing against my ass.

If he thought we were doing part two this morning, he was dead wrong.

My laugh was nervous, my tone high-pitched. "Yes, me, Suzy Homemaker."

His hands skimmed my bare stomach, under my half T-shirt, and he rotated his hips, pressing his morning wood against me. "Last night was the best movie I've ever made." He chuckled against my skin, his warm breath sending shocks lower and lower that I felt in my core. "Let's reenact it. I don't think I've perfected the scene."

Oh boy, that is an understatement.

Breathe. I just needed to breathe.

I disentangled myself from his arms. All I knew was that I couldn't get too deep. Who was I kidding? I was knee deep in Jordan shit, and there was no way in hell a replay of last night could happen because I'd get more attached than I was now.

I reached for the empty plate beside me, pushed the bacon and eggs onto it, and hip-checked him out of my way. "Although I'd love to do Jordan part two," I sassed, "I can't. I've got a busy day ahead of me."

My heartbeat rang in my ears.

Pound. Pound. Pound.

Harder. Harder. Harder.

He followed me toward the table where I placed the plate of bacon and eggs and two table settings. After I served us, I focused on my plate of yellow and burnt red like it was the most interesting thing on the planet. I couldn't breathe. I couldn't get the next breath into my lungs. I was the freaking girl who could breathe freely. I owned the air. It made way for me as I passed.

What the hell is happening in my life?

Automatically, I stood. "You know what? I really need to get my day started."

I needed to breathe. I needed air. At this point, I was gulping, semi-hyperventilating.

He stood, too, his eyes cautious. "Is something wrong?"

"No, no, no." I frantically shook my head. "I just I really ..." *Breathe.* "... really need to go." And then I snatched my keys off the counter and bolted toward my own door, running to the elevator, down to the first floor, and past my doorman in my pajamas.

Once outside, I inhaled deeply, dropping at the waist and taking in air like there was a shortage.

It took a few seconds to finally think clearly, and I half-ran to my car, shutting myself in and driving to nowhere in particular.

I'd just done the walk of shame. But for the first time ever, it was from my own condo.

I drove for thirty minutes. I was in booty shorts and a half T-shirt that showcased a lot of skin. I couldn't get breakfast because I was half-naked, and I'd stormed out of my apartment with nothing other than keys. But at least ... I could breathe.

I ended up in front of Angie's place because there was nowhere else I could go.

The doorman recognized me. Hell, we owned the building. I ignored the way his eyes roamed up my legs. I would have had a snarky comment for him if I didn't have bigger problems to worry about.

I paced the small elevator until it pinged, opening to Cade and Angie's floor.

Bang. Bang. Bang.

My fists pounded against Angie's door, unrelenting in their attack. I froze when Cade opened it instead, his hair a disheveled mess, his eyes pissed off and standing only in boxers.

Anyone else would have been intimidated by his stature alone, but I knew he was harmless.

"I'm here for Angie." I stormed past him and walked toward their bedroom, shutting and locking the door behind me.

The shrill shriek of her voice had me jumping back. Half the sheets were thrown on the floor, and so were most of their clothes. She was naked, and I had obviously interrupted their alone time. Hence Cade's pissed off face.

"What the hell, Tene?" She pulled the white sheets over her bare body.

I scoffed. "Don't pretend like I haven't seen you naked. Remember when I walked in on Cade eating your—"

"Stop!" Her eyes were round and horrified.

And I did stop because as long as I lived, I would never be able to erase the visual of seeing Cade and Angie in that compromising position.

I noticed the whip and nipple clamps on the floor. "Angie?"

She followed my gaze to the toys on the floor. "We tried it. It's not our thing. Anyway, what do you want?" she demanded, a hint of annoyance in her voice.

I wasn't going to ask them questions on their sex life when mine was out of control. "I wanted to see you." I jumped over to her and hugged her over the sheet. You'd think I'd be uncomfortable, bumped up against her with only a sheet between us, but we were more than comfortable around each other.

"Omigod, what happened?" she asked as I snuggled against her chest.

The door shook with Cade's rage. One more pound against the wood, and it'd knock over. "Open the door. Jesus, Tene, what're you doing here?"

"I'll only be a minute," I yelled back. *Who have I transformed into? Who is this woman snuggling next to her baby sis?*

"Sorry, babe, just give us a couple," Angie yelled back.

I could hear the deep groan of frustration through the door, his heavy footsteps lightening.

"Now, tell me, what has gotten into you?" She adjusted the sheet and tucked one end into her side.

"Nothing." I shrugged. "Can't I come over and have a

little sissy time?" I snuggled against her side, hiding my face against her shoulder.

She pulled back, her look incredulous. "Sissy time?"

I huffed and shut my eyes tightly. "Don't ask me. Just don't ask me."

Shit, I would leave if I wasn't afraid of going to my own place because Jordan was there.

"My life has turned upside down and inside out like a bad sitcom," I huffed, peering up at her and with such desperation in my tone that I didn't recognize my own voice. "First, the spooning, then the nooking, and then the liking. How could I have predicted this?"

When her mouth opened, I groaned and fisted a handful of my hair. "I said, don't ask."

"I didn't say a word." Angie laughed, and then her eyebrow shot up. "The liking?" she whispered.

I buried my head into her side again. "I said, don't ask."

She sat up taller, adjusting the sheet cover so it wouldn't slip. "Does the liking have anything to do with a blue-eyed actor?"

I pounded my head, palm open, punctuating each word with a hit against my skull. "I hate this. I hate this. I hate this." Maybe I could beat Jordan out of my head and out of my life.

Her upbeat voice made it worse. "You like him. You like him. You like him!" She clapped her hands together and bounced on the bed. "I'm so happy for you, Tene." The way she uttered those words seemed as though it were my birthday, and I'd received the greatest gift ever.

"You make it sound like this is a good thing!" I screeched.

If this were such a good thing, then why did I feel like my life was out of control? I thought love—I mean, like—

was supposed to make the world go 'round and complete me, and it was supposed to feel like I was walking on water. I felt like I was drowning, and the water was seeping into my lungs.

"Well, it's not a good thing," I sassed. "Do you know we had sex?"

Her smile widened.

Gah! What is wrong with my sister?

"And do you know that I didn't orgasm?" I added irritated.

If I thought that was supposed to have her empathize with my situation, I was wrong because she started to laugh. A full-on giggle.

"It's not funny," I groaned. My stats on orgasming were unprecedented.

All the time. Never a fail. A-plus all the way.

Except for now, and I wondered why that was. *Why is it different now?* My brain and body were malfunctioning.

I flopped onto my back and covered my eyes with one arm.

"It'll be okay." Angie's sweet voice was meant to comfort me, but it only made it worse.

Because I knew it wouldn't be okay. How could it possibly? My grand plan of sleeping and gaining my old self back had backfired. Now, I'd never know which way was up. I'd be walking sideways for the rest of my life.

"You said you liked him? Then, talk to him," she said softly.

I jolted up, beyond frustrated with the situation. "About what? About the fact that I didn't orgasm? About the fact that even if I liked him, it wouldn't matter? We live on opposite spectrums of the universe. I'm running a business here, and he'll be off to Hawaii, filming for months." I shot off the bed. "Or the fact that I'm pretty damn sure he's still in love with his dead girlfriend? Do you know that he has her name tattooed on his chest?" I exhaled a shaky sigh, and wrapped both arms around my center.

Even if I wanted to, I could never compete with that. I'd lived my life being second best by default, and now that I had a choice, I would never be second to anyone else.

She gently touched my arm, compassion filling her features. "You have to talk to him."

"There's nothing to talk about."

That was the finality of it all. Jordan Ryder had flipped my world, but he'd be gone. Gone from Rosendell after filming. Gone from my bed and gone from my life.

Now, all I needed was for time to move faster.

When I entered my apartment, it was too quiet. I stuck my head through the door, as though I were a teenager creeping back into my parents' home after sneaking out, but this time, I was a grown-ass woman, and this was my house.

I let out a sigh of relief when the space was dead, dark, and silent. I stepped in and flipped on the lights, and just then, the non-breathing, palpitating, couldn't-get-a-breath-in reaction happened but full force.

The dirty dishes and pan from earlier were nowhere to be seen, probably washed and put away. All the seats were pushed in properly against the table. My kitchen was spotless.

But that wasn't what had me freaking out.

A dozen roses sat on the kitchen table with a card. *I had a great time last night with the most amazing girl. I'll call you later.*

My hands trembled as I held the card in my fingertips. *What is going on between us? What is going on with me?* There was an internal shift happening, one I couldn't control and one I most definitely couldn't ignore.

I closed my eyes, breathing deeply through my nose. What I really needed was a bag to hyperventilate into.

Normal. Normal. Normal. I needed and wanted my normal, carefree, calculated, organized life back. And I was determined to get things back to the way they were supposed to be.

CHAPTER 17

IT WAS NOW OR NEVER, but crap, it had to be now. I had kept my distance from Jordan for days, but I couldn't avoid him anymore because it was the first day of filming.

What I prided myself in was that I was the utmost professional at work. Armstrong Realty was our legacy, and there was no way in hell that I was going to mess up my job for a good-looking man and his hard, toned body.

There was a blockade along the streets to Wells restaurant, so I parked a few blocks away and walked to the barricades where a tall man was standing guard. I visited every tenant who moved into one of our locations on the first day. And this time, even though I had slept with said tenant, it wasn't going to be any different.

Multiple women stood by the barricades with signs and posters of Jordan, waiting for a glimpse, an autograph, anything. My insides soared. Besides all the drama with Jordan, this was the right decision. After filming, I was going to get this place rented. For good.

The publicity that this town and my property were getting was already noteworthy. The news had spread via media outlets, and our local newspaper featured Jordan Ryder on the front page, indicating that he was filming a movie at Wells.

I pushed past the women and walked straight to the security guard. "Christene Armstrong. I'm the landlord of this place."

He raised a thick eyebrow. "Are you on the list?" He had an earpiece on and a clipboard in his hand.

I hadn't talked to Jordan since the day I stormed out of my own apartment and had ignored his calls and texts ever since, pretending I'd gotten a bug. That was a few days ago, so I was pretty sure I wasn't on the list.

But I had to show up here today to make sure everything was okay because that was my job.

"No, I'm not on the list, but I'm the landlord. Ryan can vouch for me." I should have asked for Jordan—woulda, coulda, shoulda—but I didn't.

The security guard pressed his earpiece and began relaying the information to whoever was on the other line. My four-inch Prada shoes tapped impatiently against the concrete.

When I turned around, the few women had grown into a slew of women. Their chirpy, cheery voices echoed behind me.

"Is Jordan really here?"

"You think we'll get a glimpse of him?"

Jordan had fans young and old, different ethnicities, different backgrounds. Some of the women looked like they had just woken up, and, after watching the morning news, strolled right over here while some were in crisp business suits just like myself.

When I heard the shrill screams, I turned back around. Jordan walked out of the building in a white T-shirt and dark, faded blue jeans. I guessed he hadn't made it to makeup and wardrobe yet.

The roars of the women heightened the closer he came. A bodyguard I recognized ran toward him, and the women pushed and shoved, causing me to teeter on my heels.

"Hey. Watch it!" I shrugged off the shover behind me.

"Jordan!" they screamed.

I almost had to plug my ears, not wanting to go deaf. One woman shoved me to the side and jumped the barricade. Another followed.

The commotion happened so fast that I didn't have time to react.

The bodyguard moved in front of Jordan while the security guard grabbed a woman's waist. Goodness, this man created chaos everywhere he went. Too bad the commotion and havoc were happening in my heart now.

"Tene, move past the barricades," Jordan called out, getting pushed back into the building.

More security, about four burly men, approached from nowhere. Their loud voices carried.

"Move back, ladies. Anything past this barricade is trespassing and bound for prosecution."

"Jordan, we love you!" one yelled.

"Have my baby!" another called out.

I was frozen still, shocked from my surroundings when the bodyguard with the earpiece grabbed my elbow and ushered me past the barricades.

Jordan threw an arm around my waist, moving us closer to the building.

When we entered, he rounded a corner and caged me in. He clenched his jaw. The muscles of his cheek jumped. "Why haven't you been calling me? And why the hell did you ask for Ryan when you came here?"

There had been no lead-in. No hello. No, "How are you?"

My heart picked up in speed, the way it normally did when we were this close. I averted my eyes and watched people with headsets and earpieces scatter about.

The anger in his voice confused me. I wasn't sure if he was pissed that I hadn't called him back or that I'd asked for Ryan first and not him.

"He's the set manager," I answered.

"Well, I'm—" He cut himself short and gritted his teeth, frustrated.

I could guess what he was going to say, but I didn't want to confront that fact.

"You're my what? Sex slave?" I joked, trying to make light of the situation, though my heart was beating a million times a minute. I glanced back at his bodyguard less than a foot away, who had no reaction to my words. "I'm just your landlord."

As soon as I sidestepped him, he gripped my elbow and ushered me to the edge of the room, away from his bodyguard.

"We need to talk," he insisted.

"Why? Is something wrong?" I slowly breathed in through my nose, my eyes roaming the room, landing anywhere but on his eyes. My lungs seized, and in two seconds, I knew I'd hyperventilate. "I mean, the place looks amazing. Did you guys need something regarding the property?"

"No. It's not that." There was a tightness in his tone, a sharpness in his eyes.

I glanced behind him again and watched the camera crew position their equipment.

"Tene!" He grabbed my chin and forced me to look at him.

His warm breath blew against my face. He smelled of mint and cigarettes and my favorite cologne in the whole world.

"What is the matter?" he practically begged. "You haven't been taking my calls. I've been texting you nonstop." He lowered his voice when a female crew member passed us. "I feel like a stalker."

"A little ironic, right?" I laughed, playing it off. My skin was on fire, spreading from his hold on my chin, down my neck, to the rest of my body. "Since you're the actor and you have a real-life stalker out there on the loose." I gritted my teeth in a fake smile that puffed out my cheeks.

"Stop." He pushed himself against me, and automatically, my body reacted, the warmth transforming into a fire within me, my body wired.

I couldn't breathe again. I needed out.

Out. Out. Out.

He must've noticed my internal struggle, or maybe it was the fact that I was really starting to gasp. "What's going on with you?"

Can't. Breathe. Again.

Need air.

I pushed at his chest, needing room to fill my lungs. I'd given this spiel many times before, but the only difference was, this time, I was lying. "Listen, Jordan, what's going on with you?" I spat out, putting this on him. "Don't make this weird ..." I motioned between us. "... the after-sex relationship."

He narrowed his eyes, not giving an inch. "Don't fucking give me this speech. I've perfected this speech. I wrote the original after-sex, *it's not you, it's me* speech. You can't pull this card." His tone was hard, but there was hurt behind his eyes. Hurt that I'd put there.

Why couldn't this be easier? Why couldn't it just be a forgotten one-night stand?

"The infamous bachelor ..." I pushed fire in my voice, but I lacked it in my gut.

"That's my old life, former life," he growled.

I rolled my eyes. "Yeah, right."

"It's true." His neck stiffened, and the veins on his fore-arms bulged as he fisted his hands at his sides. "I can't stop thinking about you, Tene. And you not picking up my calls is driving me crazy."

Air. All I wanted was air. "So, what's that supposed to mean? When have you ever wanted a serious relationship?" I threw at him, reaching for straws, trying to ignore the desperation in his stare. "I see you all the time in those magazines. Bachelor for life."

His voice got quiet, personal. "That's a facade."

I shook my head, pretending not to buy it. "Oh, the lines you spew."

"This is different," he insisted, running one hand through his hair.

I needed to leave, to get out of his vicinity, away from this conversation, so I could have air to fill my lungs again. My eyes made it to the exit, to where I needed to be. "How is it different this time?"

His breath was a soft whisper against my cheek. "It's different this time because it's with you." His blue eyes shone brightly, unwavering, firmly fixed against mine.

I fell against the wall, and my fingers spread against my chest. I felt like a breathless girl of eighteen again.

I couldn't take the intensity of his stare, the softness in his voice, the warmth of his hands on me.

"I know something is happening here. Something more than a fling." His fingers pulled me in at the waist, and he ducked in closer, his head by mine. We were locked in this tug-of-war, his eyes open, vulnerable, almost begging.

"Jordan ..." I heard off to the side.

We both peered up to see a young woman with a short red-haired bob. Her name tag said, *Susie*.

She peeked over her clipboard, headset on her head. "We're starting in five minutes."

The moment he stepped back, I dug my heels in the ground, getting some semblance of control back.

I secretly thanked her for the interruption. I needed time to think. "Go," I said, moving from under his arms.

He pinned me with a stare. "We're not done here."

Little did he know, I was more than done. I should have been done with him the first day I met him. He'd fulfilled a purpose and helped me in renting out this property. My issues with him and this loss of control in my life would disappear once filming was over, and he was back in his Hollywood Hills home.

His hands grazed my hip before moving away, leaving a trail of heat from where he touched.

Ignore the heat. Ignore the heat.

Once he was out of my sight, I leaned against the wall and tipped my head back, closing my eyes. Finally, I inhaled deeply, taking in what felt like my first real breath of the day.

━━

When Jordan started filming, I talked to Ryan, ensuring everything was okay with the Wells restaurant and that the production crew had all they needed.

I left to tend to my other tenants. I had to get as far away from Jordan Ryder as possible. And I didn't just need space. I also needed time. But I needed more than a few days. I needed months, years, infinity to forget everything that had happened between us.

After a crazy day at work, my thoughts raced nonstop about the actor with the blue eyes who knew so much about me without saying a word. I texted Angie that I'd meet her at Allswell. It was her natural habit that she ended up there after work.

I readjusted my Armani suit and strolled out of my newly waxed car with a smile plastered on my face. I pushed through the doors of Allswell and almost tripped on my two left feet when I spotted Jordan by the bar. Filming had obviously wrapped up.

Wyatt was laughing. Cade had his hands fisted at his sides, silent but with anger brewing under the surface. And Jordan looked outright ... pissed? His feet were planted far apart, his nostrils flared, and his eyes narrowed. He was pissed all right.

My sister grimaced and averted her gaze, not wanting to look at me. I tilted my head and assessed her. She looked ... apologetic? She bit her thumb the way she always did when she'd done something wrong.

Wyatt held his belly and laughed harder. And Jordan? He charged toward me, stomping his feet hard enough that the ground shook. Angie's eyes widened, and she shuffled in my direction right behind him.

They reached me at the same time.

"You." He pointed a shaky finger. "That's why you've been acting the way you've been acting," Jordan said.

Angie reached for his arm as an attempt to pull him

back. "You heard me wrong. I think I misinterpreted the whole thing."

They bickered back and forth, and the louder their chatter became, the more annoyed I got.

I waved a hand. "What the hell is going on?"

Jordan stepped into me, and five fingers tightly gripped my waist, eyes firm with determination. "I want a fucking do-over."

"Do-over?" I reeled back. "For what?"

Angie grabbed his arm again, practically bouncing on her toes. Her eyes went wild, and her voice increased to an alarming pitch. "Jordan, it's fine. You're fine. Everything is fine. Please don't." She tugged at the sleeve of his shirt. "Please. This is all a big misunderstanding."

I sighed heavily, stepped back, and crossed my arms over my chest. "Again, what the hell is going on?"

"Why did you fake it?" Jordan spat out.

I blinked, stunned into a stupid stupor. The world stopped. The chatter in the restaurant quieted to a soft lull. I must've heard him wrong because my sister would never in a million years betray me.

The color drained from my face, probably leaving a white pasty ghost behind. I gritted my teeth and turned directly to the shorter, cuter version of me. "Tell me you didn't." I pointed the finger at her, and she flinched. "You told him?"

Her chin dropped to her chest.

"You told him!"

She apologetically raised both hands. "I swear to God, I didn't."

"Then, how the hell did he find out?"

Her voice was whisper soft, and if she had the ability to

shrink, she'd be as tall as a mouse. "I told Cade. Then, Cade told Wyatt."

I went cross-eyed, blew out a breath, and looked toward the ceiling, anywhere other than to the sister I loved so dearly because I was two seconds from putting her in a choke hold, WWE-style.

Breathe, Tene. Just relax and breathe.

It didn't work.

My fists flew to my hips. "Really, Angie? Really! Do you tell him everything? Why, oh, why, did you have to tell Cade that Jordan had missed the mark?"

"I'm still here, you know," he said, sighing heavy with exaggeration.

"And you ..." I shook my head. I most definitely didn't want a do-over. "It's fine. It happens, you know."

He pulled me to the side, away from curious stares, and then dipped his head by mine. "That does not happen to me. Ever."

Cocky, are we now?

"Like, never? Like, no one has ever in the history of your sex life faked it?" *Him and his damn ego.* "Well, let me tell you. It wasn't that good." *But, god, it was really good.*

His eyebrows flew to his hairline. Yep. Shocked him with that one.

I moved past him. I needed that drink badly. But, suddenly, Jordan swooped me up and carried me over his shoulder, causing me to face his ass.

"Jordan!" I screeched. The draft could be felt up my already-short suit skirt.

He swatted my bottom, and I yelped.

He turned toward the door where I got an upside-down view of my sister and Wyatt looking ridiculously amused at my situation. And Cade's face twisted. I thought he'd have been more pissed that we'd slept together.

"Angie!"

My sister's response to my pleas was to throw up her hands as if to say, *What do you want me to do?*

I'd remember this moment. If she were drowning or quite possibly wanted me to wax her bikini line again because she was embarrassed to go to a salon and have a stranger do it, I'd deny her. The things I did for her, seriously, and this was how she repaid me?

An older couple laughed when we passed them. Great, we were comic relief to the patrons, and right now, this was anything but funny.

CHAPTER 18

JORDAN USHERED us past his bodyguard, waiting by his SUV and down the block into the closest alley. He lightly placed me on the ground, but his firm grip on my waist was anything but light.

After I flattened my hair and straighten my suit, he tightened his hold on me, his body flush against mine. I felt his erection against my thigh.

"Where were we?"

His breath was warm against my cheek, and if I didn't have any self-control, my panties would slip to the ground and disappear.

"Do-over?" he whispered.

Goodness, I wanted him. Just the scent of him, the feel of his body pressed against mine, had my hormones running rampant.

He kissed my cheek and then dropped his head to my neck, dragging his thick, warm tongue along my collarbone. My knees just about gave out, and I let out an audible sigh.

"I've got a talented tongue. Maybe I'll make you come that way."

My mind was warring with my body. Usually, I gave in to my wants and what my body needed even though I would suffer the consequences later, but not today, not when everything screamed for me to stop. Not when my body wasn't the only thing on the line. Now, it was a fragile heart. I had more to lose.

All I'd originally wanted was to ride a Ryder, to get him out of my system, but I knew that was the last thing I could do now because one more ride on the Ryder mobile would most likely cost me my heart.

My hands glided up his hard chest. "We can't. I can't."

He peered down at me with a look of confusion, as though he was trying to figure me out. I wanted to tell him it wasn't the sex I was afraid of. I knew we'd be explosive if I just let go. It was the intimacy, the way he made me feel beyond the physical. The bigger problem was, I liked him. Not *bang him and leave him* like him, but *bang him and possibly keep him* like him. And that meant trouble.

He looked at me as though he really saw me, but then how could he when Candice's name was forever etched into his skin?

It's an illusion, Tene, a messed-up illusion because he only sees her.

Ignoring my words, he slid his hand to the back of my neck and angled me toward him, where he kissed me sensually.

His kisses were heaven and hell, sweetness and sex, war, and peace. Just pure, atomic explosion.

It took every ounce of my self-control to pull away from him. "Jordan ..." I breathed. "Stop."

"Let's start over." He pulled back and smiled his devilish grin. He stuck his tongue out and rolled it. "I've got some moves."

I shook my head. We couldn't go there. Not if I wanted to stay intact. I pressed my back against the wall of the building, feeling the roughness of the bricks beneath my fingertips. His bodyguard stood stoic just a short distance away, at the end of the alley.

I gave Jordan one forceful push and disentangled myself from his hold. "It's a bad idea."

He huffed, and confusion reigned in the sea of blue staring back at me. "Usually, girls are throwing themselves at me, wanting something from me, but with you ... the girl I like, you want nothing to do with me." He ran one aggravated hand through his hair and linked his hands behind his head. "This is worse than a blow to the ego. This is a swift blow to the fucking heart."

I couldn't bear to look at him. I wanted The End, not a Do-Over.

He rubbed the back of his neck, his eyes tormented. "Were you not into it? I'm not dumb, Tene. I knew you were into it. Your body was ready. You felt so good."

I couldn't do that to him, lie to him and bruise his ego any further. It wasn't fair.

"It was good." *Explosive.* I bit my lip, my gaze falling to the concrete to keep myself steady, to remind myself that even though my equilibrium was shot, I was standing on solid ground.

He stepped into me, his black dress shoes toe to toe with my heels. He gripped my chin and forced me to meet his eyes. There was a softness in his stare, drawing me in. "What's the matter then?" His eyebrows knitted together, and he searched my face for an answer.

Slowly, I pulled his hand down. "Nothing."

"Bullshit." There was no bite in his voice, just an underlying sadness. His thumb grazed my cheek, so lightly, so sweetly, so Jordan. "I'll try harder," he said, almost begging me.

Sigh.

"That's not it."

"Then, what is it, baby?"

His word of endearment broke me.

"Is that what you called her too?" I whispered. I swallowed back the shake in my voice and dimmed the vulnerable look in my eye. "You're not over her. I know that the ink on the upper left side of your chest, right by your heart, is her name. It's all of it rolled into the fact that you, Jordan Ryder, are not over your dead girlfriend, and I cannot and will not be second best to anyone."

I searched his face, waiting and wanting him to deny it. Deny it for me, for us, for some future I'd made up in my head.

But he didn't. His eyes widened, and he didn't say a word. And so, I pushed past him and never looked back.

He didn't call my name or chase me down the alley because it was the truth. I was not going to compete with a ghost when I knew who would win in the end. And it wouldn't be me.

CHAPTER 19

MY NERVES WERE SHOT. An hour later, I was pacing back and forth in my enormous condo, not knowing what to do. *Eat first? Am I hungry? Shower? But it's too early.*

This man had flipped my axis, turned things around until I felt so out of control that I didn't know what to do next, and even worse, I didn't know who I was anymore.

The banging on the door wouldn't relent, and I knew it could only be one person because I'd be doing the same thing if I'd been shut down.

I opened the door, and Jordan walked right in like he owned the joint with two bags of something greasy and smelling oh-so yummy.

"What are you doing here?" My tone was low, defeated, tired of fighting.

"I'm feeding you because you're hangry, and we've got a few things to sort out."

By the firm line of his jaw and his alert gaze, I knew he wasn't leaving even if I kicked him out.

I grabbed the food from his hands and placed it on the kitchen island. After getting plates from my overhead cupboard, I tore through the bags and placed what looked like disheveled gyros and fries on the plates.

His eyes burned through me as I moved across the kitchen. I didn't know what was worse, the feeling of total discombobulation when his eyes were on me or the agony when they weren't.

I was absolutely going insane. In-freaking-sane.

After I slammed the plates on the counter, he reached for my wrist. "About what you said earlier …"

"No, it's fine." I wasn't ready to talk. "Let's eat." I plopped on the stool and focused on the gyros in front of me. My stomach flipped and flopped, the queasy feeling settling in my gut. The last thing I wanted to do was eat, but I'd do anything to keep from talking about his dead girlfriend. I shouldn't have even brought it up.

"Tene," he said, his look pensive, cautious even. "Baby … just tell me what's the matter."

I slammed the gyro on the plate, tzatziki getting on the counter.

"Everything's the matter." I stood and took a good healthy step away from him. "I'm going crazy. My life feels out of control. I don't know which way is up or down. I can't make a decision to save my life. I don't know what to do next—eat, shower, sleep. I've never …" I released a heavy breath and paced the room to my couch, where he followed. "I've never, ever felt as out of control as I have recently." *And it has everything to do with you.* But I left that bit out.

I had officially jumped off the cuckoo train.

"Shit," I breathed, realizing that everything in my head had just spilled out like a bad case of diarrhea of the mouth. "Forget it."

He reached for my hand, and my fingers trembled within his.

Great. Now, he knew how he unnerved me.

My lips pinched together, and I rubbed at my brow, knowing I couldn't be vulnerable in front of him. It wasn't in my nature. I was the firstborn in my family. Strong. Resilient. Fierce. Never showing vulnerability.

The facade of a put-together woman, my shell, prevented me from getting hurt. It was what I showed my mother, what I showed the world.

The air from my air conditioner blasted in the background, and I welcomed the noise to dim the chaos in my head and the cold to dim the heat rising within me.

His facial features softened, and he leaned into me. "Everything you just said is exactly how I'm feeling."

He brought my fist to his lips, and when I tried to extract myself from his grasp, he placed another hand on top of both of mine, holding me in my spot with his hands, his eyes, the emotion pouring out of him.

"I've been going crazy, and I know it has everything to do with you," he whispered. He stepped into me and placed a light hand on my hip. "All that noise in my head ... it disappears when I'm with you."

As though he couldn't stand the distance between us, he sat on the couch and pulled me onto his lap. And even though I should push him away, I didn't resist because, in the short time we'd known each other, I realized one thing: Jordan was my weakness.

The house could be burning down, and even if my gut and mind screamed for me to leave, if he asked me to stay, I'd stay.

My gaze flicked downward. "What if I told you, the noise in my head only escalates when I'm with you?" Like a mariachi band was playing so loud that my brain might combust.

He smiled. "I'd tell you I know why that is. It's because you aren't giving in to us yet because, if you did, I swear, that noise would settle. It'd disappear." He held both of my hands in his, leaning in. His eyes so certain, his voice full of conviction.

But how could he be so sure? And what about her?

"Let me explain." His thumbs brushed softly on top of my hand.

Three words that I'd heard before—from Logan, from someone who'd supposedly been in love with me. There had been nothing to explain when I caught her mouth on his dick in broad daylight. I'd forever remember the blow to my heart, the ultimate betrayal of not knowing.

"I just need a minute." I needed more than a minute. I needed an hour, a day, an eternity.

I stared at our intertwined hands, my pretty pink manicure perfectly done. Probably the only perfect thing in my life.

"Tell me. Tell me what you're thinking," he urged.

I swallowed. He ducked into my line of sight, but there was no way I could look at him because he'd read all the vulnerability written on my face.

"Are you still in love with her?" It slipped out before I could stop it; before I could sugarcoat it; before I could lie and tell him that I didn't care. You would think by saying it out loud that my fears would dim, but it only heightened them.

His face crumbled. He dropped my hand and straightened. After a slow breath, he ran one shaky hand through his hair.

The air choked my lungs as though thick black smoke was coming through the vents.

No words needed to be spoken to understand his answer. He wasn't over her.

Ice flowed through my veins, a direct link to my heart, freezing all the arteries. "You don't owe me anything, Jordan. You don't have to try to explain. It's none of my business."

I stood, needing to leave. Once again, on the verge of walking out of my own condo.

"Yes, I love her ... loved her."

The words, the way they stuttered out of his mouth, were like a sledgehammer to my chest. It was his truth, but it didn't hurt any less. He loved her, and it gutted me.

I didn't want to hear what he had to say.

"I'm going to go ... or maybe you should leave." I refused to run from my own place again. This was supposed to be my sanctuary.

"I love her," he said firmly, making me listen. "But I'm not *in love* with her ..."

Unable to look him in the eye, unable to get my emotions in check, unable to hear his lies, I stood from the couch, and my bare feet padded against the hardwood as I walked away.

He erased the gap between us and gripped my wrist, stilling me, holding me in my spot. "I'm not in love with her anymore because ... I feel things for you, Christene."

I closed my eyes, and my body betrayed me, reveling in the closeness of him.

His strong hands gripped my arms, and then he turned me to face him. "Did you hear what I said?"

I closed my eyes, eyebrows wrinkled, and dipped my chin to my chest. An internal war battled in me, one deep in my soul, between my strong-willed mind and my weak, passionate heart. "I want to believe you."

"Then, believe me." He tipped up my chin, his steely-blue eyes locking with my brown ones. "Believe me because it's true."

He led us back to the couch, our food and my appetite long forgotten. "You don't know my brother Wyatt as well as you know Cade." His voice softened as though he recalled a memory. "He's quiet and reserved, and he internalizes a lot. But if I ever need advice or want the truth, he's the one I go to."

He leaned in, and our hands fell between us, drawing my focus.

"You have to understand where I came from to understand who I am today." His stare became distant, his eyes clouding over with memories. "My mother died from an overdose ..."

My eyes flicked upward. I hadn't been ready for that. Automatically, my hand tightened around his, and my chest ached for his history, for his family.

"My father was in prison ... and probably still is. I went from house to house, causing worse trouble than the last place I was at." He released one shaky breath that made his entire body tremble. "There was no doubt where my path was headed. I knew I would be dead or in prison before I graduated high school. And then I met the Ryders." A small smile touched his lips. "I was still the badass I always was until ... until Candice put me in my place."

He was allowed to have a history. It made him who he was. Curiosity clamped my mouth shut, and I was determined to hear him out.

"She softened me, made me believe life was worth living, and self-destruction was not an option."

He poured out his soul, and slowly but surely, I understood him.

Candice Ryder had saved him. She had shown him love and compassion and given him a reason to live. And in my heart and the deepest part of me, I knew that I could never compete with that. At that moment, that brief moment when he was revealing his past, vulnerability seeping out every ounce of him, my heart broke, cracked in two because who could go against the woman who had made his life worth living?

"She made me believe in the future, a future with love and happiness and forever."

The hurt heightened, and I swallowed a lump in the back of my throat.

"I miss her every day ..."

Tears almost burst from my eyes, threatening to spill over from his history, from the story of his long-lost love, the story of a future he never got, the future I would never get.

"I can't ... Jordan. I just can't." As selfish as it sounded, I couldn't hear any more.

"I miss her every day, but the only time ... the only time I ever forget her is when I'm with you." His eyes were begging me to understand. "For years, all I've tried to do is dim this ache in my chest from her absence. First with alcohol, then with women, and now with work. Nothing I did would erase the loss of her." He brushed his knuckles on my cheek, and I felt it everywhere. "Until you." He paused. "Until you, Christene."

Then, he smiled a beautiful smile, one that reached his eyes. "I felt like I was cheating. Because, all of a sudden, I stopped feeling miserable. It's been years, and I was used to the pain and feeling guilty. And for a brief moment, I felt bad for feeling happy." He laughed. "Which Wyatt made me realize was just plain stupid. It's dumb to think I'm dishonoring her by being happy.

"I know we haven't known each other long, but I want to be with you, Christene." He held my chin between his fingertips, and I leaned into his touch. "We're going crazy, but the solution is obvious because we're only going crazy when we're apart."

He leaned in to kiss me, and I let him because I wanted to, because I couldn't deny myself any longer.

And just like every time our lips met before, a shock of energy surged through my body, stopping right by my heart.

"Crazy is *not* kissing you." He flicked his tongue over the opening of my lips. Grabbing my waist, he stood up and lifted me until my legs wrapped around him. "Crazy is *not* doing the things I want to do to you, to your body." He walked us back to my bedroom, peppering kisses down my neck and nibbling on my earlobe. "Crazy is *not* spending every waking second with you because I want to, need to."

He gently guided me on my back, where I was staring up at him and his Adonis body. He lifted the back of his shirt, where ink spanned the upper part of most of his body. I closed my eyes, afraid to look, terrified that it would ruin the moment.

"Crazy would be not giving you an orgasm—or worse, you faking it." A deep, masculine chuckle made his chest rumble. "But, I'm about to rectify that right now."

He peeled off my clothes one by one, starting with my skirt. Then, after trailing kisses up my stomach and to my neck, he slowly and seductively unclasped each and every button of my blouse until I was naked for his taking. "This is my do-over."

CHAPTER 20

THE CLOCK on my dresser said four thirty-five as I lay on Jordan's hard, muscled chest. The scent of passion lingered in the air. Talk about mind-blowing, spine tingling, wall-shaking sex.

My body was bone-tired, but my mind ... it was wired with random thoughts. Random thoughts of us.

When I'd truly let go, only then had I experienced the full orgasmic experience.

I liked this man, more than any other Tinder-swiping man I'd met or anyone I'd dated before.

Jordan Ryder could very well be a keeper, and for once, I'd give in to the emotions I was feeling.

We were both awake, and I doubted we would get any sleep. His fingers traced circles along my thigh, a touch I felt everywhere. More and more, the awkwardness between us fizzled. Lying next to him, in the silence, was so familiar; it felt so right, perfect, and complete.

The sexual tension I usually felt in Jordan's presence was dimmed by our openness and replaced by a nice, comfortable, full feeling—fully satisfied, happy, and elated.

"Why hasn't anybody snatched you up yet?" he asked in the dark. "Why don't you have a boyfriend?"

I rested my chin on his chest, staring up at his baby blues. "How do you know I don't?"

Laughter rumbled through his chest and warmed me. "I'm serious," he said, brushing his fingers through my dark locks.

"I'm serious too." My tone was devoid of any humor. In another life, I could've been an actress or a con artist.

The moonlight shone through my window, highlighting the sharp planes of his jaw, his straight nose, the stubble under his chin.

When his smile faltered, I poked at his side. "I'm kidding."

I was going to say I was too busy for a relationship, which was the typical excuse I gave Angie and my father and Nana or any other person around me. My mother probably thought no one would ever fall for me, but that was a different story entirely. When I'd been with Logan, even though life had been hectic and work had pulled me in all different directions, I'd made time because it was important, because I'd been in love.

"I'm waiting for the right one," I whispered, honesty leaking out of me.

I could've put up a front, but what was the point? And with Jordan, I felt safe, like I didn't have to pretend anymore. We'd crossed some boundary tonight, and I would try my hardest to move forward, not backward.

He nodded, his eyes searching mine. "So, tell me about your ex. You know about mine."

I hated talking about my failed relationship even though I didn't take the blame for it. Still, I liked to succeed in all aspects of life.

"I wasn't always this man-eater." Nervous laughter escaped my lips, and I averted my stare, thinking of my last heartbreak. "You met him," I said quietly. "Logan was my last relationship, and I was utterly in love with him. He worked in mortgage and financing, and we were a match made in real-estate heaven."

Pedigreed family, Ivy League degree. He'd been perfect. At least, I'd thought so.

"But ..." I paused, recalling memories that made my chest ache. "... our relationship was a lie." Saying it out loud was like a punch in the face, a slice to my heart. I rolled my eyes like the breakup didn't affect me, though it still hurt to think about it. "He was still in love with his old girlfriend, the girl who was with him when you met him."

He held me tighter and pulled me closer, which gave me the courage to continue. "I was the rebound girl who lasted a little too long, and I didn't want to be the second choice anymore ... so I left."

I bit my bottom lip and dropped my gaze. The memories bombarded my mind like scenes from a bad movie. "He promised me things—the future, that I was his one and only." I rubbed at the center of my chest to dim the pain. "I thought we were it. Everyone thought we were it." I held my breath. "And then I caught him cheating, which you know already."

The anger and betrayal I'd felt at first were replaced with utter devastation. I had put everything into my relationship with Logan. I'd invested time and energy and had given my heart to someone who had been only half in. I remembered denying it till the very moment I'd caught them with his dick in her mouth.

"I'm sorry." He tenderly kissed my forehead. "So, so sorry that you ever had to go through that."

"Don't be. I had given him an out so many times. I asked a million times if he was still in love with her, and I realized he was lying to me when we accidentally bumped into her at a restaurant. It was written all over his face."

I was used to that look, the one that said, *You're not my number one*. It was evident in my mother's stare. The way she regarded Angie versus the way she glared at me. I worked my hardest to stay on top at my job, with my life, and I refused to settle for anything less. "Even then, I didn't want to believe it. I think my bullshit radar had been blocked because I was so in love with him. It wasn't until I was hit in the face with the image of them together, literally catching him with his pants down, that I realized we were over."

The air was thick with emotion, with our passion, with our broken past. There was no doubt that I'd had my share of heartbreak, and Jordan had his too. But his ... his cut deeper.

"Your turn," I said, needing the attention off me and wanting to know more of his history. "Tell me about Candice."

His small smile tightened, and he looked past me, randomly playing with the ends of my hair.

The change in his tone and the nostalgic vacancy in his eye told me he was thinking about her. And though it hurt me to hear, curiosity ate at my insides. I wanted to hear about her, know why he had been so enamored with her. I wanted to know what she'd had that every Victoria's Secret model didn't.

The corner of his lips tipped upward like he recalled a memory. "She was kind, beautiful ..." He tilted his head and then paused, eyeing me. "You know what? I don't want to talk about this anymore."

I frowned. "Why not?"

He held my chin within his fingertips. "Because I don't and because you'll think it's more than it is."

My mouth slackened. "No, I won't." I motioned with my hand for him to continue. "Sometimes, Cade will talk about her, and I'll get glimpses of how alike they were."

He laughed. "Yep, they were. She was a badass in a softer, gentler way." His breathing slowed almost to a stop. "But she taught me real love. I had never experienced that before her. I never had parents who loved me or foster parents besides the Ryders who cared. They took me in, cared for me, adopted me." His eyes turned glassy, and there was a look of longing and regret in his eyes that frightened me.

"What happened?"

He gulped hard. "You don't know?"

If he thought Angie had told me everything, she hadn't. She'd given me hints into what had happened with Candice but not the whole story.

That was part of Cade's secret past that she never shared in full detail, only that an accident had taken Candice's life and their father's, leaving their mother paralyzed from the waist down.

"She ..." He inhaled deeply, and a shiver ran through him. "She killed herself."

The world stopped, and I became vividly aware of my surroundings—his body next to mine, the blast of my air conditioner in the background, the peeking of the moonlight through my windows. I wanted him to repeat it because a freak accident had taken Cade's sister, Jordan's old girl-friend. Not this. The wind was knocked out of my lungs, and my sharp intake of breath cut through the room.

"She was so high that she drove into oncoming traffic on

the other side of the road, killing our father in the process." He closed his eyes and rested his arm against his forehead. "She physically died that night, but her life had been taken way before that—by the asshole who'd attacked her. She had a stalker at school. Real messed up kid obsessed with her. When I found out, it was too late."

His body began to tremble, and I wrapped my arms around him, to minimize the ache, to warm the chill.

"After that attack, she was never the same. She tried to dull the pain with drugs, alcohol, anything she could get her hands on. I tried my hardest to help her, but I wasn't enough." His voice shook, and his body tensed, his muscles tight like a wire. "I almost killed that fucker," he spat out. "If it wasn't for Wyatt putting himself between us, I would have shown that douche his maker, the Devil himself."

And he'd have been locked up at the end of it.

He clenched his fist, his eyes narrowed as though the person who had taken Candice's life was physically in the room. I cuddled closer, wanting to erase his pain, his horrific memories.

"I hate talking about it. Every time I do, it brings me to a dark place I'd like to forget."

"I'm sorry." My hands moved up and down his shoulders in a comforting motion. My pain was nothing compared to his, what he'd endured as a child in the foster system, what he'd endured with Candice.

I kissed the tender part of his neck and rested my head against his chest, feeling his heartbeat against my cheek. "I get it. Not wanting to talk about things. You're like the king of avoidance, and I know how that is because I'm the queen."

"Yeah." His breathing was steady, slow, normal now. "Is

that why you avoid any questions about you and your mom?"

I sighed. "She hates me. That's what's up."

He pulled me up, so I was straddling him and angled his head toward me to meet my lips. "She can't possibly hate you. Who could hate you?"

I smiled. "She's the one exception."

"You're always on the defense with her," he carefully pointed out.

"No, I'm not!" I cringed when the words flew out of my mouth because those exact words sounded defensive. "Nothing I do is good enough."

"Has she uttered those words exactly?"

My eyebrows pulled together. "No, but ..."

"But nothing. Listen to her next time. Listen to the questions she asks you: *Were you guys hanging out? Was Christene showing you around? Do you think you can rent Wells after filming?*"

"It wasn't like that," I countered.

"That might not be what you heard, but it's exactly what I heard."

I shifted from his hold, wanting to get off him. He didn't believe me. No one did. I was always the one being blamed.

Ease up on your mother. Why do you have to take that tone with her? My father's and Angie's voices rang loudly in my ears.

Now, Jordan was on board.

"I'm done talking about my mother."

Everyone was trying to fix our relationship, but the problem was, it couldn't be fixed. I'd tried to please the woman, wanting and needing her affection, but at some point, I had given up. There was no saving us now, just living through it.

He pulled me closer and cupped my cheeks. "Just listen, baby."

I loved how he called me his baby, like that one term of endearment could melt me into a puddle of mush.

"Listen next time to what she's asking you, and before you blow up, just answer her question. Have you ever wondered if maybe she takes that tone with you because you take that same tone with her?"

I pulled his hands from my face. "I told you, I don't want to talk about her anymore." I filed through my memories, trying to recall a time when my mother and I were okay, where there wasn't this tug-of-war always between us, but I came up short. I simply couldn't remember.

He licked the seam of my lips. "Fine with me. I don't want to talk about my ex-girlfriend anymore, either."

I thought we were going to have a long, drawn-out make-out session, but he pecked me one last time before pulling me against his chest and tugging the covers up to encase us in. I nestled against him, my head by the crook of his neck. We were totally nooking, and I was enjoying every bit of it this time.

"Sleep, pretty girl." He gently guided me to my side and spooned me from behind. "Just sleep."

And I did. I slept soundly for the first time in what seemed like forever and had the best dreams that night.

CHAPTER 21

THE SHEETS RUSTLED against my legs, and the chill of the morning cut through my bones. My hands felt along the space beside me, looking for warmth, but when my eyes slowly opened, I realized that Jordan was nowhere to be found. Half the sheets were on the floor, the rest at the corner of the bed, on my ankles. I did sleep like a crazy person. Sometimes, my bed would be disrobed, the fitted sheets and down comforter on the floor. One time, I had seen them chucked across the room, as though I'd gotten up in the middle of the night and thrown them, baseball-style.

I sat up on the bed when the scent of food filtered through my room.

Mmm, bacon grease.

I inhaled deeply, slipped on a T-shirt and shorts, and strolled into the kitchen to find Mr. Domesticated cooking by the stove. His bare back and all his muscles and ink were on display for me to drool and ogle and admire.

Is this a dream? Because I could stay here forever.

He hadn't heard me come in because he was belting a Britney Spears song that was playing on my iPad.

All I did was grin at the scene. There was no urge to flee or jump off the balcony at the sight of him in my kitchen. Not today.

I approached, hugged him from behind, and kissed his shoulder. "What's cooking, good-looking?" I asked.

He met my morning-breath lips with a chaste kiss. My hair was a matted mess, and I had no makeup on, but I didn't care because this ... we ... felt right for once.

His sexy-ass smirk was on display. "I've got the sausage. You've got the eggs?"

He kissed my neck, turning to wrap his arms around me.

"You have a bit of underlying dork in you. Did you know that?" I chuckled.

His face lit up, and then he playfully pinched my side. "Never been called that before, but I'll be your dork." He swatted my butt. "Go set the table, woman. Breakfast is almost done."

I sauntered to his left and stood on my tiptoes to reach for the dishes on the top shelf. My pajama shorts hitched up where my cheeks were almost hanging out, and I pushed out my bottom a little, hoping to catch some blue-eyed boy's attention. My T-shirt drifted higher, revealing a little of my waist, and I bit my lip to hide my smile.

I could feel his eyes searing through my skin, scanning the backs of my legs and the span of bare skin at my waist.

He groaned, turned off the stove, and pushed me against the counter in one swift movement. His front toward my back. His head dropped to the crook of my neck. "You're doing that on purpose, aren't you?"

"What?" I said, playing innocent.

"You know what you're doing." He placed sweet, tiny kisses along my neck, bringing me flush against him.

I closed my eyes, my body filling with want and need and pure, unadulterated lust.

If we started, we'd never finish, and I'd call in to work for the first time in forever.

First, the cuddles. Then, cooking me breakfast.

I was in deep with this man, like cotton-candy goo, and I was undeniably smitten. And *smitten* was a word I had never used.

"I'm feeding you breakfast and then feasting on you for dessert." His rich, throaty voice resonated deep in my belly. "Want my redo." He bit at the tender part of my neck, sending shocks of pleasure everywhere.

I turned to face him, eyes wide. "Redo? You did and redid and re-redid, and I swear, I don't know how I'm still walking."

He'd wanted to make up for my lost orgasm, and he'd done that in earth-shattering spades.

He turned me to face him, and our lips met.

"You're something I can't get enough of." His fingers slipped in my shorts, and he grabbed my bare asscheek.

"What are we doing?" I whispered, our heads barely touching.

He lightly kissed my lips, staring down at me. "I don't know what we're doing. Do I like staying here? Yes. Do I like playing house?" His hands moved to the small of my back, dipping me slightly. "No. I hate playing house, but for once, I don't want to play anymore. I want to stay in that house—live in it—furniture and all."

The intenseness in his eyes seared through me, touching a place I had in my heart that I usually kept caged.

"I like you. And for the first time in a long time, I want more than one night with someone. I can feel you pulling away, and I need you to stop." He dropped his forehead against mine. "Christene, you're strong, you're fierce, you're beautiful. And I can't get you out of my system—I don't want to."

My hands held on to him for support, as I felt like I might fall to the ground at the way he'd just uttered my name.

"All I want to do is touch you. All the time." His lips dropped to my cheek. "And kiss you all the time." He dropped a kiss to my neck.

I knew what I felt in my gut, in my mind, in my heart, and I was afraid of everything that was going on. "We're alike in so many ways. And this ..." I motioned between us. "... scares me."

He smiled a devastatingly beautiful smile—not the one he smiled for the cameras, not the one that was plastered in grocery store magazines, but the one filled with adoration and sincerity and honesty. "I kind of knew it. I kind of knew you had a crush on me."

I tilted my head back and rolled my eyes. "Please, you fell for me way before I fell for you."

He silenced me with another chaste kiss on the lips. "Now, I have to ask you something."

I stiffened at the intensity in his stare. "Yes, you can take me on the kitchen counter. That is allowed."

He chuckled. "No. Will you be mine?"

My heart stopped at the lightness in his voice and the glimmer in his eyes.

"My girlfriend."

Girlfriend. I mentally tested the word out.

The last time I had been someone's girlfriend, it had ended in the worst possible failure.

Still, my cheeks hurt from my smile because I couldn't dim my amusement at the question boys used to ask me in grade school. And I wouldn't let fear prevent me from taking chances.

He held both of my hands in his. "Seriously, Tene. I haven't done this in a long time."

I concentrated on him, our intertwined hands, his open honesty to keep me steady and prevent me from freaking out. "I haven't done this in a long time, either."

I'd built a cage, a wall of false confidence around me. It was in everything I did, the way I walked, in how I handled business. My outward appearance protected me from hurt. Only very few people had the key to this cage I'd built because the more people I let in, the more vulnerable I became. I had never liked feeling out of control. But as I searched his face for any indication that he was kidding, I saw none.

I cupped the side of his face, and the fluttering in my stomach turned into a flock of butterflies. "Yes. Yes, I'll be your girlfriend." *There, I said it.* Cheesy and corny but the truth.

He bent down and closed the gap between us in a soul-crushing kiss I felt to my toes.

"And now, you can take me on the kitchen counter," I said, lips meshed together.

I pulled at his boxers and inched backward, my come-hither smile planted on my face, but he swatted my butt and tipped his head toward the stove where the bacon and eggs and pancakes were probably cold.

"Go eat first."

I pouted while he took our food to the kitchen table, but when the first bite of bacon filled my mouth, I forgave him.

Good-looking, great cook, master in the bedroom, and he has a job. I sighed.

Jordan took out some papers and laid them out in front

of him, stuffing forkfuls of eggs in his mouth. I could watch him eat forever. It would be my new pastime.

"Production starts tomorrow, which is going to be a little nuts. When word gets around, and the trailers and production crew start filling the streets of downtown Rosendell, it's going to be little Hollywood here."

I clasped my hands together and bounced in my seat. "It's going to be crazy and great for the businesses downtown."

"Now that we're together, your life is going to be more of a circus," he warned. "You're never going to be alone." He placed his hand on top of mine, his thumb brushing over the top of my wrist. "Paps are going to follow you everywhere. But if it's okay with you ..." For once, he looked sheepish. "... I don't want to keep us a secret. I don't want to talk about us to the press either, but if I want to go out with my girlfriend, I will." He leaned in, his eyes almost pleading. "You're okay with that, right? With the chaos that will come when people find out?"

I flipped my hair over my shoulder. "Have you seen me? I thrive on being the center of attention. That's how it is in our family. If there's anyone who can handle being your girlfriend, it's *moi*." I pointed a thumb to my chest.

Jordan tipped up my chin, amused. "I'm glad you're up for the task."

Then, he pressed a kiss to my lips, and I melted all over again.

CHAPTER 22

THE PUBLICITY of Jordan's filming in town intensified. The papers and local televisions were covering it as though it was world-breaking news. And to our small town of Rosendell, this was world-breaking news.

Everyone was excited, except for most of my family. Dad was simply annoyed, Mom hated the attention, and at times, Angie would have little anxiety attacks at the photographers being too close for comfort. Me? I loved it—the attention it was giving our small town, the energy that filled the air.

The chaos of work only allowed me to see Jordan in the evenings, and I hadn't stepped onto the set since that very first day.

My hands pressed down my skirt suit as my heels clip-clopped against the sidewalk. The closer the barricade of fans came into view, the faster my pulse ticked against the inside of my wrist.

The atmosphere was different than the day before. More people. More chaos. More security.

Guards were everywhere, and Jordan's detail had

doubled to four. I'd asked him what the latest news was on his stalker, but all he could tell me was that everything was fine, and she hadn't been spotted in the vicinity.

The closer I came to Wells, the louder the roar of the crowd became. The screaming of his adoring fans drowned out all the thoughts in my head. Women, teenagers, and even a few ladies who looked to be about Nana's age had Jordan signs and posters of his last movie as they stood behind the barrier, screaming, waiting, basically panting.

A broader male, security detail from the day before, recognized me, and when I lifted a pass that was hanging around my neck, he walked through the crowd and ushered me past the barricade and straight to Jordan's trailer in the alleyway.

Having this street blocked was a disruption to the normal morning rush, but my surrounding tenants didn't mind because they were all benefiting monetarily from the filming. Their clientele was up, everyone visiting the next-door coffee, doughnut, and book shop just to see if they could get a glimpse of the infamous Jordan Ryder.

I stepped up into the trailer and was blasted with the bright lights on top of a mirror that spanned one entire wall. Jordan's eyes were closed while the thin, tall blonde with a pixie cut airbrushed his face. His chest rose and fell in a slow, steady rhythm, and if I didn't know any better, I would think he was sleeping.

"Hello," I said as the door shut behind me.

"Baby," Jordan cooed. His eyes remained closed, but he motioned me forward with his hands. "Jenny, Christene. And that's Susie, the best PA in the whole fucking universe. This is *the girlfriend*."

I didn't think I'd ever get tired of hearing those words.

My fingers met his outreached hand, and he brought it to his lips.

"Your makeup," Jenny, the artist, snapped. "I just airbrushed your lips."

Susie stuck out her free hand to shake mine. "Hi, Christene," she said in a cheery voice to match her cheery personality and bright red hair.

Susie looked no more than twenty, dressed in boyfriend jeans and a white T-shirt tied to the side. She had two coffees in a coffee container and a box of doughnuts resting on her arm. Her earpiece was slung around her earlobe, no doubt to bend to Jordan's every command.

"I have an extra cup of coffee here if you want it."

I grabbed one of the cups from her container and opened the top, watching the steam rise before taking a careful sip. "Thank you." The coffee was hot, and it warmed the back of my throat as I swallowed.

"I have to bring this one to Ryan. Tootles! Jay, be out on the set in thirty. And if I come back here to get your butt, it won't be pretty." She waved at me and practically skipped out the door.

"Jay? I kinda like that." I sat on the couch opposite his makeup chair, taking another slow sip of my coffee. "She's a spunky one."

"You can say that again. Half the time, I think she's on blow because she's got so much energy. But she's organized and timely, and she keeps me in check."

"Stop talking," Jenny ordered. She continued to use the machine to airbrush his face.

I watched in awe as she evenly covered every inch of skin, his neck, and then his arms and hands with the stroke of the brush. Jenny marred his cheek with fake skin, dried blood. She had darkened some of his body with a purplish-blue tint to highlight his bruises.

For a moment, I had to tell myself he was safe, that it wasn't real. The makeup was all for show, but it was eerily believable.

They were filming a dire hostage-takeover situation at the restaurant, and Jordan looked like collateral damage. I wanted to go over there and bandage him up and kiss all his scars and make him feel better but without the audience.

Twenty minutes later, when Jenny was done, she tipped her head in approval and proceeded to put away her high-end makeup sprawled out on the counter. I swear Jordan was sleeping. His eyes remained closed, his breathing slow and steady.

"Wake up!" Jenny roared.

I laughed when Jordan jumped from his seat, eyes open.

Then, in a softer tone, she said, "You have to be on the set in five." She smiled at me. "No kissing or other things that could get in the way of his face, please." Then, she turned her attention back toward him, her smile disappearing. "Don't make me redo your makeup, Jordan, or I'll be thoroughly pissed, given that I spent hours on you."

He waved a hand and pointed toward the exit. "I don't have to use my face to do what I want to do. Now, go get your second cup of coffee. You're much better when you've had caffeine."

Jenny threw him the middle finger and strolled out the door.

"Everyone is in a mood," I said.

"Well, everyone—me, included—has been here since five a.m."

I frowned. "I know. I missed you when I woke up this morning."

He motioned for me to come over, and I complied. When I was within reaching distance, he gripped my hand and pulled me onto his lap, snuggling closer.

"Your makeup," I scolded.

Jenny seemed nice enough, but I certainly didn't want to be blamed. My fingers lightly etched the broken skin at his temple.

"I know. I won't mess it up. I'm just going to hold you."

"Yeah, while your erection is poking me in the ass." I laughed.

He shrugged as if his boner weren't poking into my butt.

His hands slid up and down my thigh, sending a direct shock down my spine.

"Don't start something you can't finish," I said, pushing my ass against him and rotating my hips, taunting, teasing, tormenting.

Now, he'd be walking on the set with a hard-on. It would be hilarious to see him execute his fight scenes with a big-ass boner the size of Mt. Olympus.

"I have five minutes. I can make you come in two." He wiggled his eyebrows in a promise of success.

I touched his chin, where the fake flesh depicted busted-open skin. "Your imperfectly perfect face." I pouted.

He took my palm and kissed the inside of my wrist. "You know what I was thinking?"

"What?"

"We've got to tell Cade and Angie about us soon, about us being together. It's been days, and I hate keeping this from them."

He was right. Over these past few days, I'd been trying to answer Angie's questions without lying because I hated liars, had been burned by one and didn't want to turn into one. It was exhausting, skating around the truth to my best friend, my sister, day in and day out. I ended up sending all her calls to voice mail.

I exhaled a breath full of worry and anxiety because telling them would mean telling my mom. And she had specifically ordered me not to complicate my sister's relationship. If Jordan and I didn't work out, that would be a big complication. My stomach turned at the thought.

One day at a time, Tene. I had to take this new relationship one day at a time.

"Fine." I sighed, giving him a pointed stare. "Let's tell them, but it's your balls, not mine."

He laughed. "He didn't think I'd be using my balls with you again after you told Angie, who told him that I had problems performing in the bedroom."

The annoyance of Angie spilling her beans rose my irk meter to a ten. That had been between us, something sacred between sisters. What was the point of telling your sister something in secrecy if she didn't keep her trap shut?

"It wasn't you or us ... I was too much in my head at that moment. Your Candice tattoo ... Cade." I shook my head and bit my lip for spilling my guts to this man. *Great, just great.* I'd just revealed that Cade was basically on my mind while I was riding him like I was at a rodeo.

Just when he opened his mouth to speak, Susie popped her head inside.

"Hey, hey, hey, Jay-Jay, what did I say? On the set." She snapped her fingers. "Quick, quick, quick. Hanky-panky later." She waited expectedly, impatiently.

I placed my fingers on his lips. "I've gotta go anyway."

His eyebrows rose. "We're not done talking."

"I know," I said. "Want to meet up after your shoot?"

He placed a chaste kiss on my lips, totally breaking make-up protocol. "Yes. Plus, Wyatt's in town again. But can't you watch me in action for a little bit?" He wiggled his eyebrows, playing for cute.

I rolled my eyes with exaggeration. "Fine. I guess if I have to." I hopped off him, still aware that his boner was saluting at attention.

He groaned when he stood.

Susie blushed when she noticed, coughed, and turned away from the door. "Don't make Alex come and get you. Better me than him."

"The director," Jordan answered my silent question, all the while peering down at his boner. "Are you going to take care of this real quick?"

I made my way to the door, grinning naughtily. "Why don't you let Alex take care of that?"

He shook his head in disappointment. "You're terrible to your new boyfriend."

He strolled out, limping, while I half-skipped to the set, ready to see my new boyfriend in action.

I left during the second set and decided to go home after the trying day I'd had at Armstrong Realty.

I walked to my car, the breeze hitting my bare legs. There was a tiny skip to my step, a lightness in my heart, and I knew it had everything to do with Jordan Ryder and the anticipation of seeing him tonight after he was done filming.

I had it bad.

When I slipped into my car, I was still on cloud a million and nine. My smile could not be dimmed. I opened the visor mirror to check my makeup, and a little white piece of paper dropped into my lap.

It was folded in half.

I opened it, and three words had ice pumping through my body and the world around me halting to a stop. My clammy fingers shook as I read the note, slower the second time.

Leave him alone.

Immediately, I dropped the paper in my lap like a fire had torched my fingertips. My head jerked up, and I scanned the area around me. My heartbeat thrashed in my ears, and my hand flew to the lock on my door.

There was a woman walking her dog down the street. A couple on a work break, carrying their briefcases. Media and fans stood by the barricade. She could be anywhere.

His stalker.

She had been here.

In my car.

It could only have been her.

Nothing usually shook me. On the outside, I might seem delicate, all woman, someone who didn't want to break a nail, but that was when the saying, *Looks can be deceiving*, came into play.

It took me ten seconds to get it together. The sun was shining brightly through my windshield. It was the middle of the afternoon. People were everywhere. Nothing could happen in broad daylight, right?

I stepped out of the car, and my eyes perused the area more closely. I studied every passing man, woman, and child, memorizing their features. I lifted the piece of paper in plain view for the culprit to see if she was truly watching me. Courage stiffened my shoulders.

You leave him alone.

Game on!

I reminded myself that this woman had a restraining

order against her, and if she was in the vicinity of Jordan, she could very possibly go to jail and soon.

Instead of getting back in the car, I did the opposite of what the white piece of paper had instructed. I walked straight back into Wells to watch Jordan finish filming. Work could wait. I didn't have any appointments I couldn't cancel. I'd make sure he was safe and tell him what had happened in person.

I wasn't afraid for my safety. I was afraid for him.

CHAPTER 23

FILMING ENDED at eleven thirty in the evening.

"Bright and early tomorrow morning," Alex yelled out to all crew members.

My legs itched; my body ironically wired from the long day of doing absolutely nothing but sitting. I took note of everyone in the room, the stuntmen and extras with their gear and guns. Anyone in here could've written that note too. Maybe he had more than one stalker. But he had body-guards. Dex and Larry followed Jordan everywhere. I wouldn't be surprised if one whipped out his dick and the other helped him take a piss.

I waited while Jordan said bye and chatted up the production director, the lighting crew, the camera guys, and practically everyone else on set.

I waited until it was just the two of us because I didn't know who was involved.

After a few minutes, he finally approached. "Sorry, babe."

He kissed my lips and grabbed my hand before jetting

us through the back door. A few fans stood outside behind the yellow barrier.

He released me and stopped to sign some autographs. I stood back and took in the scene. When he bent down to take a picture with a shorter woman who reminded me of Nana, I stiffened. Anybody could be the culprit. Even though someone looked innocent, they could very well be hiding a weapon—a knife, a gun. My shoulders tensed.

"Jordan!" they shouted.

The crowd grew bigger—getting louder, booming.

"We love you, Jordan!"

He was adored by so many, loved by the majority of the female population. And in the craziest of ways, it was almost unbelievable that he was with me.

He took his time, making sure he had signed his autograph for every single one of the people who had probably waited the whole day to get a glimpse of him.

"Thanks, everyone, for coming. I love you too," he yelled back.

A girl in pink went in for a picture. When she leaned into Jordan, the hairs on the back of my neck stood at attention like pins on the back of a porcupine, and when she reached into her jacket, I didn't think. I just reacted.

"No!" I jerked him away with enough force, jumped the barrier, and shoved her to the ground.

Commotion erupted. The bodyguards moved past the barriers and pushed us behind them.

"Tene?" Jordan was shocked, his eyes wide and assessing the area, noting the woman on the floor. He pushed me behind him.

"She was pulling something out of her pocket! She has something in her pocket!" I pointed at the culprit, and her eyes went wide.

Larry pulled the woman off the floor.

When she reached in her pocket again, I gripped Jordan's sleeve in a tight vise. "Let's go! You need to get out of here."

Then, she pulled out a pen.

A whoosh of air rushed out of me, and I blinked, momentarily stunned. "I swear, I thought ..."

Jordan grabbed my arm, and his bodyguards ushered us into the black Escalade. The adrenaline rushed through me, and when the door shut, Jordan's whole body faced mine.

"What's going on with you?"

"I thought she had a gun." My voice was shaky, my nerves on end.

"A gun? It was a pen." He ran one hand through his blond hair, making it stand on end. "Dex and Larry, they have everything under control. But you can't be doing that. With all these lawsuits from fans and paparazzi, you just can't. Don't worry; I won't let anything happen to you."

"Me? I'm not worried about me. I'm worried about you." I reached into my back pocket, pulling out the note, and placed it in his hands. "I found this in my car."

He opened it, and his whole face hardened. "Shit." A visible shiver ran through him, and in the next second, I was in his arms. "You're fine. Everything is going to be fine." He kissed the top of my head and reached for his phone. "I'm texting Cade."

"It's late."

"It doesn't matter. If this woman has gotten to you, who knows if she's been in contact with your sister or my brother?"

I blinked, bile rising to the top of my throat. At the mention of my sister, I closed my eyes. This was getting out of hand. She'd already gotten to me, and there was no way in hell I'd let her reach anyone else I cared about.

I needed her behind bars.

———

Larry stood directly outside the door of Cade's apartment, and Dex was stationed inside, his big-as-boulder arms crossed over his massive chest as though he were protecting a billion-dollar diamond. They were both in suits and wore earpieces, looking like they were part of the Secret Service, standing stiff and stoic against the window. The light, bright floral curtains that I'd helped Angie pick were up and draped over the floor-to-ceiling windows. The colors blended into an array of flowers from a garden—sweet, vibrant, and opposite to the mood in the room.

"Have you seen her?" Cade asked, pacing, his gaze menacing like the stalker was in the room. The muscle in his jaw ticked and ticked and ticked.

Wyatt sat on the plush leather couch, his eyes narrowed, and he was stealthily silent, but I could read the worry in his features.

"No, I haven't seen her since the last time, in court. And before that, at my place, half-naked."

I gripped Angie's hand tighter, as we were squished on the love seat, watching Wyatt, Cade, and Jordan contemplate the next steps.

"This is crazy. Just ask them to take her in," Wyatt said.

"On what proof?" Jordan threw his hands up. "Tene didn't see her, but I know in my gut that this is Jordie."

"Jordie?" Goose bumps formed on the back of my neck. "Sorry, her name is Jordie?" *What kind of name was that?*

He sighed. "I don't know what her name was before, but

she changed it to Jordie." His face turned a shade darker. "Jordan and Jordie."

I shot up. "She's crazy." I placed my hands on my hips. "What you need to do is get your studio on the phone and tell them what's going on. Track that witch down and put her in jail."

What girl would change her name to match his? A psycho, the kind you only saw in movies—that was who. One who was insane enough to possibly do anything to have him—and if she couldn't have him, then no one could.

"Crazy is an understatement," Cade said. "She has multiple tattoos of his face and name on her body."

"I hate this." Angie rubbed her temple, her knees bouncing with agitation. "I hate that there are so many people in town, and we don't know which one is her."

I patted her hand once and then stood.

Bile rose up my throat, and my stomach tightened. "I just can't." I paced the room with both hands on my hips and then faced Jordan straight on.

Why the hell were we still in this room, doing nothing? We should be at the police station, filing a report.

"You're in danger. You need to take this seriously. We need to get the cops involved," I said.

"We don't." Jordan's tone was firm, his facial features unmoving.

Was he already desensitized by this danger, by this nonstop stalker girl who kept coming up in his life? He had to take this seriously.

"What?" My hands waved above me like a banshee. "What do you mean, we don't? She may still be in the area. Last time, she showed up at your place without shame. Who knows what she'll do now?"

What was it with men and their calm facades? My father

was the same way. The house could be burning, and they would maintain their composure and slowly walk out from the burning building while the women would be running out.

"Calm down." Jordan's eyes softened, which made me want to slap him upside the head to knock some sense in him. "You're worried about me, but she was in *your* car. She knows we're together. You're the one in danger." His gaze grazed my face.

He was constantly concerned about me, but I only cared about his safety.

All eyes were on us. Now, they knew we were a couple.

Cade's eyes were unreadable, but my sister looked as though she had stepped into a Wilton bake sale, where all their accessories and baking items were seventy percent off.

"You're together?" she whispered, standing from the couch.

"Yeah, we are," Jordan answered for both of us, but his stare was locked with Cade's. "You can beat me up like you did all those years ago for dating your sister, but I'm not giving Tene up."

He squeezed my hand and stared down at me with such reverence that my heart flip-flopped. Goodness, I could fall for this man.

"And I haven't been this happy in a long time."

It was a declaration of his feelings for me, and my insides soared like a rocket ship on its way to Venus, the planet of love.

Silence spanned the room.

Then, Wyatt stood and clasped a strong hand on his brother's back, bringing him in. "If you've found someone who can finally deal with your ass, then I'm happy for you."

Angie practically bum-rushed us, her arms tightly

weaving around Jordan and me. "I'm so happy. This is so crazy. I just knew it. You're too alike to ever be apart."

She couldn't have spoken truer words. Where she and Cade were polar opposites, Jordan and I were like twins separated at birth. And maybe we'd never settled down before because we hadn't found the right person. Now, we had each other.

Cade's eyes were tight, his face closed off. When he walked toward us, Jordan sucked in a breath. Through the challenge in his eyes and the way his posture stiffened beside me, I knew that Jordan wanted Cade's blessing, and inside, I secretly prayed for it too.

"This was one of the things I was afraid of. Bringing your Hollywood drama to this small town," Cade said.

"Bro, chill out," Wyatt piped up.

My eyes took in all of Cade Ryder, a wall of muscle, the hard planes of his face, the narrowing of his eyes.

"Last time this happened, when you told me you were dating my sister, I beat you to a pulp." Cade tipped his chin. "And make no mistake, she's basically my sister, ever since I started dating Angie."

When Cade's gaze made it my way, Jordan stepped in front of me. My sister gripped the edge of Cade's shirt, but he didn't budge. Their stare-down, brother to brother, swallowed the air and space of the room. And when Cade took one more step forward, I stepped in front of Jordan, between them, to break the tension.

"I don't have a say in this because Lord knows, I've tried." Cade's dark-as-night brown eyes locked with Jordan's blue ones. "I want to know you're ready. You've moved on. You're healed."

Cade was talking about Candice, and I understood his

concerns. If Jordan wasn't over Candice, then he couldn't fully be with me.

Jordan squeezed my hand harder and lifted his chin to meet Cade's gaze. "It took me a long time to get here. And time and time again, I've lied to myself and others, telling everyone that I was completely healed—that I was ready to move on." He brought my hand to his lips, staring deeply into my eyes now. "But I am. Because I wouldn't be with you if I wasn't ready—if I wasn't all in." His proclamation hit me directly in the chest, and I melted into him.

When we turned to Cade, his eyes were intently focused on Jordan, studying him—debating, maybe.

Cade took a step forward, and I held my breath. I thought everyone was.

"You'd just better treat her right. But judging on your past relationship, I have no doubt you will."

A whoosh of air rushed from everyone's lungs, so loud and all at the same time that we all began to laugh.

"Yay! We're now basically all related," Angie cooed, pulling me into a hug.

"That sounded wrong," Jordan said.

My little sister squished us together in a little bubble of love, her love, my almost-love.

Then, she began to jump up and down until the hardwood shook beneath us.

Boom!

The sharp, piercing noise shattered the celebration.

My heart jumped to my throat.

At once, the men in the room were alert, faces tight, necks taut. Then, Larry busted through the door, gun out of his holster, and we realized what had been the cause of the noise that made the house shake.

With all the jumping next to the side table, the vase that

held the mini orchid had fallen off the edge and onto the hardwood floor.

We let out a laugh, this time less carefree.

"We're all on edge," Jordan said, his features devoid of any humor. "And I'm going to settle that sooner than later."

CHAPTER 24

THE NEXT DAY, after the long day of filming was over, Jordan and I headed to the suburbs to have dinner with my family and the boys.

The leather seat of my BMW clung to the backs of my legs as I peeked at Jordie's picture on the dashboard.

Jordie Stein.

The stalker had a name, a face, and a plan. A plan to be with my man. Little did she know that was never, ever going to happen.

The day before, I'd watched my boyfriend pace the room and talk to numerous people from the studio about Jordie and her little note for me. Jordan had made sure I knew what she looked like, her style of clothing, and what she drove. I cringed when Jordan showed me numerous pictures, showing her at various events.

"You need to memorize what she looks like. From every angle, even when she's wearing a hat or a disguise. And if you ever see her, you need to run in the other direction."

"I know." I plucked the picture off the dashboard and

flicked it to the floor. "I don't want to look at that face anymore. Every time I do, I want to hunt her down."

I didn't want to think of Jordie. I wanted to think of food, of filling my belly, of laughter with Nana, and of hugs from my father. Not this shit. This was the last thing I wanted to think about.

When we stopped at a red light, Jordan bent over and picked up Jordie's picture, shaking it in front of me. "Are you listening? This is important."

"I know! I wish you'd stop worrying about me. I'm scared shitless for you."

He sighed. "I told you ..." He brushed a tender hand down my cheek, pinching the bottom. "... don't worry about me; I'm a big boy."

"And I'm a big girl," I countered.

The light turned green, and he pressed on the gas. His lips were in a thin line, his jaw tight. "She's dangerous, Tene. And crazy smart. I have no idea how she got through my gated community, past my security, and into my house. Who knows what she's capable of?"

Chills ran down my spine and to the end of every one of my nerves. "Did your studio call you yet?"

"Not yet. They'll be on this. They will locate her. The studio has people who work on this kind of stuff."

The ringing of my phone in my purse diverted my attention. "Hello?"

"Where are you?" Angie asked. "Dinner is ready, and you're twenty minutes late. You know Mom ..." Her voice trailed off.

That was the understatement of the year. Of course, I knew my own mom.

"And, Tene, make sure when you enter the gates, no photogs are following you. They were outside the restaurant today when I went to visit Cade. I swear, they could've followed me home."

"Shit, Angie. I'm sorry."

"I know. I stayed in the car for an hour until Cade got me. They get me all nervous. I hate these people disrupting our town."

Angie was the anxious type, so I could empathize with where she was coming from, but because crowds and attention didn't bother me, I focused on the positive—the thriving of businesses around the Wells property due to the new attention my boyfriend was bringing to our small town.

"It'll be over before you know it. Anyway, will be home soon. Jordan was on the phone with the studio and local law enforcement, which is why we're late."

"What happened?" Angie's voice heightened, and the worry in her tone was evident. "Did you find out anything new?"

"I'll fill you in once we get there."

I hung up the phone, and my gaze flickered toward my boyfriend, whose steel-blue eyes were distant while he was deep in thought. We'd talked and argued and debated on what was to be done about Jordie from when I found that note in my car and into the morning after leaving Cade and Angie's and to now. My body ached. My brain hurt. Even though our minds raced, right now ... it was time for the quiet.

———

Warm, pale-yellow walls beckoned us in, but as I stepped into the foyer of the house I'd grown up in, I cringed, knowing my mother was just around the corner, and I wouldn't hear the end of it because we were late.

This house. I loved this house. The couches, worn leather from all the jumping and plopping and just plain sitting. The colorful pillows against the couches that I used to drool on. The pictures of every stage in our lives hung neatly along the wall of our family room. The plasma TV mounted on the wall and Dad's recliner, which was older than me, set in the corner of the room.

We walked down the hall and paused before we entered the dining room.

I stilled hearing my mother's voice.

"When will filming end? All this hoopla has interrupted my grocery shopping. Did you see the traffic today? It took me an extra fifteen minutes to get downtown."

"I know. I know. Thank God all of this won't last forever. Once filming is over, I assume they'll follow him to his next location," my father added.

"It's not that bad," Nana chimed in.

Of course, Nana would be eating this all up.

"At least they're not following your every move. Well, actually, they're stalking Cade, him being the brother and all, but I'm still collateral damage," Angie whined. "But I agree; at least it'll be over soon."

I exhaled a heavy sigh. Over soon? Once everyone got wind that I was Jordan's girlfriend, it would never be over. Angie would be the Pippa Middleton of the United States. Our lives, what we did on a daily basis, would be scrutinized.

"Don't say I didn't warn you," Jordan said before pulling us into the room. "But it'll be fine." He squeezed my hand hard.

But would it?

I didn't want to move, and if he moved here, he'd bring the mass of chaos that always followed him. This was the difference between men and women. Women thought ahead. That was just in my nature—to plan. The men of the world just worried about the now.

Why couldn't things just be simple?

"Hey, guys!" Jordan stormed into the room, and everyone waved in greeting.

We were hugged by Nana and my father first. My mother had dinner set on the dining room table, a room we only entertained in. She hadn't looked up when I entered and continued to straighten the already-perfect table setting.

I made my way down the long mahogany table fit to sit sixteen, where Cade, Angie, and Wyatt were seated. I half-hugged each of them as I went down the line.

"Glad to see that you made it." My mother's voice seethed with sarcasm.

I wanted to plop on the floor, throw my arm over my eyes, and say, *I give up.* That was the kind of day I was having.

"At least she made it in safe and sound." My father pulled out Nana's seat and then dropped down next to her.

I didn't even have the energy to think of a snappy, smart response. I took my regular seat at the table, but Jordan stood straighter, his hand resting behind my chair. I pulled at his shirt to sit, but he didn't budge.

"I'm sorry we're late, Mrs. Armstrong. I was tending to a stalker who has been following me around the nation, even showing up in my apartment. And now, she's left a lovely note in your daughter's car." Then, he sat down as though he hadn't just thrown a hand grenade on top of the green beans.

The gasps of my mother and Nana echoed around the

room. Then, a commotion erupted, coupled with a slew of questions.

"Where? When did this happen?" my father piped in.

I could kill the BF at that moment. Talk about inappropriate dinner subject.

"Are you okay?" Nana asked, her aged eyes round with worry.

Great. Now, he was going to give my eighty-five-year-old grandma a heart attack.

"Where is the stalker now?" My mother's hand was pressed to her throat. She dropped in her seat as though she couldn't hold her own body up.

Was that genuine concern in her tone?

"Everything is under control," Jordan said above the ruckus. "I have the studio tracking down this woman's whereabouts."

Cade added, "And I've beefed up security at the restaurant."

Cade's eyes were laser-trained on Jordan. Guess I had someone else on the strangle-Jordan team.

"Tene's place is secure, and building security knows about the situation."

Cade gripped my sister's hand fiercely above the table, and when their eyes met, his smile was tight with worry.

"This is crazy. Why is this happening? Why are they targeting Tene?" My mother's voice heightened with hysteria. "How do you know that we don't need security too? How do you know that you didn't lead her to our home?" She gripped the armrests, her knuckles white from the tension.

"Mother, calm down," I said, trying to keep my voice even. *Of course, she's more worried about herself.* "It's never going to get to that point."

Her face turned to me, one shaky finger pointed my way. "Don't tell me to calm down. Why is Jordan's stalker after you?"

Her eyes lay deathly intent on my face, and I swallowed.

"Because she wants Jordan." *Duh. Isn't that obvious?*

"So? What does that have to do with you or Angie?"

"Mrs. Armstrong ..." Jordan swallowed, and he placed one strong hand on top of mine. "This stalker's aggression is geared toward Tene because ... because we're together."

Bomb number two dropped.

Way to silence the room.

My gaze dropped to the tablecloth and the silver napkin rings set on top of my great-grandmother's china. Everyone's eyes burned through me, but I wasn't ready for this—for everyone to judge me and my decisions.

The last and only man I had taken home to meet my parents had cheated on me. The constant questions about Logan, where he was, what had happened between us had been never-ending, which hadn't helped my state of mind at the time. That time had spiraled me into a depression that took a good part of my heart, my self-esteem, and my self-worth.

And here I was again, opening myself to vulnerability.

I knew I'd said I wouldn't date Jordan. My mother had warned me off him, but there was no way I couldn't at least give this ... us ... a chance.

He ducked into my line of sight, and longing and pure fierceness poured out of him. "And because she's mine, I'm never going to let anything happen to her. Ever."

My sister openly sighed on the other side of me. When I turned to face her, her smile was blinding, super-cheese to the max. I bumped my shoulder against hers. If only I had the same reaction from the rest of my family.

My mother's reaction was stoic, but my father's and Nana's matched Angie's. Both of them exuded happiness. Laugh lines were etched on the corner of Nana's mouth. My father's eyes crinkled.

"So, my eldest daughter has a boyfriend now." My dad grazed his white beard with one hand, his fingers twisting at the ends, and his eyes landing on Jordan's face. "She's a special girl, and she needs to be treated right."

Jordan's eyes flickered between my father's and mine, and he squeezed my hand on top of the table. "I don't think she'd have it any other way."

"I know how that is." My father chuckled, and his gaze landed on my mother's. "Like mother, like daughter."

Being compared to my mother was like being compared to the Queen of England and Mother Teresa, all in one— proper, respectful, and perfect. You'd never live up to their expectations. I didn't want to be compared to my mother, even if I always was because I looked most like her.

She playfully slapped his arm, and he reached in, grabbed it, and brought it to his lips. My father always lightened my mother's mood, lit it like a candlewick. He had a knack for doing that, for making her smile when she rarely did, for easing up her seriousness when she needed it.

Wyatt spoke up beside me, "And don't worry; you're safe, Mrs. Armstrong. So are Tene and Angie. You should see the precautions made for Angie because of Cade's crazy protectiveness." The side of his mouth quirked up, and it made me pause for a second, noting the unnatural lightness in his tone. Wyatt tended to stay in the quiet, serious box.

Was that his form of a joke?

"It's my job to take care of the people I love," Cade said in defense.

"That's my job too." Jordan's eyes grazed my face, scouring it, our eyes never breaking contact.

I held my breath. For one, two, three seconds. *Did he just nonchalantly proclaim his love for me?*

I averted my stare, my chin lowered toward the food already getting cold on the table. "And let's eat, shall we?" I didn't know how to process what he'd said or hadn't said or could possibly mean. And I didn't want to read too much into his words.

I didn't want a repeat of the past. I needed someone to press the brakes and slow us down.

"Can you pass me the potatoes?" I tipped my chin toward Nana in an effort to divert attention and get the eating started.

Dinner was filled with tons of food and laughter, mostly by the men. Wyatt, Cade, and Jordan's banter was refreshing, and it changed our family dynamic of mostly women.

"Jordan, remember when you thought girls had vaginas and boys had pizzas?" Wyatt laughed.

"Inappropriate, bro," Cade said, but his chest shook from his chuckle.

"Well, if we're going way back, all the way back, do you remember when you thought everything was yours to pee on? Even the damn dog."

Wyatt chuckled and rubbed one hand down his growing beard.

The whole table burst into laughter, and Wyatt lifted both hands. "What? He was always lifting his leg on every corner to pee. I thought it was about time for him to learn his lesson."

"With all the peeing and pizzas ... I think it's time for

dessert." My mother smiled and shook her head, obviously amused. "Angie, will you help me bring in the dessert?" When my mother stood, Angie followed her to the kitchen.

Jordan's hand rested on my thigh, giving it a little squeeze. Wyatt and Cade continued with their banter, but Jordan simply leaned into me and said, "You think you're up for some pizza later?"

My brows furrowed, and a mischievous grin crept up his face.

"You know, my pizza." His chin gestured downward.

I rolled my eyes and then leaned into him, resting my hand in between his legs. "Didn't you know? Pizza is my favorite. Especially this kind."

—

"Thanks for having us." Jordan, with his sweet ways, lightly kissed Nana on the cheek and then hugged my mother next.

They were both smitten with him. I mean, who wouldn't be? He was beautiful, handsome, and undeniably charming.

Nana hung on his arm, her short stature causing her to lift her chin to peer up at him. If Nana were forty years younger, she'd give me a run for my money.

"Come over for dinner tomorrow night," Nana said, eyeing my mother for her approval. "Right?"

My mother laughed beside him. It was refreshing to see her so lighthearted, to hear the joy in her voice, to experience this side of her. "Yes, Jordan, please come over for dinner tomorrow night."

Amusement lit his eyes. "We're on the last leg of filming, so I'll be doing a few more long nights before it's over, but we're having a cast party when we wrap up. I'd love for you all to come."

Nana leaped in the air, overjoyed. "We'll be there."

"Nana ..." I scolded, afraid she'd break her hip.

My father shook his head. "Mom, it's not like you've never seen a famous person before."

She cocked her head. "Well, we haven't. Except for this young, handsome gentleman in front of us." She winked at my boyfriend. Seriously winked.

"How about George, our neighbor who was in that car commercial?" my father asked.

She waved a hand. "Not the same thing."

I wanted to laugh. Obviously, not the same thing. There were C-list actors and Jordan Ryder, who didn't need an introduction.

Dad threw an arm over Jordan's shoulder. "Take care of my girl. She may seem tough on the outside, but she's just a sweet princess." His hold tightened around Jordan, a mostly benign but slightly menacing look in his eyes. "Don't mess with my princess."

Princess. It was the name he'd called me since I was a little girl when I'd sit on his knee. Sometimes, every now and then, when I sealed a deal, closed on a new property, filled in a vacant location with a new tenant, that word *princess* would slip from his mouth, and I'd smile big or roll my eyes, pretending I was annoyed, but inside, I lived for those moments. The moments that reminded me I would always be Daddy's girl.

"Yes, sir." Jordan's smile widened into an almost grin. That cute little chin dimple was widely on display. "I'll treat her like the princess she truly is."

Dad tipped his chin in approval, stepped back, and plucked a blank paper from his back pocket. "Hey, so I have this golf buddy, and his wife is a major fan. Can you just sign this really quickly for him? He wants to use it as a way to get him out of the house for more time on the green."

Smooth. Real smooth, Dad.

Jordan chuckled. "Sure thing."

I eyed my sister from the other side of the room, and we shared an amused glance.

After we all said our good-byes, Cade, Angie, Wyatt, Jordan, and I strolled out the door and down our circular driveway to our respective cars.

"I think I've replaced you as the favorite boyfriend," Jordan said, tipping his chin toward Cade.

"Pfft. Yes, favorite actor boyfriend who has gained his girlfriend a stalker," Cade growled, rubbing his forefinger at a vein throbbing at his temple.

Angie slapped Cade's side. "That's mean."

"Low blow, bro," Wyatt said.

"I think I sense a little jealousy in the air." Jordan opened my passenger door, but not before I caught a little scowl on Cade's face.

"Bye, Angie," I said, blowing her kisses. "Call you tomorrow."

We hopped in the car, and he held my hand in silence as the quiet suburban night and lights of the highway passed us by. My mind wandered to dinner and the interaction of both of our families that seemed to simply just fit.

Fit was the appropriate word. It was light and effortless, just how relationships should be—minus the stalker talk.

"Are you worried?" Jordan asked, his voice quiet.

I blinked and faced him. The moonlight highlighted the creases between his eyebrows.

"Because the studio left me a message when we were at

dinner. She just flew back home to California." His eyes went to the road, but I sensed the relief in his tone.

My stomach dropped to the floor and then kept going. So, it had been her. "She was here." I guessed a big part of me refused to believe it was true.

"Yeah, and though we don't have proof she's the one who placed that note in your car, I know in my gut it was her." His jaw tightened, and I stared at the shadow of his hardened features—his square jaw, the sharp planes of his nose, and the scowl on his face. "But we'll know when she comes back in town. Then, I'll snap pictures, and she'll be detained like she was before."

"This is crazy." My voice was soft, reserved, opposite to my rapidly beating pulse.

"I'm used to the craziness. I'm just not used to having someone else all up in my craziness."

He reached over, intertwined our fingers, and squeezed my hand. I loved it when he did that. It was in the simplest of touches that I knew he was with me.

"I hope that's a good thing."

"It's a very good thing," he said, his eyes briefly meeting mine. "I love your craziness."

"I guess you attract the crazies." I shivered at my own words, and my smile diminished.

The truth was, there was someone unstable out there who'd contacted me, and none of us knew what she was capable of.

CHAPTER 25

WHEN I AWOKE the next morning, I heard the shower running, and the bed was empty beside me. My skin rested against the soft hotel sheets, and it felt like heaven.

After turning over, I buried my head in the pillow, inhaling deeply and taking in the scent of my boyfriend mixed with our passion from last night.

Sigh. Boyfriend. I hadn't had one of those in a while. And I had to admit, it felt wonderful.

The ringing of Jordan's phone brought my attention to the side table. The old Christene would have checked messages and listened to his voice mail. The new, improved Christene flipped over, grabbed the pillow, and placed it over my head, wanting to revel in my blissful state. I never wanted to get up from this bed—ever. I never wanted to go to work. Never wanted to do anything but lie here and be with my boyfriend. I drowned out the ringing of his phone with happy thoughts of us last night and then again this morning.

The room went silent, but in the next moment, Jordan's phone rang again and again and again. I peeked over at the black cell, and then it went silent again. My head was about to drop onto the pillows when another round of ringing started. This must've been the fifth call. It had to be an emergency.

What if it was the studio or one of his brothers with news of the stalker?

The running water from the shower continued, so I yelled out his name. There was no way he was going to hear me, but maybe if he did, he'd stop the shower and pick up this annoying phone.

When the sixth cycle of ringing began, I reached for the phone. "Hello?"

The screen of his phone popped up with a number. It wasn't programmed with a name.

"Hello?" I repeated.

"Hello." The female voice leaked sugary sweetness one second and fiery coal the next. "Who is this?"

"Christene. Who's this?" I didn't like her sharp tone.

"Where's Jordan?" she snapped.

The rudeness in her voice heightened like an alarm bell, but I maintained composure. She could be someone from work or a friend from home, a cousin ...

"He's in the shower," I answered, voice tight.

"Well, you tell him Bianca called. He'll know who I am, and I know he'll want to call me back." She sounded so sure.

"Are you from work?" I couldn't rule this out, but her tone, her low voice, didn't scream business.

"Work?" She had the audacity to laugh out loud. "Work? Oh, honey." The high-pitched, witch-like laughter gave me goose bumps but not the good kind. "Just tell him to call me. After the time I showed him in Las Vegas ... well ..." Her voice lowered. "... he will."

Then, she hung up, not giving me a chance for a witty comeback.

What the living hell? Ahhh. The nerve of some women!

I gripped his phone, lifted it above my head, and was about to chuck his very expensive cell to the far corner of the room until something deep in my gut told me not to. Only someone who'd been hurt before in a prior relationship, someone who was insecure, would do that, and I was better than this. He wasn't Logan, and this relationship was not like my last one.

The edges of the phone dug deep into my palm, making an indentation in the middle of my hand, and I brought it by my side.

My eyes flickered to the bathroom door. The water was still going ... and I debated for two seconds, but curiosity won out, so I checked his phone. The texts were innocent. Mostly from his brothers, some from the studio. Some were from girls that had gone unanswered. I scrolled and scrolled and hated myself for even doing this, and yet, I couldn't control myself. I was the wounded animal checking the hunter's gun for bullets. I needed to know what I was up against.

I placed the phone on my lap, staring at the picture of his brothers with their mother, and then I scrolled down through other photos.

My pulse stopped when one particular picture popped up.

Candice. In my gut, I knew it was her, it was in her features that she shared with her biological brother, Cade.

Beautiful, young, and vibrant.

One of them at the park, her sitting on his lap. One where she was hugging him fiercely, kissing his cheek with her eyes closed.

There were endless pictures of them together, and a constant smile lit up Jordan's face. I curled into myself, watching their love story play in front of me.

A lump formed in the back of my throat, and I stopped at a picture where he was staring at her as though she was the most beautiful thing in the world, so much love and adoration in his expression—a picture-perfect love story that you'd see on greeting cards.

My eyes fell shut, and then I gritted my teeth and put the phone down.

She was dead.

Gone.

I had to worry about the ones who were healthy, alive, and wanted him in the flesh. Not his dead girlfriend.

She couldn't hurt me now. *Could she?*

I let out a long, shaky sigh. If a man was going to cheat, he was going to cheat. I just needed to trust him. Jordan Ryder was the hottest male to walk the planet. I couldn't be with him all the time. I had a life, and my life didn't involve running around the nation after a man to keep tabs and make sure he was faithful.

The door to the bathroom flung open, and Jordan came out with a towel wrapped around his waist, drying his hair with another towel. Beads of water ran down his well-defined chest. Right by Candice's name.

I threw his phone on the comforter. "Bianca called," I said, my tone heavy with defeat. "She wants you to call her back."

I threw my arm over my eyes, already tired from a day I hadn't even started. And to think, I had woken up in such a good mood.

The bed dipped, and the scent of his aftershave wafted my way. "Hey."

"Hey," I said, not moving, barely breathing, and just annoyed as fuck.

He pulled my arm from my eyes, his own gaze serious and tender at the same time. I hated it when he looked at me like that, as though everything would be right in the world; it made me feel guilty that I didn't have enough confidence to believe it.

"If there's something you want to ask me, just ask, okay? I'm pretty much an open book, straightforward and honest to a fault. It's a redeeming and damning quality of mine." He tipped up my chin with the lightness of his fingertips.

I sat up, back against the headboard, direct with my question, unable to bite it back. "Who's Blanca?"

His gaze didn't waver. "A girl I met in Vegas. Yes, we had a temporary fling. No, I'm not into her. Yes, she keeps calling me, though I never pick up her calls or listen to her voice mails. Anything else?"

I gulped and tried to let it go. He'd not been doing anything any other healthy, fine-ass, single male wouldn't do. Hell, I'd done the same thing. No-strings-attached relationships. That was what I'd done before him, but why did it still sting to hear it?

He pulled me into his lap, my cheek against his hard chest. "I'm not a man-whore like those tabloids make me out to be, but I'm not a saint either."

"I'm not either," I said softly, turning things over and over in my head.

I didn't want to know his number, how many women he slept with, and I didn't want him to know mine, either.

"What are you thinking?" He pulled me up to where I had to face him and ducked in closer, pausing to examine my expression. "Whatever it is, just say it." He cupped my cheek and brushed his thumb against my cheekbone. "If you don't, it'll be the end of us. I've been there before." His eyes narrowed, and for a brief second, it was like he was somewhere else. "I don't want that to happen again, so, spill."

My voice was small, vulnerable. "Why was she so sure that you'd call her back?"

"'Cause she's a freak in the bedroom."

I shoved at his arm. "Rude."

He laughed. "You asked. Remember, honest to a fault?" Then, he reached for my hand and kissed it. "But I'm not into her. I'm into you. I'm with you."

He tugged closer, but I refused to give in.

He hadn't done anything wrong. Yet.

As soon as that word registered, I pushed it out of my mind. He wasn't my ex-boyfriend. But if I fell into the comfort of Jordan's arms, then I'd forget my worries. There would be a false sense of security, and I wasn't sure if I was ready for that. The more you gave, the more vulnerable you were, the more susceptible you were to hurt. And I'd been hurt so much already.

"Why are you so damn stubborn?" One more tug and I was in his arms again. "Ask me anything."

"Were you in love with any of them?"

"Them, as in the women I briefly dated? No."

There was no point in holding it all in, so I peered up at him. "If you feel the need to cheat or give in to temptation, just let me know." He was going to speak, but I raised a hand and locked eyes with him. "Never say never, okay? 'Cause unless you're a psychic or you have a crystal ball, you can't tell. I've been in the dark before. For a long time."

When Logan had cheated on me, I hadn't known for months. Besides the obvious ultimate betrayal, I'd never felt stupider. All the signs had been there, but I'd refused to see it. And I was not dumb.

"You're right," he said, angling closer. "I've done a lot of shit that I said I'd never do. I don't have a crystal ball. I wish I did. Then, maybe I could've stopped a lot of shit that happened in the past." His eyebrows pulled together. "When Candice was going through some issues, she blocked us all out, me included. She had all these doubts in her head, about me, mostly about herself. We could have helped her get the support she needed because she was emotionally and mentally tortured by what had happened. But I swear, if she hadn't blocked me, Cade, or Wyatt out, she'd be alive today." He shook his head. "I can't have that, okay? I can't be in a relationship where you don't tell me if something is bothering you."

"I won't." I nodded. "I won't block you out. Not if I can help it."

He rested his forehead against mine and then brushed my bottom lip with his thumb. "I don't know my future, but right now, at this moment, I know that I want a future with you in it."

I released a breath ... or maybe it was a sigh. Who knew?

"My life in Hollywood, it's all a facade." With the tips of his thumb and forefinger, he lifted my chin. "But this ... you ... us ... is the most real thing I've had in a long time. And I wouldn't jeopardize that for anything."

Then, he brushed his lips against mine, and I relaxed against him, needing his words to be true, needing to believe them.

———

There was a difference. A difference between the random women he'd been with and the one girlfriend he was possibly still in love with. I'd compete with the random women, but I couldn't compete with the girlfriend who'd first won his heart.

I aimlessly slipped out of the car and shifted my purse to my shoulder as I walked into Allswell.

She was beautiful. I could still picture her staring at me through the screen of Jordan's phone. Her dark locks, her brown eyes, her smile that seemed to shine through the photograph.

"Hey!" Emery said, waving me over from a booth. Her blonde ponytail was pulled up high in her signature hairstyle.

She and Tara had been my roommates in college, the only real friends I still kept in touch with.

I smiled, breaking myself from my Candice trance. I'd have to confront Jordan later. There would be no secrets between us. That was what we'd promised each other. I could have done it this morning, but then he would've known I was snooping, and after the Bianca call, I hadn't been in the mood to fight.

"Hey, girl." I pulled her into a half-hug, squeezing her tighter.

Emery was a ball of light, a burst of energy. She worked for JobOps, a nonprofit organization that she'd started herself, helping the homeless get on their feet and find jobs.

"Thanks for doing this again, Tene." She pulled her ponytail to the side, readjusting the black elastic band that held the strands together.

"No problem. I'm just mad that I didn't think of this sooner."

"It's okay." Her blue eyes sparkled, a contrast to her white T-shirt. "I'm just happy to get more restaurants on board with my plan. I mean, it only makes sense. If they're going to throw out the food after these big corporate functions, they may as well donate it to us, so I can feed those who need it." A fire flared in her eyes.

Emery would always be Emery. She wanted to save every stray and adopt every little kid who needed a family, one of the many reasons I loved her. Where I was trying to build up Armstrong Realty, Emery wanted to save the world. And she was looking mighty fine doing it.

"I hate you," I said without a bite in my tone. I gestured to her adorable outfit. "Look at you. You don't even have to try. In jeans and a T-shirt, you're stunning."

Emery was a stereotypical blonde-haired, blue-eyed babe. But her upbringing had been anything but typical. She'd had a rough life, similar to Jordan's in the foster care system.

She rolled her eyes. "Please, Tene. I'm just lucky I don't have to get dressed up in a suit every day." She slapped my shoulder. "And what are you talking about? You're drop-dead gorgeous."

I sighed. "Emery, I have to get up an hour and a half before I leave to look like this. You, on the other hand, roll out of bed and look like ... that." I motioned to all of her.

She waved a dismissive hand. "Whatever."

"You can never take a compliment. Anyway, let me introduce you to Cade."

I led her back behind the bar and into the kitchen of Allswell. The place was already buzzing with the lunch hour rush. Food sizzled in the frying pans. Stacks of plates had been set on a stainless-steel table in the middle. The scents of spices and meats filtered through my senses, and endless rows of cakes and desserts tempted my belly.

Emery linked arms with me, licking her lips. "I'm getting hungry from just being in here."

When I approached Cade's door, I knocked and waited.

Memories of the last time I'd entered without warning stilled me. It was not something I wanted to repeat, so I waited to be welcomed in.

"Come in."

After pushing open the door, I stepped in. "Hello, hello, future brother-in-law of mine."

You'd think he'd be annoyed every time I teased him, but I'd noticed he liked this specific nickname.

"Cade, this is Emery." I gestured to my beautiful, bombshell blonde friend.

He stood at his full almost-six-feet height, smiling professionally. "Cade, the future brother-in-law."

After brief introductions, they chatted up the logistics of a partnership between Allswell and JobOps, Emery's company.

I walked around Cade's small office. Against the shelves were pictures of his family and him and Angie in black-rimmed frames. I noticed one of the whole family—Cade, Wyatt, Jordan, his parents, and Candice. The boys were skinnier, all clean-shaven, but what had my attention was Candice. She was beautiful with her long, flowing dark locks and olive skin, and for the life of me, I couldn't stop picturing her and Jordan together, the pictures of them on his phone, the display of their love story unfolding. Unwelcome jealousy surged through my veins. I couldn't help it.

I had no pictures of my ex. Hell, I'd burned that shit during the breakup party. *Why did Jordan still carry pictures of Candice around on his phone?* One could argue this was worse than his wallet because a phone was more indispensable. *Is he not over her?*

I rubbed at my brow. *Damn it. This is perfectly understandable, right?* They had a history together, and she was gone. And in not so many words, he'd said she had saved him. But still ... I couldn't help how I felt.

"Thanks, Cade." Emery stuck out her hand, breaking me from my thoughts. "You have no idea what this means to me, to the people I'm trying to help."

Cade shook her tiny hand in his huge one. "I think this will be a great partnership. Our next big corporate event will be the wrap party. You should come. Then, after, you can take the leftover food and desserts. Jordan's studio has gone all out on this one."

"Emery will be there," I answered for her.

Emery made a face, her eyebrows scrunching together. "I ... I don't know. Fancy shindigs are really not my thing. I'm more of the pick-up-after-the-party kind of girl."

"You'll have to go. How are you going to meet my boyfriend?" I asked with a playful grin.

"Wait. What? Boyfriend?" She clasped her hands, and her smile widened. "Oh, goodness. Who has tamed the infamous Tene Armstrong? I didn't know you had a boyfriend."

"Yeah, it's Cade's brother. You might know him." I rested my hip against Cade's desk. "Jordan Ryder."

She blinked, her smile faltering. "Who?"

"Yes, Emery." I nodded proudly. "I'm dating *the* Jordan Ryder." I plucked that picture frame from the wall and showed her the picture of the brothers.

Her mouth dropped open. Her reaction was epic. And for a moment, I let my worries about Candice go.

――――

Emery and I had lunch afterward. We were seated at a booth. My Cobb salad was almost done while Emery's burger had been devoured.

She seemed deep in thought for a minute, lost in her own beautiful head.

I snapped my fingers in front of her face. "Emery!"

Her eyes widened, and she laughed. "Sorry. I totally blanked out."

"What's the matter?"

She paused for a second, and her forehead crinkled. "That picture ... back at Cade's office. One of his brothers looks so familiar."

I laughed. "Yeah. Of course, you've seen him. He's only been voted the Sexiest Man Alive, two years in a row."

She shook her head as though that wasn't what she meant. "No I was talking about the other brother." She waved a hand dismissively. "Anyways that's crazy. I'm still in shock that you're with him." The only item left on her plate was a half-eaten fry.

"I know. Seriously, me too. It just happened so fast that I'm trying to comprehend it all." I poked my fork into the lettuce, now regretting that I hadn't ordered something more fulfilling than a salad.

She tilted her head and assessed me. "You look different, Tene ..." She picked up her fry and pointed it in my direction before popping it in her mouth. "Different good. Happy."

"I am." I genuinely was. But could happiness exist with doubt? "Can I ask you something?" I pushed my plate to the side and reached for my glass of water.

"Of course—anything. You know that."

And I did.

"If you found ..." My fingers played with the tip of my straw.

I couldn't even get the words out because I didn't want

to voice my doubts out loud. Somehow saying it out loud sounded more ridiculous than in my head.

"Is it normal ..." I stopped myself again, not sure how to word it without sounding crazy jealous of a dead girl.

Still, I couldn't help my unsettled feelings. I just didn't get it. Maybe he wanted to honor her. A picture in a frame or a picture on the wall. I thought I would've been fine with that. But pictures on his phone that he'd taken from the physical photos? That felt more intimate. And an endless amount of them too.

"Would you be disturbed if your boyfriend had pictures of his ex on his phone? I mean, a whole album dedicated to them together." I rubbed at my brow, dropping my gaze. The table linen seemed very interesting at the moment. "Of course, you'd be disturbed. Actually ..." I raised a finger. "... I'm not disturbed. I'm annoyed."

Emery being Emery, the most even-keeled practical woman in the whole world, said, "Just ask him. Don't get me wrong, but maybe ... maybe there's a reason he still has those in there." But she sounded uncertain.

I had to laugh because she wasn't sure either.

I didn't answer. I stayed stoic and silent and simmered in my thoughts.

"Stop thinking and just ask," Emery said with a sweet smile. "Maybe he forgot they were in there."

I lifted my gaze and quirked an eyebrow, and she merely laughed again.

"Okay. Then, you put him in his place," she said.

I stabbed the salad with my fork. "That's the thing. I can't put him in his place without sounding insecure and inconsiderate. I purposely checked his phone." I shook my head. "If I bring this up, I'll seem like an insecure witch. How do I ... how do I tell him that I don't feel comfortable with it? It's hard because she's kind of ... dead." I rubbed at my brow, hating that I was feeling this way.

Shame filled my gut, and I cowered into myself. He'd loved her, and I needed to understand that they had a history.

The businessmen in the next table stared at me, making me realize that I'd spoken too loudly. Automatically, my eyes searched the bar for Cade, glad he was out of hearing distance because I didn't want him to hear me complaining about his deceased sister.

Emery placed a hand in mine. The touch was sweet and much needed. "That's fine. Anyone in your situation would feel the same way you do. It's okay."

"It's not," I whispered to myself. My voice trembled. "I'm scared." I revealed my innermost fear.

She leaned over the table and took both of my hands in hers, giving it a little shake between us. "There's nothing to be afraid of." Her voice was soft and kind and gentle, and I didn't deserve it, especially after snooping. "He's your boyfriend, and from what you told me, you are both so into each other. Just don't keep this inside. You need to ask him. It's a justifiable question. He'd feel the same way if he were in your situation. Don't be scared."

I took a deep breath. *Is knowing better than not knowing? What if the truth hurts?* I didn't know if I could bear to hear it. Especially since I'd been on this ultimate high since we'd been together.

"What can you possibly be afraid of?" she asked.

My heart stuttered. "That he's still in love with her. In love with a ghost, in love with the first girl who showed him love. And how do I compete with that?"

And even though he'd denied it, a very deep part of me still didn't believe him.

CHAPTER 26

I SLIPPED into my car and almost vomited. The stink from something foul punched me in the nose, and I couldn't breathe. It must have been my latte that I'd left in the back. This was worse than curdled milk. Febreze wouldn't help this situation. I needed a full-on overhaul, a new car, a detail. Something. Anything.

I reached into my purse, plucked out my bottle of Chanel No. 5, and turned to spray the whole bottle into my backseat when I screamed.

Blood.

Everywhere.

I jumped out of the car, falling on the sidewalk in the process, scraping my knees. My feet couldn't catch up to my racing heart, the adrenaline rushing in my veins.

I pushed through the doors into Allswell, still screaming hysterically. Everyone's eyes were directed at me, but I didn't care. I didn't think twice. Panic rushed through me.

"Cade!"

His head peeked up from the bar, and he rushed over to me, his hands gripping my elbows. "What happened?"

My whole body trembled. Sweat crept up my neck to my brow. "It's ... it's dead."

I couldn't breathe. I couldn't think. I couldn't get my next words out.

Dead. Dead. Dead.

"What?" he asked, worried and confused.

"In my car," I panted. "The cat."

I rushed past him and into the restroom. The scene I'd just seen played back in my head, and I dry-heaved into the sink.

I splashed water on my perfectly contoured face and took a deep breath through my nose and out my mouth as though there was a shortage.

The stink.

The blood.

The knife.

The dead animal.

My hands covered my mouth as I rushed into the handicapped stall. Dropping to my knees, I vomited everything that was in my stomach. I couldn't get the stink from my nose, the vision out of my head. I covered my eyes, seeing darkness. But the black became the background, the image of the cat, a lifeless, innocent animal.

I stood, but my legs wobbled, the earth beneath me unsteady. I braced myself against the wall, concentrating on the cream ceramic tiles, the grout between each square.

After a few minutes, I emerged, one hand holding my stomach. My feet dragged like dead weights attached to my ankles as I approached the sink. When the restroom door opened, I jumped and ignored the stares.

An elderly person slipped into a stall, then washed her hands beside me, and slipped out of the restroom. Once alone, I stared blankly at the mirror in front of me, letting the hot water flow through my fingertips, forcing warmth back into my body.

Then, it hit me. Like a rock against my hard head.

Jordan wasn't kidding; she was dangerous. This could only be her. His stalker had killed a living animal and placed it in my car.

I needed to call Jordan, but my purse was in the car, and I didn't want to again see the blood and knife in that poor cat's body.

But I needed to get to him. After I wiped my mouth with a paper towel and patted my face dry, I staggered toward the door when it opened and slammed against me.

"Sorry." The voice was quiet but so high-pitched and screechy.

I had to lift my head to see if it matched the person it was attached to. It sounded like the voice belonged to a middle school girl.

"It's fine," I said.

When she didn't move, I tilted my head and angled closer to meet her gaze. The world tipped on its axis, and I froze, unblinking.

I'd recognize her in my sleep because she haunted my nightmares.

The blood drained from my face.

It was Jordie Stein.

Every impulse in my body screamed for me to run, but my feet were bolted to the floor. I couldn't move, paralyzed by the realization that this was her.

Jordan had made sure I'd know her if I saw her in any disguise, with any new haircut.

Of course, I recognized the dark-as-night irises—the signature crazy gleam in her gaze—and her dyed dark brown hair, her blonde roots showing.

My body snapped back to attention, awareness pushing to the surface. I forced myself to smile. "Excuse me."

I sidestepped her, but she still didn't move.

I evened out my features. Maybe if I pretended I didn't know it was her, she'd let me pass, but she had to see the recognition in my eyes, notice the pause, the shock in them.

"Christene." Her voice was no longer quiet, her tone firmer, as though there was no doubt it was me.

My pulse raced into overdrive, and I concentrated on steadying my breathing, though I wanted to gasp for air, swallow it in large, overwhelming gulps.

"Sorry?" I tilted my head, blowing out one silent breath. "Do I know you?" I locked my knees to stop myself from visibly shaking.

"No." Her lips lifted into a menacing grin.

But what had my stomach turning was the vacancy in her stare, as though she wasn't all there.

"Well, can I pass?" I asked with a bite. "My friend is waiting for me right outside the door."

I begged for Cade to come to my rescue. After seeing the dead animal in the car, he'd have to know I was in danger, or, at a minimum, know something was wrong.

What is she doing here? Is she crazy?

Of course, she is!

She didn't care if she got caught, and she didn't give two shits if she went to jail. The unstable didn't care about their life, only that they got what they wanted.

She took two steps farther into the restroom, and I automatically backed up. After she slipped her oversized purse from her shoulder, she took out a jimmy and then jacked it against the door, so it wouldn't budge.

"What the hell are you doing?" Panic seized control of my lungs, and this time, I lost all focus, all composure. My whole body tensed, preparing to fight. I would not go down without throwing a few punches.

At one time, a long while ago, I had been that girl in the schoolyard, beating up anyone who picked on Angie. That was a long while ago, but here and now, I had to channel that girl to survive.

"You know who I am, don't you?" She kicked her purse against the door. "I know you do."

She waited for me to respond, but when I didn't, she continued anyway. "Don't worry. I won't hurt you," she said calmly, as though she were reciting the weather, but it was the eerie calm before the storm.

How could I tell? It was her semi-formed smile as she simply fed off my fear.

When I backed up two more steps, she advanced toward me.

"If that's the case, why did you just lock the door?" My arms clutched my stomach, holding me upright.

"I just want to ask you a couple of questions." She tilted her head to the side as though she had a crick in her neck. "Just a few questions."

Her smile widened, and I swallowed down the bile forming in my throat.

My eyes searched the area for a weapon. Anything. But besides some paper towels and the soap dispenser, there was nothing that could protect me, and who knew if she had a gun or a knife with her?

She smiled, all teeth this time. "Do you love him?" she asked, her high-pitched, screechy voice reciting the words in a singsong tone.

I blinked, carefully picking my next words. "Who?" If I pretended and played dumb, maybe she would believe me.

"You know who I'm talking about."

Her gaze flickered to the right above me, almost making me turn around to see what she was looking at, but I couldn't afford to take my eyes off of her. Tiny spider-like tingles crept up my body, my arms, into my throat, choking me. She approached the sink, studied her reflection, and used her pinkie to swipe at the corner of her mouth.

"I love him, too, ya know? He thinks I'm crazy, but I just want him to realize I'm not." She rapidly blinked at me and remained silent as if waiting for me to confirm that she wasn't crazy.

I leveled my stance, planted my feet on the ground, and forced myself to calm down and think logically. Panic would not do me any good at this moment.

I didn't know what to say. Any word could set her off, could be used against me, so I remained silent, biting my tongue and thinking of my next step. There was no way I could run past her, remove the jack, and get out the door without her stopping me first.

She flipped around, leaning against the sink. "I just want to talk without any disruptions."

The eerie gleam in her eyes remained, and the hairs on my arms stood at full attention. She wasn't taller than me, but she was twice my body size. I debated on whether I could take her down, and if it came to that, I'd do what I needed to.

I had to think of a solution, a way out of this situation. If I started to scream my head off, who knew what else was in her purse? Also, she'd jimmied the door. I could be screaming for several minutes until someone busted through it.

Maybe I was the crazy one, but I wasn't afraid of her. I wasn't afraid to die. Deep down, all that mattered was that everyone I loved was safe.

"I know he loves me." She smirked, and I noticed the thick film of yellow on her teeth. "It just hurts when he works so much, and we have to be apart."

I blinked, staring at her with no emotion on my face. This woman was delusional, not angry. But those were the worst kind of psychopaths because there was no distinction between reality and fantasy. In her mind, she and Jordan were together; they were one.

She fluffed up her hair, crossing her legs at her ankles. "The least he could do is pick up my calls. But I'm understanding."

She peered down at her chipped, manicured nails, and then her stare turned icy cold when her eyes met mine. I felt the chill hit my veins and enter my bloodstream.

"It hurts to be the second choice, doesn't it, Christene?"

Do not respond to this delusional witch.

I bit the inside of my cheek, and my hands clenched.

"For Jordan to love someone other than you, and no matter what you do, you can't compete."

In her fantasy mind, she was first, and I was second. I swallowed back the words I was going to say because I knew she couldn't be reasoned with. She only saw what she wanted to see, what she believed to be true.

Seconds ticked by, and I prayed that Cade would bust through the door. It must've been at least five minutes since I'd been in here.

He would've called the police and then ... shit.

Angie. He'd call her next.

Angie couldn't come in here. I wouldn't allow my sister to be collateral damage. I needed this to end. I was the queen of manipulation, and I needed to amp that power up now.

"I know he's with you, but you'll never be his first," she repeated, her eyes taunting.

She wanted a reaction. That was it.

I lowered my head in fake resignation but kept my eyes on her the whole time in case she tried something. "It hurts." I forced a desolation in my tone, and my voice quivered. "All the time. But I'll take what I can get." I decided to play the part, appease the crazy.

I saw sympathy register in her eyes, and when her shoulders slackened, I knew she believed me.

"I'm sorry."

She stepped forward and placed a gentle hand on my forearm, and it took all my energy to stay stoic and still, unmoving when every fiber of my being screamed to jerk back from her hold and punch her, a closed fist to the face.

"I feel the same way. I love him so much." Her breath stank as though she hadn't brushed in a week, and I swallowed back the bile that crept up my throat. "But I'll never compete with Candice."

Candice?

My eyes dilated, and I couldn't move, couldn't speak. Shock registered through my system. *How did she know about Candice?* I shook my head to focus. Of course, she knew about Candice. I didn't doubt there was anything this crazy lady didn't know about Jordan's life.

I staggered back, which forced her hand to drop.

"You have to know about Candice, his first girlfriend. His one and true happily ever after." She rapidly blinked again, her telltale sign she wanted a response for me.

Ringing initiated in my ears. Beating louder, pounding harder.

"He has her name written on his heart."

My breathing came in slower, shallower, hurt filling me

up, confirming my doubts. Jordie's smile widened, turning sinister.

She knew she was getting to me, twisting the knife, forcing all my insecurities to the surface. I pulled at the end of my ponytail, trying to steady my breathing, trying to school my features, trying to pretend her words didn't affect me.

She could've found out about his tattoo anywhere, right? He'd been pictured shirtless enough, but to know what the characters stood for ... who was etched in permanent ink over his chest ...

She cackled, straight out of a horror flick. "You thought I was talking about me?" She placed a hand on her heart. "That I was his first love?" She swatted the air and laughed. "Not me, silly girl. Candice. Second best—that's all you'll ever be."

I flinched as though I'd been hit. She'd hit a nerve, a nerve tied to history and all my insecurities about not being good enough, about having someone favored above me. The issues with my ex and my mother surfaced, and I couldn't shake it. I couldn't dim the anger, and sadness balled into one knot in the pit of my stomach, a knot that made me want to throw up because I wanted to scream ... *Not again!*

"He'll never get over his first love. I get that. I accept that. I can live with that, given the fact that she's dead. But he still wears her chain around his wrist. He made it into a bracelet. Talk about obsessive."

The irony of her words didn't shock me as much as hearing her revelations about Candice.

I inhaled deeply, her words seeping into my skin.

She's crazy. I pounded those words over and over and over in my head. *A crazy lunatic who has a restraining order against her. Don't believe her. Don't believe anything that flows effortlessly out of her mouth.*

But as hard as I tried to convince myself that she spewed lies, I realized I did. I believed her.

Because if she knew about his tattoo, the rest could be credible.

"He celebrates her birthday. Visits her grave and brings her flowers. Roses are her favorite." She twisted her dead brown locks with her fingertips. "It means true love, after all. He's not over her. Probably never, ever will be."

She shoved the words in my face, each sentence like a jab in the jaw.

"Sometimes, he orders her favorite meal in addition to his when he's alone. I wanted to be like her. Dreamed I was her." She nodded rapidly, her head bobbing up and down as though she was a rag doll, her smile wide, her eyes still eerily blank.

Right then, everything clicked. I put two and two together, remembering seeing a specific picture of Candice on Jordan's phone. Jordie's blonde roots peeking out of her dyed dark locks. She had colored her hair to look like Candice.

"He still wears the same cologne she bought him in high school. Can you believe that? Talk about crazy." Her eyes rolled to the back of her head, and she laughed hysterically.

My shoulders tensed at her reaction and because my favorite scent in the world wasn't signature to him. It belonged to *her*.

Jordie shrugged and sighed, her animated self dying down. "But if this is all we get, we have to take it, right?"

I lifted both eyebrows, eyes steady on her, about two seconds from decking her. My cup was full of her shit, and I was about to pour that cup right on top of her head.

"Second best is better than no best." She laughed, and all my composure disappeared.

All self-restraint gone.

She was placing us in the same playing field, the same sandbox. I was done.

"We'll take it, though, right?"

She slugged my shoulder like we were pals, and I pushed her off.

"Get away from me, you crazy bitch!" I shouted, my inner street fighter coming out.

She flipped the loco switch, and she straightened to almost my height. "I'm not crazy." Her voice dropped abnormally low, almost robotic sounding. Her eyes were unfocused, the look straight up from a horror film.

I didn't think. I simply reacted. I maneuvered around her, but she gripped my wrist. I bit down hard on her hand, feeling my teeth dig deep into her soft flesh and sinking into her skin.

When she screamed and yanked back, I rushed to the door, kicked the jimmy, opened the door, and ran.

I face-planted into six feet of muscle, running right into Wyatt's football frame. My breath came in and out in huge puffs. I was hyperventilating.

"Tene?"

One hand flew to my chest, and I pointed to the restroom. "Jord ... Jordie." I tried to catch my breath.

"What?" Then, Wyatt's eyes widened with realization. He rushed past me toward the restroom.

A few seconds later, a few officers followed, and then Angie was by my side.

"Are you okay?" Her eyes scanned my body, looking for any proof of violence. Thankful there hadn't been, in the next second, she pulled me into her, hugging me fiercely.

There could've been multiple weapons hidden in her bag. She could've conjured up different ways to torture me. But that didn't affect me. What rocked me to my core was what Jordie had said about Candice.

"Okay?" I rested against Angie, her small frame carrying my body weight. I shivered as though it was below zero, the adrenaline now slowing. "No." My voice shook. "No, I'm not okay."

Angie tried to shield me when they walked Jordie out in cuffs. But she couldn't hurt me. Not physically anymore.

But I still couldn't get her words out of my head.

"He's not over her."

CHAPTER 27

IT HAD BEEN hours since the incident. It could've been worse. At least, that was what the police, Cade, Angie, and my parents had said.

I tucked my knees under me and rested against my couch, but even curled into a ball with my wool blanket wrapped around me, I couldn't dim the chill that ran through me.

My mother paced my apartment in a fit of worry, and Angie was doing her best to calm her down. But I couldn't hear anything other than the ringing in my ears, the ache in my chest, the weakness in my legs.

When my door flew open, and Jordan stormed my apartment, I shot up to a sitting position, blinking. His face was bloody and torn and wrecked. Panic rushed my insides, and I threw the blanket to the side and stood.

"Are you okay?" I touched his face, realizing it was makeup. The fear from earlier clouded my mind. Of course, it was makeup.

"Am I okay? Am I fucking okay?" His face contorted,

making his wounds seem genuine, fresh, real. "Are *you* okay?"

I pressed a finger at the fake flesh at his brow as he scanned my face, down my body, touching every part of me, as though he was checking for damage.

Then, he began to strip all of the makeup off and wiped at his face with his sleeve. He cupped the back of my neck and kissed me, full-on, lips closed. A tremor passed through him, and then he brought me to his chest and wrapped me so tightly against him that it was as though we were one. A shaky breath escaped him, and he squeezed me tighter.

He held me for minutes. Long enough that the room cleared. Everyone had left us alone.

"I'm so, so sorry, Tene. I thought everyone had this mess under control. I thought the studio had located her." Then, he pulled back, rubbing his thumbs at my jawline. "I was filming and didn't have my phone on me. We were doing take after take, trying to finish up. I didn't know what was going on until Wyatt rushed to the studio to tell me what had happened. I'm so sorry, baby." His words broke at the end. "So sorry. I never—"

My fingers met his lips to silence him, and I gritted my teeth, afraid true tears would flow. I couldn't remember the last time I'd cried about anything other than the latest episode of *This Is Us*.

"It's fine," I said, but it wasn't fine. Everything was far from fine.

Jordie's words rang loudly in my head as though she'd pounded it into my flesh. *"He'll never get over his first love."*

He'll never get over Candice.

I bit the inside of my cheek long and hard as he held me. Pain. I wanted to feel physical pain. It was better than emotional pain. It hurt less.

"I swear, she's not going to touch you. No one is going to hurt you. They have her at the station, and I'm going to make sure she goes straight to jail, where she can't harm you."

He searched my face, his thumbs trailing up and down my cheeks. His eyes were so dreamy, so blue, so endless. And I knew in that second that I loved him. I loved him, and I couldn't do this anymore. I couldn't be all in when only half of his heart was available.

"Tell me everything." He pulled me to the couch and into his lap.

"She confronted me about you," I whispered. "She talked like you guys were together." I blew out one slow, jagged breath. "She talked about how you were too busy for her because of work, but she understood, understood you still loved her. She was delusional and confused."

"She's sick," he bit out.

I nodded. There was no doubt about that, but she knew. She knew the truth.

I pushed myself off his lap, threw my legs over the side of the couch, and sat straighter. I closed my eyes and tried to muster enough courage to end this. End us.

"Tene, everything will be fine." A warm hand landed on my thigh.

And as soon as those words left his mouth, I knew it was a lie—because how could everything be fine when he still wasn't over Candice.

When he reached for my hand, I didn't deny him because I wanted him to touch me. He made me weak. He was my crutch, my kryptonite, but I couldn't live my life like this.

"She asked me how ..." I swallowed. I focused on our intertwined fingers and how my soft hand fit perfectly in his rough one. "How it felt to be second best." My eyebrows knitted together as my focus dropped to the bandage on my knee. I had refused to go to the hospital, and after giving the police officers my statement, I'd left.

"See?" He threw both hands in the air, his tone seething. "She's crazy. Second best to her? She needs help. I never gave her any indication that I was even remotely interested—"

"To Candice." My voice was quiet and broken. "Second best to Candice."

His mouth shut, and I peered up, studying and searching his face, wanting him to say something, anything.

One.

Two.

Three.

"She's crazy. She has no idea what she's talking about."

It had taken him three seconds to deny it. Three seconds too long.

Liquid filled my eyes, and I tore my gaze away. I didn't swipe at my face. It would only give away that I was crying. So, I blinked the tears back, swallowed, bit my cheek, and willed them to stop.

"Tene ..." With light fingertips, he lifted my chin. "... you're not. You're not second best. You're the only one. The only one I want to be with."

I pulled his hand down, my insides trembling. "Why did you hesitate?"

"Because everything I say about her, about my past, hurts you."

His scent wafted through my nose, filling my senses. A scent I'd once wanted to drown in, bathe in, but it wasn't really his. It was hers.

"Is that the cologne she gave you?"

He blinked, momentarily stunned. "What?"

"The one you're wearing now."

"How did you know that?"

"Jordie," I whispered. My heartbeat slowed to a sluggish beat.

So, it was true.

I fingered the chain that I hadn't noticed before, wrapped around his wrist. "This was hers, wasn't it?"

His whole body went rigid, and he swallowed.

"She knew that too." The hollowness in my chest widened.

She hadn't been lying. It was all true. Jordan's reaction only confirmed it.

I didn't doubt he visited her grave every birthday or ordered her favorite meal in addition to his own.

Immediately, I stood and walked to the kitchen. I had too much pride to be in this type of relationship. And above that, I couldn't handle any more heartache.

"I can't do this," I said, my voice quivering. I gripped my island with two hands, and my head dropped back between my shoulders.

"I have issues, okay?" he said, his voice breaking. "But they're issues I've dealt with, issues I've talked through— before I went all in with you." He blew out a small breath. "I'm trying here. The first step was allowing myself to be happy and not feel guilty about it. Everything else will follow. It's just ... everything from the cologne to putting this bracelet on ... it's been routine for fucking years, and now ... I need to change, but it's hard."

"Why do you have a montage of her on your phone?" Not just a few pictures, but a whole slew of pictures saved on his cell.

He gritted his teeth, true, unhidden emotion displayed

in his features. "Because I can't delete them," he admitted, his shoulders slumping and his body going slack.

I nodded through tear-filled eyes because I understood that. She was gone, and to erase her would be like pretending she hadn't existed. It wasn't like I wasn't trying to understand where he was coming from. I was really trying ... but failing.

He stood and gripped my shoulders, his lips so close to mine. "What we have ... it's great. It's amazing. It's more than I ever thought I'd have with anybody. I'm doing things slowly. You don't see it. But I'm taking baby steps to make this count, to make us stick." He peered down at me with such soulful desperation. "I need you." He gulped. "You're it for me. I swear it."

I wanted to believe him. My heart wanted to believe him, but my strong-willed mind, my pride, my stubbornness, my fragile self-esteem wouldn't let me.

"I can't get rid of her ... she's a part of me."

He rubbed one hand down his face, and I took a step back, creating some distance between us.

He shook his head, his eyes firm and locked on mine. "But what you have to understand is that she's my past, and you can't erase the past; it makes me who I am. You wouldn't have wanted the man before Candice. He was half the man standing here today. He was a liar, a thief, broken in pieces that were angry at the world." Both of his hands cupped my face while he rested his head against mine, gently tapping it. "Without her, you wouldn't have me, right here, right now, being the most truthful and honest man, telling you that Candice is my past but you ... you, Christene Armstrong, are my future."

I could see my reflection in his blue irises—vulnerable and heartbroken.

"I already got rid of things that you don't know about—like the little monkey that used to travel with me. Candice had given it to me. I'd had it since high school, but I shipped it off to my mom's. Just give me a chance." He kissed my lips, then my cheeks, and then each tear streaming from my face.

I couldn't bear to see him beg and break down, but here he was. Here I was. We were vulnerable, naked in front of each other while remaining fully clothed.

My fingers threaded through his hair, and our eyes locked.

Unspoken words passed between us. And because I very much wanted this to work, to give him a chance, I leaned forward and captured his lips in mine to answer his question.

Because everyone deserved a second chance, and I was one of them, needing to work and get past my insecurities.

CHAPTER 28

THE NEXT FEW days passed by in a whirl. From being interviewed at the police station to the nonstop nagging of my sister and mother to make sure I was okay, I was utterly exhausted.

Except for going to work, Jordan was with me, and when he wasn't, he had detail on my tail, following me and reporting back to him. He had low-key stalkers—none that he had restraining orders against, but those the studio liked to label as overzealous fans. Still, Jordan was not taking any chances with me.

When he wasn't filming, he was stuck to me like rice on chopsticks. And I loved every single minute of our Netflix-and-takeout evenings and forever-lovemaking nights.

We bonded over our love of *Game of Thrones* and day-old pizza. We talked about everything from how we had been when we were younger to our goals and dreams and aspirations.

Day by day, little by little, my relationship with Jordan blossomed.

The wrap party was tomorrow night, and I couldn't be more excited.

With Jordie no longer a threat, being held in a psychiatric hospital back in California, Jordan was proving to me that maybe, quite possibly, we could work. I was trying to be more patient, which wasn't my strong suit. I needed to be more patient with Jordan and let us happen organically and not force things. Because of my new revelation, my life was turning over, becoming brighter.

I poured myself a tall cup of coffee, adding cream and sugar, while Jordan placed our breakfast on the table.

"So, you'll be home tomorrow, before the wrap party?"

"Yes." He kissed me and then slipped a pancake onto my plate. "I have to grab a few things and pick up Mom, but I should be back tomorrow, late afternoon. It'll be a quick trip."

Jordan's mother was at an assisted living facility. When Candice had hopped in the car, doped up, her parents had jumped in to prevent her from driving. Though Candice and her father had died, their mother was paralyzed from the waist down.

Their mother, their matriarch, was strong, resilient, and beautiful. When I had met her months ago, she'd exuded love and strength and everything a mother should be, and I couldn't wait to see her again.

"I have the security detail on you while I'm gone."

I set my mug down, the steam lifting from the brim. "What? Why?"

"For precautions." He reached over for my mug and took a sip of my coffee.

"Okay, I get it. But really, am I in any danger?" I rubbed at my brow, annoyance creeping up my back.

It would be okay if I didn't see the guards because then I

could pretend they weren't there, but that was not the case. They checked out every room I entered before I could walk inside.

"No. Now that they have Jordie far away from here, you're not." Then, he smiled before cutting up a piece of pancake and eating it. "But it would make your boyfriend feel better."

"You're coddling me like I'm a child." And although it was cute, I was feeling crowded. "You're just like my mother."

He looked slightly offended. "You dislike your mother."

"I do not," I argued weakly.

His eyes narrowed. "I saw you send her call to voice mail."

"Yeah, but only because she's coddling me."

"But *that's* only because she's concerned about you."

I could read what he was thinking on his face. I lifted an eyebrow, challenging him.

"Fine," he conceded. Then, he reached for my hand and pulled me into his lap. "If I'm coddling, it's because ..." He kissed my nose. "... You're precious cargo."

My body melted into his touch. When he said such sweet things, I was a puddle of mush, porridge, oatmeal—all of the above. But I was scared. It wasn't that I wasn't feeling all that Jordan was about our relationship, about us. I just wanted to feel secure and not like this relationship could vanish at any second, that it was temporary. I wanted to know in my gut that this was real, not fleeting.

I wrapped both hands around his neck. I was in utter bliss, him living with me temporarily, waking up to him every morning and sleeping next to him every night.

Our relationship was on a high-speed train, and I told myself I'd enjoy the ride, let this take me wherever it was going to take me because, for once, I was letting my insecurities take a back seat. I wanted to learn to trust again, and slowly, I was getting to a place I wanted to be.

"What's the sad face for? I'll be back tomorrow before the wrap party." He nipped at my bottom lip, and I could taste the sweetness of the maple syrup.

I inhaled deeply, noticing that his scent—that masculine cologne I still loved—was missing. He smelled of laundry detergent, fresh, clean, still masculine.

"Your cologne ..."

He nodded and then fingered a lock of my hair. "Slowly, but surely. Plus, I figure I should upgrade from the current cologne to something more sophisticated. Can you help me pick one out when I come back?"

I smiled. "Sure, baby. Sure."

"But, I leave you with this." He bent down and kissed me deeply, passionately, endlessly until my whole body warmed, and my mind was mush.

"I love you, Christene Armstrong," he whispered against my lips before pulling back.

I peered up at him in a daze, pretty sure I had heard him say it but wanting him to repeat it again.

"You don't have to say it back ... yet. But know that when I'm not with you, I'm counting the seconds to get you back in my arms."

I wasn't ready to say it yet, but I knew I was very much there. Very much in love with Jordan Ryder, Hollywood's heartthrob.

After Jordan left and I met with a few contractors to redo

one of our buildings to accommodate a hair salon that wanted to sign a five-year lease, I headed to Allswell.

The day was beautiful, the sun shining brightly above me. Jordan was done filming. The wrap party was tomorrow night, and he'd be off for a few months until the filming of his next movie in Hawaii. I could visit him. Take a vacation for once since I never did.

I pushed through the revolving doors of Allswell and took in the transformation of the restaurant. It was a black-tie affair, and everything was decked out in black linen and white cloth napkins. A red carpet split the room between the round center tables and the booths.

Angie was at the far corner with Susie, Jordan's PA, placing black linen over a long table.

"Hey," I said, approaching. "I'm confused. Isn't the party tomorrow?"

"Yes, it sure is!" Susie said in her normal chipper voice. "But 'preparations ...'" She placed her fingers in air quotes. "... Take a while. I figure I'll be here all night long."

I lifted some bags on the floor. "What are these?"

"Party favors," Angie said. She nodded to the door where there were boxes upon boxes stacked Cade-high.

I peeked into the bag beyond the tissue. There were candles, face masks, colognes, and perfumes. The bags were color-coded, black and white.

"Who is coming to this shindig? I thought it was just the cast and some close family members."

Susie's head was deep in her party bags, her voice muffled. "Yeppers, peppers, it is. It's the whole cast, not just those who did the reshoot. Not to mention, the whole production crew. Crazy. The sponsors gave great gifts today. Check this out."

She lifted a small bottle of champagne, and I blinked up at Angie.

"How many people are coming?" I wondered if this would be up to code.

If the inspectors happened to come in for a random check, Cade could be heavily fined, and our license could be revoked.

Angie opened up a bottle of lotion and dabbed some on her inner wrist. "One-fifty, maybe?"

I exhaled a sigh of relief. The restaurant could hold that amount.

"Jay coming back tomorrow?" Susie asked, smiling. She placed the finished bag in a box and retrieved another, placing tissue inside.

"Yes. He went home to pick up his mom."

"In Kritell?"

Kritell was their hometown, where they had been raised.

I nodded in response.

"Why didn't Wyatt just go get her?" Angie flattened the sheet over the table. "Jordan's butt should be here, helping us."

"He's an actor, not the help." I peeked over to see what else was in the bag of goodies. "No offense."

"None taken because this help ..." Susie pushed a thumb into her chest. "... gets paid, and it's not too bad, being the help."

"Hey, guys. Need help?" Wyatt strolled over, dropped his book bag on the floor, and made his way over to Susie.

Is she blushing? Definitely blushing.

She hadn't lifted her head, but her cheeks flushed.

"Just put me to work," he said in his deep, baritone voice.

Wyatt—with his big brown eyes, a fully-grown beard, and his soft demeanor despite his stocky build—was more introspective than his siblings. There didn't seem to be a violent bone in his body, which was strange, given he had grown up with Cade and Jordan, who were over-the-top vocal and just plain crazy at times.

"I don't even know what's going on." I motioned to the commotion coming from the two busy bees in front of me. "Susie and Angie have some sort of organized chaos happening over here. I'm afraid I might mess up their bag-packing, table-fixing cycle. Carry on, fine people. Carry on." I waved a hand, knowing that I wouldn't be of any assistance, and walked to the bar to get a drink. I raised a hand. "Tall Long Island, please." I flashed Cade's cute bartender a smile.

"Tene!" Emery burst through the kitchen doors, her skin flawless, her face gleaming with her natural glow.

I wished I could bottle up some of that goodness for myself.

She practically skipped to the bar.

"Em, you coming tomorrow?"

She half-hugged me and then pressed her cheek against mine. "Yes, most definitely, and Cade was so nice to hire some people from the center. They can put tomorrow's job on their résumés, and it'll help them get employment faster."

This was a win for Emery. Partnering up with Cade was the perfect match. She would be able to feed people in the shelter that she worked with and find them jobs to get them on their feet.

Her smile was blinding. "I'm so grateful." She clasped her hands together. "My team is just so excited to see Jordan and be a part of this." She motioned around the room. "This will lift their spirits. I know Cade was originally going to hire out some temps, but … gah!" She squealed. "I just picked up this paperwork from him." She reached in her purse and chucked out a manila folder. "It's the nondisclosure agreements my staff has to sign." She jammed them back in her purse and half-hugged me again. Her buttery sweetness and over-the-top cheer was so contagious that it had me smiling. "Cade is so kind."

"Eh, he's okay." I laughed. "Yeah, I guess my sister is a lucky woman."

"And the apple doesn't fall far from the tree." She bumped her shoulder against mine. "Given your crazy-lovesick smile, I'm betting Jordan is the sweetest thing too."

I sighed. "He is." I raised my hand to the bartender, ordering for Emery. "Ginger ale, light ice." Then, I turned to Em. "Shoot. Is that what you wanted?" I knew she'd liked it in college but wasn't sure if her drink tastes had changed.

She plopped down on the stool next to me. "Exactly what I wanted. So, where's Jordan now?"

"Picking up his mom back home. She wanted to see her boys, so he's going to bring her here." I didn't want to go into the details of how his mother was paraplegic, and that was why she couldn't drive herself. Everyone would find out soon enough.

"And so …" She leaned into me as though she were going to let me in on a little secret but then asked, "Are you in love, Christene Armstrong?"

My ears burned. Wild butterflies stirred in my belly. Then, I reached for her hand and squeezed. "I am. Truth be told, I'm scared shitless. But I've never felt a love like this, Em. Never."

She patted my hand with gentle ease. "Don't overthink this, okay? I know how you are." She tapped my temple with a light fingertip. "You're thinking that some big ball will drop, that it's too good to be true. But good things always happen to good people, and you're the best person I know."

I released a long, jagged sigh. She was right. In relationships, I'd always been cautious. But I had to trust Jordan and was working on any doubts I had. This relationship business was new territory for both of us, but he'd said he'd prove he loved me, and so far, through his honesty and his actions, he was.

"You're right. I haven't been this happy in ..." I smiled. "... well, never."

With a slight shake of her head, she said, "I still can't believe it. *The* Jordan Ryder."

"And you get to see him tomorrow night." I bumped my glass with hers.

After we chatted, she drank up her ginger ale and left to get back to work. Emery was always on the go, on the hunt to save the world. The Emerys in the nation were one in a million.

Angie and Wyatt approached the bar, laughing.

"Susie is a little firecracker, isn't she?" my sister said, motioning to the other end of the room. "We weren't packing fast enough for her, so she decided to do it herself."

"She practically does everything for Jordan," I said.

She was in charge of his schedule and completed the menial tasks that he was too lazy and too famous to be seen doing.

Who had bought him a jockstrap? Susie. Deodorant? Susie. Got his early morning coffee? Susie.

She did it all and always picked up Jordan's call on the first ring.

"Who was that?" Wyatt asked, his face thoughtful,

glancing toward the door where a flurry of blonde hair exited.

"Who?" I almost got whiplash from his abrupt change in subject.

"That girl you were just talking to."

"Oh, Emery?"

"Emery," he repeated.

Cade emerged from the kitchen, making his way to the bar. He must've heard me because he said, "Yeah, Emery was here." He smirked. "Same girl you were asking about a few days ago." He tipped his chin toward his brother.

Wyatt averted his gaze and reached over the bar for a beer. "Real smooth, brother."

Cade's smirk widened. "Shit, bro. I think Tene needs to make an introduction."

Wyatt tipped back his beer. "Nah. That's okay." He shifted uncomfortably in his spot.

By the little change of color in his cheeks, there was no doubt who Wyatt had a little crush on.

"She's a pretty little thing, isn't she?" I asked, baiting him.

Cade threw me a sideways, amused glance.

"Yeah." Wyatt scratched at his brow, a man with the fewest of words.

"Not only is she beautiful ..." I straightened in my seat and picked a piece of lint off my skirt. "... but she also owns her own nonprofit organization, helping the homeless find jobs."

He plopped down in a stool next to me with his beer in hand.

I thought he'd ask me for information, yet he didn't press me further, so I continued. "She came from the system too."

His eyebrows lifted.

I had his full attention now.

"She had foster parents and bounced in and out of homes until she was adopted at fifteen. Her adoptive mom is the kindest woman you'd ever meet. Emery and I've known each other since freshman year in college."

"How is that girl single?" Angie asked.

"Well ..." I thought of her asshole of a boyfriend. "... she's not really single."

"Oh," Wyatt slipped out. Then, he let out a sarcastic laugh, a sound I didn't hear from him often. "Figures."

I bumped my elbow against his arm. "You're lucky 'cause I want her to dump that ungrateful ass."

Angie popped out a hip. "Hey, we're not wrecking any homes today, Tene."

Then, I winked at Wyatt. "Not today, but maybe tomorrow night."

CHAPTER 29

I MISSED HIM. Terribly. I had it bad. I missed his warm body in my bed. A comfortable bed that was suddenly uncomfortable without him in it. But when my phone rang the next morning, and my booty-call ring played, I reached over and almost fell in the process.

"Hello?"

"Picking up on the first ring." He chuckled. "You usually let me wait right before it goes to voice mail."

I laughed. It was true. Now, there was no way I could hide my anxiousness. "I might ... miss you a little." Goodness, I was turning into a sap, one of those girls who waited by the phone and swooned and awed and broke a sweat every time they heard their man's voice. "Where are you?"

"With my mom, running errands."

"What time are you getting here?"

"Right before the party. Just head out there without me, and I'll meet you. I've got to take care of a few things here."

A disappointed sigh escaped me. "I wanted to *party* a little before the party ..."

He groaned. Then, he lowered his voice and whispered

into the phone. "Party after the party? I'll make it up to you, I promise."

"You'd better," I said, running my finger across my neckline. Just thinking of the after-party was turning me into a horny mess. "It's okay. I have tons to do today anyway."

Wax down under. Get my nails done. Get my eyebrows done.

"Tene?"

I released a soft sigh. "Yeah?"

"I miss you."

I was glad he wasn't in the room to witness my super-cheesy smile. "I bet you say that to all the girls."

"Only you." I could hear the smile in his voice too.

"I'll see you tonight," I replied. A girl had to save some of her pride.

"Bye, baby."

After daydreaming of our night to come, I pushed off the bed and got ready. My uniform of the day was a crisp white button-down, knee-length, fitted black skirt, and stiletto heels that could be used as weapons. Besides prepping for tonight like I was walking the red carpet at the Oscars, I had real life work to do.

I had a tenant moving out and another moving in at one of our vacant properties. Good customer service was important which meant I was going to meet them on their first day at our location.

And tomorrow, I had a handful of potential tenants wanting to see the Wells location for their businesses. My plan had worked. All I needed to do was seal the deal, have them sign their multiyear lease, and tell Daddy I'd done it.

There was swagger in my walk, a lilt in my voice, and a stirring in my chest that I couldn't deny as I strolled into Denali's Bar. The blue neon sign for my tenant was up, just like I'd ordered it weeks ago. The walls were coated with fresh cream paint, and the decor was magnificent—from the blue-and-green borders etched on the walls to the paintings of the Amalfi Coast in Italy.

"Christene!" The owner, Janel, sauntered over, one hand in the air and in her red Louboutins that matched her ruby-red suit jacket. "The place is perfect. I can't wait for opening night."

"Everything is looking really good."

Her booths and tables and lighting all matched her Middle Eastern motifs. Deep blues and yellows and greens highlighted the linen in an intricate pattern.

I plucked the folder from my purse. "I'll be here for the opening."

"You'd better." She winked.

I slipped her the paperwork and then headed out the door. My heels tapped against the sidewalk all the way to my car. Once inside, my whole body relaxed against the warm leather seat.

I closed my eyes, ticking off everything that needed to be done before tonight's black-tie event. Cameras would be everywhere, and tomorrow, I would be on the cover of some fancy grocery store magazine. This made my skin tingle. I didn't mind the attention, but I knew I didn't want this type of attention where everyone in the country would have an opinion about the girl on Jordan Ryder's arm.

Wax. Pluck. Pamper.

That was today's agenda.

My phone pinged with a message, and absently, I reached into my purse, plucking out my cell, still in a daydream state of mind. The text was from an unknown number.

When I swiped at the screen, my whole world stood still.

A heavy weight settled deep in the bottom of my stomach.

It was Jordan, undeniably so.

He stood tall in all his handsome beauty, carrying a dozen red roses, towering over a headstone. The picture had been taken from afar. The time-stamp was today.

A sudden coldness hit me. The second picture was of Jordan, kneeling, hands in front of him, head downturned as if he were crying, broken, as though her funeral had been today.

I sat there for a few minutes, just staring at the images. *Who cares if he was visiting his dead girlfriend's grave? Maybe he was visiting his father too? What was wrong with that?*

I bit my thumb, telling myself over and over that this was no big deal.

Who sent me these photos? Jordie was locked up under observation. It couldn't have been her.

Damn it.

Who the hell cares?

He wasn't with his mom now. Maybe he'd seen his mom in Kritell, and he was on his way back with her, but it obviously wasn't the only reason he'd gone home.

The scent of the cologne she had bought him filtered through my senses. It lingered in my car, or maybe I was imagining it. But whenever I was close to Jordan, I'd be reminded of a woman I was always comparing myself to.

My forehead fell against the steering wheel, as I felt

defeated, while the soreness in my lungs spread to my throat, choking me, suffocating me.

I tapped my forehead against the steering wheel. One, two, three times.

Why? Why isn't love in the cards for me?

CHAPTER 30

HOURS HAD PASSED.

I changed my mind. Wait for me. I want to walk into the restaurant together.

Hey, baby. Did you get my other text?

Testing.

Bothering you again. Is your phone dead?

Everything okay?

He'd texted me earlier, and through five texts and three missed phone calls, I hadn't answered the phone.

It was party time, and I was dressed to the nines, now waiting in the car ... simply thinking and rereading his texts.

After a long while, I finally texted him back.

I texted that I'd meet him at the party. I didn't want to speak to him. I didn't know what I was going to say. I even debated whether I should go to the cast party at all, but if I didn't, my whole family—Jordan included—would be searching for me.

My body sat idle in the car, waiting, wishing, wanting for something that I knew I had already lost, a loss of security.

All that pampering and waxing felt meaningless now.

A line had formed in front of the Allswell, a red carpet laid out and ready to receive the countless staff and stars and media. The paparazzi stood right behind the roped-off area, cameras in hand, flashing at people heading into the restaurant.

My hair was curled to perfection, not a smear of makeup out of place. On the outside, my appearance was immaculate, all put together, a typical Tene facade. But on the inside, my broken heart ached.

I'd talk to him. Ask him what he had done over the last couple days. That was what responsible people in a relationship did. We talked things through and worked things out. He'd tame my insecurities, just like he had before. But the pictures ... I sighed. Him on his knees, with a bouquet of flowers, his head downturned ... they looked so intimate.

The banging on my window made me jump and jerk my head up.

It was Angie.

Her hair was up in a high ponytail with soft curls cascading down her back. She motioned with her hands for me to get out of the car, so I did.

"Hey, the party has started." She pulled me into a half-hug, and for a brief second, I leaned into her, letting my body sag against her.

Take it away, Angie. Just like you defuse fights with Mom and me and how you consoled me with Logan. Please, Angie ... take this hurt away.

She loosened her hold, but I wouldn't release my tight grip on my little sister. I breathed her in one last time and then took a step back.

Her eyes widened, taking in my ensemble, a black halter-top dress that swished against my ankles and shimmered in the light. The stunner was the slit that sliced the dress to my hip.

"Look at you, sexy thing. I'm assuming, since you're wearing that, you're not planning to stay long." She grinned.

My fingers gripped the satin shimmer at my sides. I'd bought this dress specifically for Jordan, for us, for the first time we'd be seen together as a couple, our *show the world we're in love* moment.

My chest tightened, and my gaze dropped to the ground.

"Tene?"

"Hmm?"

"Are you okay?" Concern lay heavy in the creased line in between her brow.

No.

"I've just had a long-ass day," I said, never letting up on my death grip on my dress.

Maybe this had been a mistake, taking a chance on Jordan, knowing that everything we'd done would affect Cade and Angie. People would pick sides. Though we wouldn't want them to, they would.

My mother had been right. I could hear her disappointed tone ringing in my ears, loud and proud.

"Aw, poor baby." She patted my shoulder. "Working a long day for once after your staycation with Jordan."

I took a deep breath, preparing myself. "Let's go in," I said. I reached for her hand, squeezing it tightly.

"Tene?" she whispered, looking confused. "Really ... are you okay?"

She stopped to face me, but my focus was behind her, to the line formed in front of Allswell.

I nodded, lying through my teeth, "Yeah. Let's go."

I swirled toward the restaurant, afraid she'd be able to read my face.

There was a barricade in front of the roped entrance. The crowds and spectators of Rosendell had their cameras out, their black-tie attire on—suits and ties, designer dresses, high-end purses. Everyone was all dressed up, all waiting for a glimpse of Jordan and the rest of the cast.

"Is Jordan here?" I asked.

"No, he hasn't arrived. Susie says that's just how Jordan is. He likes to make a grand entrance at these things."

Once we were in line, I took in my sister's sexy ensemble. I had been too much in my head a minute ago. Angie's tube-top dress was new and so unlike her with the amount of skin showing, but it was still classy, like Angie Armstrong.

"I think you're the one who's planning to leave a little early." I chuckled.

Her cheeks turned a darker shade of pink, and I pinched her side.

"Tene." She slapped my hand out of the way.

There was no way Jordan and I could end badly. I knew these were my insecurities, but still, a real deep part of me believed Jordan and Candice weren't over. If it came to that, I would let him down easy for Angie and Cade's benefit. I couldn't give in to my emotions, especially when it would affect our families. Just thinking of the possibility of seeing him at holidays, family functions, their wedding ... I clutched my stomach, feeling unsteady.

I was still wondering who'd sent me the pictures. Probably one of his crazy flings.

It didn't matter. The pictures had slapped the reality back into my life.

We walked into Allswell, and the aroma of meats and

spices filtered through my senses, making my stomach clench with nausea. Prime rib, T-bone steaks, chicken cordon bleu, and smoked salmon were all on the menu. I adored food; eating was one of my hobbies—eating good food—but the thought was far from my mind at the moment.

Allswell had transformed. Black linens covered the normally white circular tables. Tall pilsner vases filled with fluffy white hydrangeas were placed in the center of each table. Gift bags that Angie and Susie had prepared lined the table on the far end. The bar was stocked with cold cuts and cheeses. Waiters in white suits moved through the crowd and served appetizers on silver trays.

Almost everyone held a drink in one hand and an hors d'oeuvre in the other.

Emery waved from across the room and then stood from her chair at one of the center tables. Her hair was braided to the side, and an elegant V-neck black dress hugged her figure.

"Well, well, well. Look at you, hot thang." I went in for a hug.

"Tene," she squealed.

She had the asshole with her. Fernando the Jerko. I'd thought she'd be smart enough to get rid of him. But alas, love could be blind. She had fallen hard for Fernando's nonprofit ambitions and with helping the less fortunate. That had been the before; this was the now, where Fernando was only working and earning and looking out for himself.

Fernando's eyes wandered everywhere in front of him, so I ignored him because he was obviously ignoring me.

Emery's smile was blinding, and she had me automatically smiling even though my heart still ached.

A light sheen of gloss coated her lips, and there was a natural blush on her cheeks. Emery never needed much to look immaculate.

"Fernando, this is Christene's sister, Angie." Emery motioned toward the greasy guy in a suit, who shook my sister's hand.

I tipped my head toward him and avoided touching him. Unfortunately, we knew each other already, and fortunately, he knew I didn't care for him. There was classy and classless, and Fernando embodied the latter.

"Hi, Tene," he uttered.

I scanned him from head to toe, letting my disapproval show. "Hey."

This was the self-made man who treated his girlfriend like shit. They'd met years ago, and I knew in my gut something was off about him. Late-night hours and overnight trips to God knew where, doing God knew what, but Emery trusted him, and what could I say to that? But it went above that. Fernando never came across as genuine, only pretending to care about the less fortunate and pretending to want to make a difference. Now that one of his businesses had taken off the ground, his true colors had shone.

I didn't know what Emery saw in him. I'd already told her how I felt about him, but I wasn't in their relationship, and it was her life.

"I swear, this is the biggest thing that has come to Rosendell." Emery's eyes widened with awe as she scanned the area, taking in the people dressed to perfection—women wearing fitted designer cocktail dresses, men in full-on suits or tuxes.

"Yeah, probably." I flicked my hair to my back. "Nothing happens here. Well, besides that infamous murder at Wells that put us on the map."

From the corner of my eye, I noticed Wyatt's eyes were trained on Emery like a laser light on a target from across the room. Oddly enough, he was in the corner as though he were hiding. What he should be doing was storming here and introducing himself to Emery, front and center. Like that would happen, given how shy he was.

Maybe Fernando could leave early, and I could introduce them. God forbid, Wyatt come over and make a pass at her. I tapped my chin, debating on how I could slyly play matchmaker.

Suddenly and as though in slow motion, the crowd roared, and everyone's attention turned to the door. I followed everyone's line of sight to see Jordan stroll in, dapper and handsome, and all the things my heart wanted and couldn't have. He was in a tux, the bow by his neck perfectly tied. The blond in his hair glimmered in the light, and his eyes, those intense blue eyes, scanned the area.

He waved and bowed with exaggerated Hollywood grace as he passed people he knew, and then he found me. His eyes were trained on me.

Alex caught his attention by the bar, and he laughed at something he'd said, but his eyes never left mine. My stomach clenched with nerves, and I wondered if I could go through with it. Leave him for good.

He said something to Alex and then marched toward me, briefly acknowledging the people trying to get his attention but never stopping until he was right in front of me. He smiled, dimple on his chin and all, gripped my waist, and pulled me into him, kissing me firmly on the lips. A kiss I felt from the roots of my hair to the soles of my feet and everywhere in between. And against my will and my inability to think clearly, I melted into his kiss, this kiss.

"I've been wanting to do that for days." His head rested against mine.

Our eyes were shut, our breathing even, and the love of my life was right here.

But through the darkness, all I saw was him standing over Candice's grave with a dozen red roses in his hands and sadness and love and longing in his eyes. My hands moved up his chest and slowly pushed him away.

Cameras flashed all around us, but we ignored them all.

"Mmm, I missed you, baby." He squeezed my hip. "You look beautiful. And that dress ..." With a slight shake of his head, he leaned in and said, "It's too bad I'm going to rip that off with my teeth tonight." Without shame, his hand dipped lower and squeezed.

"Where's your mom?" I took a step away from him, needing distance between us. My eyes scoured the place, searching for the matriarch of the Ryder family.

He gave me a questioning look. "She wasn't feeling well and decided not to come last minute."

My breath hitched. "You drove all that way to pick her up and not bring her back?"

"Yeah, I really wanted her to come." He shrugged as though it wasn't a big deal.

Liar, liar, pants on fire!

Suddenly, nausea hit me, and I moved to expand the distance between us.

"Jay!" Susie called out, approaching.

I was glad for her interruption because I had been about to say something I'd regret and cause a scene, which wasn't what I intended to do. I hugged my middle, trying to keep myself together.

"Get over here. Alex and Jayson and Cynthia want to talk about opening night in a month. What do you think of the place? Do you like it?" Susie beamed at her restaurant transformation.

"Excuse me, I want a drink," I said, ready to leave them to their business. I needed away from this place, away from him.

Jordan's head tilted. He raised an eyebrow and gripped my forearm, stilling me. "Everything okay?"

"Yeah, sure," I said, my tone dry and tired. "Why wouldn't it be?"

"Something is wrong." He ducked in, all humor erased from his features. "What's the matter?"

"Nothing." I closed my eyes, not wanting him to see the emotions running rampant.

"Jay," Susie urged.

"One second," he told her. He maneuvered me to the side with a twist of his wrist. "I think I know you well enough to know when you're lying."

I took a deep breath through my nose. "Well, I definitely don't know when you're lying. I have to actually catch you in a lie."

He jerked back, and his face twisted. "What are you talking about?"

Everyone's attention was on us. Their stares ping-ponging back and forth and forth and back again.

Breathe, Tene. Not here. Not the place. Not the time.

"Nothing." I shook my head and jerked my hand back. "Just go. Deal with your shit."

He ran a rigid hand through his hair. "What the hell, Tene? What happened to straight-up honesty?"

My eyes fell shut, and I blew out one exaggerated breath. I used extreme focus to keep myself calm and steady, concentrating on my breathing, on the snugness of my dress, on the people around me. Anywhere but the man I wanted to call out and confront in this instant.

"Tene." He tilted his head, examining me, his expression pinched.

My boiling blood coursed through my veins. "Jordan," I sassed.

"How are we going to make this work when you can't tell me what's bothering you?" he whisper-yelled.

We're not.

He obviously didn't care that we were causing a scene, so why should I?

My nails bit into my palms. "Honesty? You want honesty? How about you lying to me about going home to pick up your mom?"

"What?" He blinked and threw up his hands. "What the hell is that supposed to mean?"

There goes not causing a scene.

"Surprise, she isn't here."

His jaw tightened. "She's sick."

"You're lying to yourself and to me." I shoved my finger into his chest, pushing him back an inch. "Tell me you didn't drive all the way home to visit Candice."

His mouth fell open, and he jerked his head back.

My chin trembled because his reaction was so open, so honest. He had gone home specifically to see her.

"Deny it," I challenged him.

He blinked, and it took him a few seconds to speak. "Tene, let me explain."

I swiped at my now imperfect face, unable to hold the tears in. "Answer me. The truth this time. Tell me you didn't go back home to see her." My whole body went rigid, and he went lax. "Tell me, did you go home specifically to see Candice?"

He dropped his head, his shoulders hunched, and with a nod of his head, I had my answer.

"You want the truth?" My body shook. "We're done." My hand flew to my lips, but still, a silent sob escaped. "Because I won't settle for less."

"No. Don't go." He gripped my wrist, his eyes feverish and bright. "Listen, let me explain. Yes, I went to see her, but—"

"No buts! Stop lying to me. Stop pretending you're over her because you obviously aren't." Heat flushed my body.

I had everyone's attention. Every single cast member. And now, my family, who had just walked in. My mother included. But I didn't care anymore. Jordan had wanted this to happen now, so here we were.

I pounded a fist against my thigh. "I saw you at her grave, with a dozen roses ..." My voice trailed off, my heart tightening.

He shook his head, confused. "How?" Frustration was evident in his tone.

"Someone sent me pictures."

He lifted a hand and then leaned into me. "Who?"

I shook my head over it all. "It doesn't matter. I saw you. Everything was written on your face. A thousand emotions I wished were meant for me." My hands fell to my chest, and a whimper escaped me.

He stiffened. "Who sent you the pictures?"

"Are you not listening to me? It doesn't matter! You lied. You're not over her. Now, let me go." I stormed past him and past Angie, who called out my name, to the open outdoors, past my car and down the street, into an alley. I wouldn't be able to get into my car and out of this place fast enough, given the traffic jam. And knowing my apartment would be the first place he'd go, I wanted to be anywhere but there.

Heavy tears flowed down my face, like an endless stream. The warm night air couldn't dim the chill in me. I slid down to the ground, feeling the bricks scrape my bare back. The hollowness in my chest was vast, wide, endless.

Why did I let my guard down? I should've known better. I should've listened to my gut.

I swiped at my cheeks, hating the warm tears, hating that I showed emotion, hating that I had let my vulnerability shine in front of my family, in front of the world, in front of Jordan.

It hurt. I rubbed at my chest with the heel of my palm, needing the pain to dim, but I knew with experience, nothing would dim the pain but time.

I'd been here before. Long ago, but this hurt went deeper. Because I had thought … for a brief moment, I'd thought he was it. We were it. Forever.

My phone vibrated in my purse, and I reached in and went to silence it when a text appeared. It was from the same number that had sent me the pictures.

Now, you know the truth. Now, you know that he never loved you.

Goose bumps prickled my back, creeping up my neck. She was here. At the cast party.

"Hello, Christene."

I peered up from my phone.

And gasped.

It was Susie.

Pointing a gun directly at my chest.

CHAPTER 31

"AREN'T you going to say hi?" Her cheery demeanor was long gone. She was a different person altogether. No smile on her face. No heightened intonation in her voice.

I stayed utterly silent and pressed my elbows into my sides, cowering into myself.

There was no blankness in her stare, where there had been in Jordie's. Her gaze was laser-focused, sharp, calculating, and that frightened me that much more.

The gun was directed toward my chest.

"Don't move. I have good aim. I should know. Going to the gun range is my weekend hobby." Her laugh was without humor, short and cunning.

I stood and froze, my feet rooted to the ground. I could run in heels, but there was no way I could outrun a bullet.

"Turn around." Her voice was firm, strong.

I breathed slowly, and when I didn't move, she shoved the gun into my chest.

"I said, turn around."

"You're going to shoot me in the back." It was a statement, not a question.

And my whole life—happiness and regrets—flashed before me. I wasn't ready to go. Not before telling the people I cared about that I loved them.

"You think I'm going to let you die that easily?" She shoved my shoulder, forcing me to turn, and pushed the gun into my back. "Now, walk." She had one forceful hand on my shoulder, the other on the gun.

I bit the inside of my cheek, telling myself to focus and take note of my surroundings. We took a sharp right into an alleyway. Brick walls of the building caged us in. My body trembled with fear, but if she took me to a second location, I was as good as dead.

I debated taking her. Taking her down to the ground. My insides were built with steel. At least, I'd thought so until the cold barrel of the gun was at my back, and my whole body trembled with fear.

She walked me to her car, down the dark alley. She had me positioned by her, smiling like the psycho, fake, cheery person she was. I would not go down without a fight, and I formulated a plan.

As soon as she opened her car door and before she shoved me in, I'd grab the gun and kick her with my four-inch stilettos. I was waiting, counting the steps to the car, fear choking me with every second that passed, but resolve settling in my gut to at least try to obtain the upper hand.

Only a few more steps and I would turn, grab the gun, and use the bottom half of my body to take her down while I gained control of her weapon.

But I didn't get a chance to because the last thing I remembered was feeling the butt of her gun against my skull, the searing pain that spread down my neck, and the depthless hole of blackness that took me under.

———

Thud. Thud. Thud.

The rough edges of something pushing at my side brought me back to consciousness. She was kicking me with the point of her high-heeled shoe.

Blood trickled down my cheek to my mouth. The metallic taste of blood against my lips made me gag. If I had to guess the source of my wound, it was from the blunt jab of her gun against my head.

Pain radiated through my scalp to the back of my neck and down my spine. For a moment, I thought I might be paralyzed, but I wiggled my toes and fingers to confirm that wasn't the case.

My hands and feet were duct-taped together. The rough edges cut through my skin, leaving my hands purple and my arms numb, but my mind was awake, alive. The adrenaline coursed through my body now that I was conscious.

It took me two seconds to realize where we were. We were in the kitchen at the Wells property. The cold linoleum floor chilled my bare back, my naked legs. The light bounced off of the hood over the stovetop, and the sound of droplets from the faucet pinged against the stainless-steel sink.

"So, Sleeping Bimbo is awake?"

Her smile was evil personified, and her whole cheery demeanor that I was used to was gone. She had transformed. I could see it in her eyes, the depthless soullessness, and the fiery red in her hair reminded me of hell.

"I hear the owner butchered her husband, cut him up into pieces, limb by limb, finger by finger." She walked slowly around me, like a lioness ready to pounce on her prey. Her eyes were stone-cold hard, and the gun in her hand waved back and forth as she spoke. "Maybe that's what I'll do after I empty this gun into your pretty little head."

Anxiety tore through me as I took in my surroundings. The phone was against the wall, too far for me to reach, especially bound up. The Exit sign burned a bright red, but there was no way I could escape, tied up on the floor.

Susie rubbed the edge of the gun against her shirt and continued to pace the linoleum floor. She stroked the underbelly of the gun against her cheek, rubbing against it as a cat would do against its owner's leg. I shivered and not because I was cold.

"I spent hours upon hours making sure that party was perfect. You think he noticed?" She shook her head and sneered, "You think he could say *thank you* for once?" A sinister laugh escaped her lips, and her hand bounced at her side, the gun now turned toward my direction. "No, especially not when you're in the room. I'm sure he notices now. Now that you're gone."

She bent down right beside me and tapped the gun at my temple, taunting me. I flinched, gulping down breaths to keep quiet. Every fiber of my being wanted to scream and kick and fight, but I knew it would be useless.

There was no one here.

The cold barrel of the gun pressed deep into my temple, and she smiled.

This is it. The end.

In that moment, the people I loved the most flashed in my eyes. It took one second for all my regrets to push through. I found myself begging for my mother's forgiveness. For not loving her as best as I could and not forgiving her for the things that she'd done to hurt me. For our constant fighting and our back-and-forth disagreements. Because none of that mattered anymore. Not when I was on the brink of death. I'd die today without telling her that I loved her and that I was sorry that our relationship had not been better.

Tears sprang from the corners of my eyes. Not from fear, but from heavy-hearted regret. I wasn't scared of dying. Everyone was going to die eventually. But I hadn't expected my time to come so soon. I was scared of leaving this world without telling the people that mattered most that I loved them.

"You have nothing to say to me?" Her nostrils flared, her eyes growing wild. "Nothing at all?" She nudged the gun at my head again, more forceful this time. "At least this will be quick, and I won't be cutting you up in the back."

"Why would you do this?" My tone turned to panic, heightening with hysteria. "Why would you risk your job, your freedom for this? What do you want?"

Maybe I could reason with her, but there was no point in reasoning with the unreasonable.

She clicked her tongue. "What I wanted you to do was go away, disappear, leave him alone. But you couldn't do that, could you?"

She tapped the gun against my temple again, and I flinched.

"You just couldn't take a hint. Even after I placed that note in your car. Even after I sent Jordie your way."

Jordie.

Her words rang loud and clear in my head. She had sent Jordie. My vision blurred at the realization.

"You think that stupid bitch was smart enough to kill that cat?" Her laugh was cynical, evil even. "She's so stupid that I had to practically drive her to Allswell to find you and get to you. Did you really think she knew all that information about Jordan?"

Of course, she hadn't. How could Jordie have known that Jordan ordered an extra meal at dinner or that he still wore the cologne that Candice had given him? Only someone who had access to him on a daily basis would know such information, someone he trusted and shared intimate details about himself. It hadn't made sense before. I'd blown it off in the height of everything that had happened.

"Jordie was meant to scare you off, but since you can't take the hint, I'll get rid of you permanently." She stood, the hand holding the gun going limp at her side. "Funny, isn't it? We both want something that we can't have. We want him, but he'll never be ours because he will forever belong to her."

She knew and had accepted that fact, and I'd been wondering and in pain about it. Still, even on the floor, broken and bloody and beaten, her truthful words sliced through me.

But none of that mattered anymore either.

I wished I hadn't left the restaurant angry and annoyed with Jordan. I wished I could take back all I had said. Because those words would be the last I ever said to him. They'd been said in the heat of the moment, and that was how he would remember me.

More regret. More pain. More sorrow.

If he were here, I'd tell him that I loved him. I'd thank him for making me feel alive and loved and cherished when I hadn't felt that in so long.

I could hear his voice over the ringing in my ears, as though I were dreaming.

"Susie," someone called out.

I heard Jordan's voice, as though he was literally in the room, as though I'd wished him here.

I lifted my head as Jordan entered the restaurant, and I blinked to see if I was hallucinating, to see if he'd disappear as quickly as he'd appeared. But he didn't. It was him.

Fear permanently settled in my gut, even as the gun tilted to the right. Jordan's hands were up, his normally composed face panicked. For a brief moment, he gave me a once-over as if to check if I was breathing, had broken bones, or worse ... was dead. Then, in the next second, his panicked face flipped to a composed expression, actor-trained.

"So, you got my letter?" she snapped, her hold on the gun steady, ready to shoot if she needed to.

No emotion showed on his face, and his voice was quiet yet firm. "Just put the gun down, Susie."

"No." Her voice shook the room, shook my center, shook my world.

My fear turned to resounding hysteria because she turned the gun in Jordan's direction. I wriggled my hands together, trying to see if I could loosen the duct tape, but the pain pushed against my skin.

"I've worked for you for years. Watching you date a new slut each and every week. Maybe if you had picked someone who was worthy, I wouldn't care, but every girl fit the same damn profile. Busty and dumb." Her eyes turned feverish, and her hands shook uncontrollably now that she had the gun directed at Jordan.

"If I'd only known." He slowly approached her.

My whole body went rigid, my breathing bursting in and out in one-millisecond puffs. All restraint and fear within me heightened as he advanced toward her. Fear crippled me with silence.

He didn't falter, even as she repositioned both hands on the gun, her eyes darting between me and him and back again.

"Let's just get out of here. Anywhere you want to go, I'll go."

Then, slowly, with the steadiest of hands, he reached for her face and brushed a strand of red hair away from her cheek. The gun was pointed at his chest, the barrel flush against his tux. Death by trigger was only a second away, but I knew she believed him because she leaned into his touch.

He could've grabbed the gun, but he kept his hand steady on her face. "You never gave me any indication. What was I supposed to do? Hold my breath? Confront you about my feelings?" he whispered. "I was afraid you wouldn't feel the same. I was afraid you would quit and sever our relationship."

Her face softened, her mouth going lax. She was falling for it. Shit, I would have fallen for it, too, if I didn't know better. If I were in her delusional, psycho mind.

"Give me the gun, baby." The words sounded so natural, as though he'd been calling her that for years. He was doing what he did best—acting. And he was killing this scene.

And then she snapped, her eyes hardening. "No, it's my gun." She tightened her hold on the pistol, her face tight, and then she distanced herself. "Why should I listen to you?"

"Because I care about you, Susie," he said with such sincerity. He nodded at me. "You hurt her, and everything is shit. We can't be together." One step closer. "Give me the gun." Another step. "And I'll go anywhere with you. We can talk about us and our relationship. No one has to get hurt."

Her mouth slackened, and her gaze became unfocused. Indecision was all over her face.

"Please." He didn't take his eyes off of her, his whole body pleading with her. "Let's get out of here." His voice turned quiet, almost vulnerable. "You and me. Anywhere you want to go."

I knew the exact second she'd decided because she straightened, squinting at him as though he was the target at the range. Then, she cocked the gun, and my whole world stood still. I started to scream because pure panic set in. She was crazy, and insane people didn't value life or the calamity that they caused around them.

I started squirming and kicking and shouting and doing everything possible to divert her attention to me.

And it worked.

She kicked me hard and kept on going. In my gut, in my legs, at my side. The point of her shoe jabbed against my body like a tiny dagger against my flesh.

"Shut up! Shut up! Shut up!" she screamed.

"Stop! Susie ... stop!"

I heard my body crack from the impact of her heel and tasted blood on my lips.

She trained the gun in Jordan's direction, and his hands were up, the mask of a composed man gone like ashes against the wind. Pure terror tore through his features. Then, she pointed the gun directly at me.

"Stop! Please, just stop!" His face crumbled, and then he dropped to the ground. "Shoot me. Take me. Just let her go."

Her laugh was evil, sinister, the devil with the red hair.

"Oh, how I almost believed you. I almost fell for your

lies, Jordan Ryder. I knew I'd never be number one—no one would compare to Candice—but I can't settle for third or fourth or fifth best. I refuse." Her gun flipped back and forth between us, as though she were waving a pointer finger. "Go. Go to her. I'll allow you one last kiss before I kill her."

When he didn't move, she screamed, "Do it! Or else I'll kill her now!"

He ran and then dropped to his knees, crawling to me. I tasted the saltiness of my tears and blood, a toxic mixture of pain and regret.

He cupped my face and then leaned his forehead against mine. "I'm sorry," he said, locking eyes with mine. "I'm so sorry."

"Kiss her," she taunted.

He bent down, and the wetness of his cheeks meshed with mine. He cupped my face and placed a chaste kiss on my lips. "I love you," he whispered, only loud enough for me to hear. "You'll never know how much." Determination was set heavy in his eyes, a decision that scared me. "I promise you're going to be okay."

He kissed my forehead and sat back on his heels, resolve written on his features.

"This ends now, Susie. No more violence." He stood in front of her and pounded his chest with one heavy fist.

After he took one step toward her, she lifted her gun, pointing it directly at him.

"In about two minutes, this place will be swarmed with cops," he told her, his voice firm, sure. "They know I'm here. They know you're here. I texted my brothers right before I got here."

"What?" Susie's eyes flew to the window, her eyes going wild, her body rigid.

He didn't give her a chance to think through her next

plan of action because he rushed toward her and tackled her, their bodies clashing together before they tumbled to the ground.

Their legs tangled like branches on a vine. Susie sat on top of him, straddling him. They fought to gain control of the weapon, both of their hands on the gun.

I pushed my hands against the duct tape, struggling to escape, but pain and friction hit hot and hard against my skin. I'd never felt so helpless, so useless.

She bit his hand, and when he loosened his grip on the weapon, she knocked him in the head with the butt of the gun and turned the weapon directly at him.

My scream could have cut glass, high-pitched, panicked, and screeching.

She was going to shoot him. Point-blank.

Chaos erupted around us.

Police charged in.

I screamed louder as three shots rang out, piercing my eardrums.

There was blood.

Everywhere.

It wasn't hers.

It was his.

CHAPTER 32

A SWAT TEAM stormed through the doors, taking her down with multiple shots. She was on the ground, wriggling in pain, moaning in agony. But so was Jordan.

Blood pooled all around him. His shirt turned dark red, like paint against a white canvas, initiating at his chest and spreading everywhere.

My vocal cords felt like they were bleeding, rough like sandpaper from all the screaming.

Two officers charged toward him. A few others rushed to my side. One burly and wide with a football frame and who sported a wiry beard. The other his polar opposite, leaner and taller, but I could see the strength of this man in his muscular forearms. Their mouths were moving, but I didn't hear a word. My eyes, my singular focus, was on Jordan. Muffled noises surrounded me, as though I were inside a cave, hearing the echoing of voices, but I wasn't able to make out the exact words.

"Jordan!" I cried. But I couldn't even hear my own voice.

They were taking him away.

The leaner officer undid the binding of my feet and hands. And when I went to stand, I cowered. The pain shot from my side to my legs to my spine, and I staggered, about to fall until the officer caught my arm. Everything hurt, but the determination to get to Jordan helped me push through the pain.

The officer with the beard held my shoulders and gently guided me to lie down. "Are you okay, ma'am? Are you bleeding anywhere? Have you been shot?" He repeated himself again, and within seconds, his voice became vividly clear. His eyes searched my body for any injury, his fingers gently touching me, assessing me. "The paramedics are here. They'll evaluate you."

"No. No, sir." Tears coursed down my face. "Jordan ..." My voice was hoarse. The back of my throat felt like I had gargled acid. When I tried to move, pain shot from my ribs.

"You need to lie still. We're getting a stretcher in here."

They handcuffed the crazy witch, blood marring her silver dress. I didn't know if she was alive or dead, but she wasn't my concern anymore. My sole focus was on Jordan.

Two medics approached. One held my arms, and the other held my legs as they placed me onto the stretcher.

"Please ..." It hurt to talk. It hurt to breathe. "Jordan ..." I felt the searing pain of her kicks from earlier. The signs of bruising already showed itself at my calf—pink and the lightest of purples.

The medic placed a gentle hand on my shoulder. "You need to relax. You might have broken something, ma'am. Please stay still until we get to the hospital, and we take some X-rays. Don't worry; we'll get you to him. They've already taken him to the hospital."

They wheeled me outside. The stars shone brightly in the dark sky above me. A crowd formed down the block, but it was roped off, closed by yellow tape. I squinted against the lights of the ambulance as we approached.

"She's my sister!" I heard Angie's voice break through the fog in my brain.

My head flipped around. An officer had her in a tight vise, his arms like rubber bands against her waist.

"Let me go! Let. Me. Go!" She fought against him, her feet dangling from the ground, her hands pushing against his chest.

Cade rushed behind her, his chest heaving in exertion. "Angie ..."

"No! Let me go."

Cade turned to the officer, his face hard, noting his hands wrapped tightly around his girlfriend. "Officer, I have this."

"You'll have to wait beyond the barricade," he said, face devoid of emotion. "This is a crime scene."

"No." She wriggled in his hold.

And that was when Cade grabbed her waist and lifted her in one swift movement, taking her from the officer.

Angie pushed out of his arms and rushed over to me as the medics placed me in the ambulance. "Tene," she cried, tears streaming down her face. She hopped into the ambulance and cowered into me. "Are you hurt? Are you bleeding?"

Cade argued with the officer. "This is her sister. She just wants to know she's not dead. Have a little compassion, man."

"I'm okay," I said, far from okay. My breathing was labored. My bones and everything within me hurt. "Jordan ... please. I need to see him." It hurt to speak, and I wished someone would just get me to Jordan, so I could see with my eyes that he was okay.

"Angie, give her some space," Cade said. "He's been taken to the hospital. Wyatt's with him." He blew out a breath. "Jordan's lost a lot of blood." He ran one hand down his face, his mouth downturned, his features grave.

Anxiety tore through me. I needed to see him. "P-please."

I heard the sounds of sirens and lights flickered in front of me.

I tried to sit up through all the searing pain, but I couldn't because I was strapped down.

"Stay still. Don't move. What are you doing?" Angie placed her hand over mine, her eyes panicked. "I promise you, you'll see him soon."

"You will," Cade confirmed before kissing Angie, and the medics shut the doors.

I wiggled my fingers and my toes and bit the inside of my cheek to confirm I was still here and that this wasn't some godforsaken nightmare. I was alive. Thank God.

Now that the adrenaline had died down, my body began to shake.

Angie fiercely gripped my hand. "You're going to be okay. Everything is going to be okay."

The pain was overwhelming, but what overrode the agony was my undying need to see Jordan, to make sure he was okay. It hurt to talk, to move, to do anything. But my comfort was in the sounds of the sirens, knowing that I'd be at the hospital soon.

The medics wheeled me into the emergency room, and the first thing I saw was my mother's face, her eyes red with tears. Relief flushed her features, and she rushed toward me, cupping my face and kissing my dried-up tears.

My tear ducts filled up again as a rush of emotions pushed through. "I'm sorry, Mom." I didn't know what I was apologizing for, but they were the first words that fell out of my mouth, and they'd needed to come out.

She brushed my hair from my cheeks as she comforted me with soothing whispers.

One medic on either side of me ushered the gurney down the hall. "Ma'am, we need to get her checked in."

When they pushed past her, my mother's hand was outstretched, my father holding her back.

"Tene-Tene," she cried out.

More tears fell from my face. She hadn't called me Tene-Tene since I was a little girl, since before the fighting started when life had been easy, and I'd worshipped the ground she walked on.

Mom, I mouthed before they pushed me past a corner, and she disappeared from view.

＿＿

The pain was unbearable, but the doctors gave me painkillers to put me at ease. I was barely conscious when they wheeled me out for X-rays.

I took in their words, watching them speak, but I was in and out of consciousness and barely comprehending what was being said.

"Fractured ribs ... weeks to heal ..."

My mind was mush, but my thoughts were on Jordan. Breathing hurt, coughing hurt, moving hurt, but I welcomed the pain because that meant I was alive and well. My body would heal eventually.

When they wheeled me into my hospital room, Angie, my parents, and Nana were all waiting for me. My mother rushed over and gripped my hand. Angie grabbed the other one.

I lifted my head through the fog—body numb but mind wide awake. "Jordan?" I rasped.

"He's in surgery." Angie winced. "Cade and Wyatt are with him."

"Surgery?"

"Nothing major." She smiled, but I could still read the worry in her eyes. "The bullet got lodged, and they need to get it out."

I nodded but couldn't help the tears that fell from my face. The answer wasn't good enough. I wanted to know he was okay, wanted to see him in the flesh, kiss him, know he was alive.

My mother dabbed the tissue at my cheeks, and I closed my eyes and did what I hadn't done in a long time—I prayed. For his safety, his well-being, for him to come back to me, whole and alive and well. I prayed until my eyes became heavy and sleep took me.

———

When I awoke, it was quiet, and the lights were dim. My mother was asleep on the couch against the wall.

The nurse wheeled in my food and placed it in front of me. "You should eat something."

I sat up, but the IV tugged at my arm, where my pain meds were being administered.

I tried to clear my dry throat. I had no appetite even though it had been hours since I had anything in my stomach.

When she placed the tray in front of me and adjusted my hospital bed to an upright position, my mother stirred and stood.

When her eyes met mine, she smiled. Then, she flattened her hair and pulled down her shirt, which had ridden up when she sat up from the couch. "It's okay. I'll assist her."

The nurse nodded. "I can adjust her pain meds once she has something in her stomach." The nurse smiled and then exited the room.

I glanced at my mother. I had so much to say, but suddenly, I had too much pride to say it. When she approached the bed, brushed my hair back, and cupped my face, I began to cry. Goodness, I'd cried more in the last few days than I had in my whole lifetime.

"I'm sorry," I whispered, finally getting out the words I'd hoped I'd be able to get out when I had the barrel of Susie's gun pointed at me and my own mortality staring me in the face.

Her normally composed demeanor crumbled. Her lip quivered. "No, honey, I'm sorry. I thought we were going to lose you."

She swiped at the tears in her eyes, and I didn't know what to do because I didn't remember the last time I had seen my mother cry.

She swallowed and then tore back the foil from the soup. Steam rose from the bowl. "When you were a little girl, you worshipped me." She stared at the soup as though she was afraid to look at me. "You wanted to do everything I did. You'd go in and wear my makeup and slip your tiny feet in my high heels." She stirred the soup with a spoon, trying to cool it down. "And I adored you. I wanted to give you everything you wanted because you were my firstborn, my little girl." She brought the cream of broccoli soup to her lips, temperature-tasting it. "I was pregnant with you before I got married," she admitted, watching me for my reaction.

What? My eyebrows flew to my hairline. It couldn't be. They'd gotten married in July, and I was born ... I tried to do the math in my head.

She laughed when she saw my reaction. "Shotgun wedding. I mean, I loved your father, and there was no doubt that it would have been us eventually." She blew out a breath. "But I wasn't prepared to be a mother. I ... I had to drop out of college to raise you."

Realization seeped into my skin, and relief flooded through me. There was a reason. A reason to explain all of this, why I believed she'd hated me so much.

"For the longest time, I was bitter and angry." She averted her stare, looking into the mix of broccoli and cheddar soup. "I loved you as a baby, as a toddler, as a child."

She blew on the spoon and angled it toward me. I took the soup in my mouth, and the motion brought me back to when she used to spoon-feed me and Angie at the same time.

"But you became very independent. And then in high school, you started making the wrong choices, and I didn't want you to make the same mistakes that I had too early." She shook her head. "Not like you're a mistake. You and Angie are the best things that have ever happened to me, my greatest achievements, my proudest joy." She placed the bowl back on the tray and rubbed at her brow. "I grew to be jealous, though, especially when you took over Armstrong with your father. At one time, I'd thought that would be me, working side by side with him." Her face crumbled again, and a tiny sob escaped her, all her remorse pushing through.

This time, I reached around and wrapped my arms around her. My ribs hurt, but I pushed through the pain. Her sobs vibrated through me, and small tears of my own tore down my cheeks. I couldn't remember a time when I'd been this close to my mother before. I needed this. Life was too short to hold grudges against the ones you loved. Life was too short to not hold the people who meant the most.

"I don't know what happened for us to get to this point, Tene. Sometimes, I wish I could go back to the days where you loved me unconditionally, where you depended on me, where there wasn't always this tug-of-war between us."

"I know, Mom," I said with full-on, sullen regret.

I ran my fingers through her dark locks, so similar to my own. There were years of hurt between us and anger and words not meant. Now, all that pent-up madness was replaced with regret, shame, and remorse.

"We'll get back to where we were." My chest bloomed with hope that, in the end, we could repair all the hurt that had happened between us.

CHAPTER 33

AFTER HOURS IN THE ER, the doctors finally gave me a rundown of my injuries. Broken ribs and bruises all up and down the left side of my body, but no major organs had been damaged.

It could've been worse.

That was what the police had said after they interviewed me—*worse*. And it could have been, so I was thankful that I was breathing and alive.

I stared at the ceiling as my mother, father, and Angie babied me, fed me, held my hand. I couldn't bear to tell them I felt crowded because my being alive gave them such comfort. Every ten minutes, I would ask for a status update on Jordan. Cade had come earlier, alleviating some of my worries and informing us that Jordan was recovering.

But the worry would not stop. I wanted to see him for myself.

"Sleep," they said. "Rest."

What a load of bullshit.

How could I rest when I couldn't confirm for myself if the love of my life was truly okay and safe?

My hand flew to my heart. Love of my life. *He was, though, wasn't he?*

Though our whole romance had been short, it was most definitely not fleeting. I cared about him ... deeply. And I was in love.

When Susie had her gun pointed directly at him, I had known, if he died right then and there, I wouldn't be able to survive. At that moment, my safety had been second to his. When you loved someone deeply, truly ... you put them above yourself, but more than that, I couldn't picture my life without him.

Yes, I was in love. It was in the undying need to see him and hold him in my arms. It was this immense heaviness in my chest that wouldn't go away. And I knew it wouldn't until I told him how I felt.

———

My heart thumped frantically in my chest, and I jolted to a sitting position, awakening to darkness with a cold sweat running down my back. The scene at Wells had played back in my head, a nightmare personified, where Susie was slowly and surely torturing Jordan, cutting him, until his last dying breath.

My father was on Tene duty, sleeping on the couch. His loud snores came in and out in a steady rhythm.

I swiped at my eyes, only then realizing that I had been crying in my sleep.

It was just a nightmare. I repeated. *It was just a nightmare.*

It'd been two nights since I'd been admitted, and tomorrow morning, they would discharge me. Every night, the nightmares intensified.

I'd had enough. All this waiting was making it worse. Now, I was afraid to close my eyes, worrying that behind them, I'd see Susie's animated face as she tortured my boyfriend.

"Dad ..." I whisper-yelled.

When he stirred, I loudened my calls.

He rubbed his eyes before peering over and pushing himself up to a sitting position. "Tene ... are you okay?"

He blinked away the slumber, and I wanted to cry all over again because I was far from okay.

"Daddy?" I called out.

With that one word, he was up on his feet, stumbling as he walked and ended up beside my hospital bed. "Are you hurting?"

He reached for the call button, ready to summon the nurse, but I placed my hand over his.

"How much do you love me?" I asked, playing for cute. I hadn't known I had it in me, but this time, I was beyond desperate.

He leaned in, and with the lightest of touches, he kissed the top of my head. "What do you need, my little girl?"

And with those few words, I knew my plan would come to fruition.

———

I had convinced my father to get me a wheelchair and push me into Jordan's hospital room.

Yes, he loved me. With Angie and my mother, everything was by the doctor's orders. With my father, everything was by my orders. Gosh, did I love this man.

No one was at the nurses' station when my father wheeled me into Jordan's room and right by his bed.

I watched the rise and fall of his chest and listened to the soft breaths escaping him. I reached out to touch his forearm, just to know that this was real, that this wasn't part of a wicked nightmare where the next scene would take us back to the Wells property.

My father leaned in and brushed a tender kiss at the top of my forehead. "See? He's fine. Just sleeping."

I nodded, and he squeezed my shoulder before slipping out of the room.

A gush of air escaped my lungs, as though I'd been holding my breath the whole time we'd been apart.

The pull to be closer was too strong to ignore, so I reached for his hand, intertwining our fingers, and then brought his hand to my lips. His hand was warm and heavy within mine.

He stirred, his eyes fluttering open.

And then he gave me his signature beautiful actor smile, dimple in his chin and all. "Hey ..."

Full-on tears fell down my cheeks—big, fat, and ugly—but I didn't care. "Hey." I lifted my chin, blinking them back, but they kept on coming, so I swiped at the waterfall trailing down my cheeks.

"Easy there. What's the sad face for?" The sound of his voice had me smiling because that meant he was well and safe, but most of all, he was alive.

"I'm fine." I wiped my cheeks. "It's just ..." I sniffled. "Cade has been filling me in. On your surgery. On your recovery." I swallowed down a sob. "I've been having these nightmares ... and not being able to see you for myself has been making it worse." I lifted my shirt and rubbed at the corner of my eye, wiping the tears away.

His thumb brushed lightly on the top of my fist. "You're okay. I'm okay. You know what would be better than okay?"

He gently tugged on our intertwined hands. "If I could hold you."

"But what if I hurt you? Where did you get shot?"

"My shoulder. And right now, all that matters is that you're on this bed with me."

As I peered up at Jordan, I realized I knew that, over the past few days, I'd mastered the art of worrying.

We both winced when I slipped right next to him, which also caused us to laugh. It took a bit to get adjusted, where I wasn't lying on him, and he wasn't hurting my ribs.

"Do you think they know I'm here? The doctors?" I asked. I'd almost bet, in about two seconds, an army of hospital workers would be in here to take me back to my room.

"Of course not." He slid his arm over my lap, lightly running over my broken ribs. "Anyway, I charmed the nurse into getting me a Coke earlier. I'll just use my charm if we get in trouble," he said, mischief heavy on his features.

Maybe his actor beauty could charm the nurses into getting us better food.

I laid my head on his shoulder and inhaled deeply. I blew out a breath, sighing, letting out my relief. He was in a hospital gown, and his bandages pushed through the thin fabric. It seemed so surreal—what had happened, how he had gotten shot, how close he'd come to death.

"It didn't hurt. Don't cry. They got it out." He angled closer and leaned into me, his hand on my cheek, peering in my eyes.

"I'm not crying." *I was so crying*. The stress of the day and the relief that we were going to be all right rushed through me like a high-speed train. Goodness, I hoped that I was not turning into a crier.

He reached up and swiped at my tears. When he adjusted on the bed, he groaned.

I laughed. "We're a mess, aren't we?"

"Yes, we are." He chuckled.

Then, his eyes turned thoughtful. With one hand, he gripped the handrail on my side, so he was facing me.

"That day ..." he began.

"I want to forget about that day."

"No. No." He shook his head, his eyes determined. "We need to talk about it. I did go home to see Candice ..." His voice trailed off, and I stopped breathing altogether, blinking up at him.

I pressed a finger to his lips. "It doesn't matter." Because it didn't. This whole daring adventure had made me realize that dwelling on the past or worrying about a future that might never come wasn't worth it. What was important was the here, the now, that he was safe, that we were both alive.

He lifted my hand from his lips and kissed me sweetly, softly. "It does matter. I went to her grave ... to tell her about you." A small smile touched his lips. "To tell her how beautiful, how kind, and how incredibly smart you are. And I know in my heart that she'd be happy for me. Happy that I was happy."

Heat radiated in my chest, moving through every part of me, causing unshed tears to line my eyes again.

He had gone there to tell her about me. About us ...

I swiped at my cheeks again. I thought I'd shed enough tears for ten years.

"I've never felt peace, ya know?" His stare was unfocused, his smile dimming. "Every time I felt happy, it didn't feel right. Because how could I be happy when she was dead?"

My head rested on his chest as he threaded his fingers through my hair. I wanted to hold him, comfort him.

"But after that moment ... this overwhelming peace took over. The sun was shining so bright, and when I lifted my head, a dove flew above me." One arm wrapped tightly against my shoulders, bringing me flush against him. "I'd needed to see her. Tell her about us because I knew she would have been happy for us. Candice was like that ... the sun, a shining light."

We held each other in silence, listening to each other's breathing and reveling in the warmth of each other's touch.

He moved his fingers through my hair, slow, drugging tugs that had me sighing softly.

"If we have to pee, that's going to be a problem," he joked.

"Yeah, it will be." The laugh that rumbled through my chest made my ribs hurt.

We both exhaled at the same time, and I knew he felt as I did, finally able to relax now that we were in each other's arms, and everything was out in the open.

"Christene," he whispered, "I'm tired."

My eyes closed, and I felt his heartbeat against my cheek and his soft breaths against my hair. "Me too," I replied.

"Christene?"

"Hmm?"

"I love you."

His words filled me with an ecstasy that I'd never known before, and I nodded into his chest again. A lightness spread throughout my arms and legs and head.

"I love you too," I said, lifting my head to take him in.

His smile was breathtakingly beautiful, just like that very first day I'd met him.

"You sure about that?"

"The surest I've ever been." I touched his face, my fingers brushing gently against his cheek.

On the brink of losing everything, I'd realized I needed to live in the present, appreciate all I had, and fully love those who mattered. If the last few days had proven anything, it was that I'd never loved anyone more than the blue-eyed man staring back at me.

"We're going to be okay?" His question was quiet, vulnerable, as he searched my face for confirmation.

"If you mean me and you and forever ..." I lifted my chin. "... I think we'll be okay."

He smiled and then followed up my words with a kiss, and we both drifted off into the first good night's rest we'd had in forever.

EPILOGUE

SIX MONTHS Later

The sun shone brightly on my beach chair as I watched Jordan from afar, hitting the waves. I hadn't taken a vacation in what seemed like forever. And here I was, on vacation in the most beautiful place on Earth—Hawaii.

My fingers flew to the spaghetti straps of my teeny-tiny bikini.

While I was baking under the summer sun, Jordan was working. Working on a movie. A love story, to be exact.

I had joined him on the last leg of filming, so we could spend some time together.

My life since I'd met him was a whirlwind. Practically everywhere I went, there were photographers. When the paps were out, Jordan would lift up our joined hands—showing them my five-karat flawless diamond—smile big like the cheeseball he really was, and pull me into him, kissing me senseless.

Jordan had proposed to me at my apartment the day after we were discharged. He'd gotten down on one knee and said because tomorrow wasn't promised, he didn't want to waste a day without me in his life. It was crazy and spontaneous and just how our lives were meant to be. He'd made his permanent residence at Rosendell, though he traveled frequently to shoot.

When filming had died down, and the thrill of having Hollywood in town was over, people in Rosendell grew protective of us, shooing paps away and even sending them on wild goose chases around town.

Everywhere else I went, people knew me as Jordan's fiancée. I was stalked, and when we were together, we needed more than Larry and Dex to get us through a crowd. We had an entourage of bodyguards.

It had taken me a while to get used to, but eventually, it'd sunk in, and I didn't care. All I cared was, he was mine, and I was his.

They were in between takes, and when I peered over at their filming destination, Jordan waved and jumped up and down like the silly man he was. I was far enough from the taping site where I could sneeze and talk and do practically whatever I wanted with no issues, and we were on a secluded island that no one else had access to. Overhead helicopters could be heard, but at least no one was on the ground, bothering us.

I brought my palms to my lips, one after the other, blowing him kisses nonstop. And he caught them midair and then stuck them in his pocket, or he pretended to catch my kisses in his mouth.

The actress, Lena Reynolds, laughed behind him.

Lena was beautiful and sexy and held all those qualities that I used to be jealous of, but not anymore.

That part of me had died. The jealous part of me that had caused me to have doubts and have an inferiority complex was gone, replaced by a love for my fiancé. Being with Jordan had brought me to the realization that no matter what, you couldn't control how others treated you or force others to love you. They simply did, or they didn't. What I could control was how I reacted to situations.

And not once did I doubt Jordan or how he felt about me because, each and every day, he made me feel loved. It was in the sweetness of his cards, the tenderness of his kisses, and the crassness of his texts.

As time passed slowly, and even though we were miles apart at times, we made an effort to make it work.

Our wedding was in a few weeks. Jordan was a hands-on planner, and with both cooks in the kitchen, you would think it would have been hard to agree on the details, but it wasn't.

We were truly alike in more ways than I could count.

We'd agreed on every little detail from the colors of the wedding to the flavor of the cake to the decor and flowers. We'd high-fived at every decision made.

I loved him truly, madly, eternally.

Hours later, the sound of the waves, the warm heat of the sun, and the gentle breeze of the Hawaii air lulled me to sleep. I awoke to someone kissing me. On my forehead, on my cheeks, on my lips.

"Sleeping Beauty." More kisses. "Wake up, Sexy Beauty."

It was my prince.

"Ready to go?" His smile was blinding, and seeing him sitting with the Hawaii sun setting in front of us made me feel like I was in a dream.

I peered up, and the film crew on the horizon was gone. I wondered how long I'd been asleep.

"We've got things to do—invitations to pick, a wedding to plan." He took my hands within his, kissing my knuckles.

"Wedding to plan," I said, meeting his eyes.

A breath escaped me, and I smiled lovingly up at him. My fingers touched his bare chest, tracing my initials etched in ink above his heart, right by a bird, free and flying. He'd gotten it on Candice's and his father's death anniversary. The brothers got a tattoo every year to celebrate their life.

Our pasts, our happiness, our hardships shaped who we were. We learned from others, and our pains shaped us to make better decisions today.

Her name was etched on his chest, right next to mine, but I was fine with that because, without her, I wouldn't have the same Jordan today. The Jordan who wanted to live every moment to its fullest, never knowing when the next moment would be our last.

His knuckles brushed at my cheek. "Cold feet?"

"No." I squinted at the sun setting in front of us. "It's just so crazy. So fast." I hadn't meant to let those words slip out; I'd meant to say them in my head.

He nodded, agreeing but still smiling, nonetheless.

"We were engaged in a month." He pressed his pointer finger to my nose. "Will be married within eight." He leaned in and peered up at me with a secret question. "Baby in twenty-four?"

I breathed in and widened my eyes. *Baby? This guy is going super-fast.* I wasn't thinking of babies. "Too fast," I whispered, feeling my pulse tick up in speed.

But then he cupped my face and kissed me breathless. I inhaled his new signature cologne, which I'd bought, and felt his large palm against the softness of my cheek, and all my worries disappeared.

Whatever happened, whatever the future held, I knew we would be more than okay.

"Crazy fast. But I wouldn't have it any other way," he said, muffled against my lips.

Crazy, madly, deeply, perfectly. That was how our relationship could be summed up.

"Thirty-six months," I whispered, extending his timeline.

With Jordan, all my plans always flew out the door.

Who knew? It might be sooner than that.

———

Did you love Jordan and Tene's journey to finding their Happily Ever After? Do you want a glimpse into Wyatt's story? Click HERE (Website: https://dl.bookfunnel.com/hlzo6eg1cg) to find out what happens to Wyatt and Emery.

ALSO BY MIA KAYLA

www.authormiakayla.com

The Torn Duet - A Rockstar Romance

Torn Between Two - Book 1

Choosing Forever - Book 2

The Forever After Series - Marriage of Convenience

Marry Me for Money - Forever After Book 1

Love After Marriage - Forever After Book 2

The Scheme - Brian's book -Forever After Book 3

Naughty Not Nice - Forever After Book 4

The Unraveled Series - Billionaire Brothers

Unraveled

Undone

Stand Alone

Everything Has Changed - Childhood friends to Lovers

Boss I Love to Hate - An Office Romance

STAY IN TOUCH

Thank you so much for reading UNDONE. There are a ton of books to read out there, but you have chosen to spend your time with mine.
And for that...I appreciate you.

Here's where you can find me. Join my reader group to stay in the loop about my most recent books.
www.authormiakayla.com

JOIN MY READER GROUP
WEBPAGE
FACEBOOK
TWITTER
INSTAGRAM
GOODREADS
AMAZON
BOOKBUB

ACKNOWLEDGMENTS

Goodness gracious, another book is officially done. This has been a year of changes, good, bad and everything. And as I finish this book, I want to thank all the people that have made writing and publishing a reality.

To God—for my creative mind that can't stay quiet and for the endless ideas he places in my head.

To the Hubs—for believing in me when I sometimes don't believe in myself. For sending me crazy motivational memes just when I need them.

To my three little girls—For giving me content to post, making me laugh, and also for your sweet notes and kisses and all the things you do to making mommy smile.

To my mom and stepdad—Thank you for helping me with the kids when I have to write and helping me with everything from copyrighting my books to the business side of things. I appreciate all you do and have learned a lot from both of you.

To my Beta Readers— Hot Tree, Alyssa, Emily, and Kristy—Thanks for helping me make this book the best it can be with your constant feedback.

To my post proof Betas—To Amy, Aisha and Norma—Thank you for catching all the last minute things to make this book perfect.

To the best people in the planet - Elizabeth and Jen. You guys keep me organized and sane and I love you for it.

Birds of a feather flock together—To Michelle, Stephanie, El, Jenny and Maya, thanks for listening me gripe about all things writerly and always being there for me.

To AF and Support and DND—Thanks for all your feedback and constant guidance in this ever changing publishing environment.

To my editors, book designer and teaser friends that has made this book package and release super awesome—Thank you Juliana, Gel, Tracy, Jovana, Mitzi, and Meghan.

Last but not least—to my readers.. I LOVE YOU and will write all the books because of you. The end.